PORT OF *Return*

PORT OF *Return*

Restored

Part 6

Mary E. Hanks

www.maryehanks.com

Suzanne D. Williams Cover Design:

www.feelgoodromance.com

Cover photos: Jack Frog @ shutterstock.com

Visit Mary's website:

www.maryehanks.com

You can write Mary at

maryhanks@maryehanks.com.

For Mary E. Simmons

In memory of my mother

A lady with big faith!

For Jason

My walking partner, projects associate, gardening buddy,

TV-series-watching pal, prayer partner, and

co-partaker in all things chocolate.

How great is the love the Father has lavished on us ...

I John 3:1

Basalt Bay Residents

Paisley Grant – Daughter of Paul and Penny Cedars

Judah Grant – Son of Edward and Bess Grant

Paige Cedars – Paisley's younger sister/mom to Piper

Peter Cedars – Paisley' older brother/fishing in Alaska

Paul Cedars – Paisley's dad/widower

Edward Grant – Mayor of Basalt Bay/Judah's dad

Bess Grant – Judah's mom/Edward's wife

Aunt Callie – Paisley's aunt/Paul's sister

Maggie Thomas – owner of Beachside Inn

Bert Jensen – owner of Bert's Fish Shack

Mia Till – receptionist at C-MER

Craig Masters – Judah's supervisor at C-MER

Mike Linfield – Judah's boss at C-MER

Lucy Carmichael – Paisley's high school friend

Brian Corbin – Sheriff's deputy

Kathleen Baker – newcomer to Basalt Bay

Bill Sagle – pastor

Geoffrey Carnegie – postmaster/local historian

Casey Clemons – floral shop owner

Patty Lawton – hardware store owner

Brad Keifer – fisherman/school chum of Peter's

James Weston – Paul's neighbor

Sal Donovan – souvenir shop owner

Fred Buckley – council member

Sue Taylor – council member

Penny Cedars – Paisley's mom/deceased

One

On the day after her marriage to Forest Harper, Paige awoke at five o'clock in the morning and began painting the same as she did every other day. Just because a man lived in her house now didn't mean she must change her routine. Although, since he was asleep on the couch in the living room, she'd try being quiet. If her morning ritual awakened him, he'd have to adjust.

There were other things she must get used to—man stuff in her bathroom, a wet towel dripping from the shower rod, more dirty dishes piled in the sink. Although, he had loaded the dishwasher last night.

His snoring? Another adjustment. Even now, rumbling sounds emanating from the other room disrupted her artistic mood. How was she supposed to focus on paint colors with all that racket?

Another distraction she couldn't ignore was the way she kept mentally reliving Forest's kiss on her cheek last night. The way his lips lingered near her ear, and she didn't pull away. Didn't tell him to stop flirting and being affectionate with her.

Since they'd agreed to an in-name-only marriage, for the time being, she informed him that there could be no more kissing on the mouth. Forest gave her such a downcast, pouty-lipped expression that she almost relented. It wasn't like she didn't want to make out with the man. But, goodness, if they kept kissing like that, as they did after their wedding ceremony, things were going to get out of hand quickly. She couldn't let that happen. They had things to work through. Past issues to be addressed before any more lip-locking, thank you very much.

Forest insisted he was going to continue kissing her cheek and holding her hand like a dating couple might do. Her being the love-starved woman she was, she agreed. However, with the way her heart hammered when he brushed his lips teasingly across her cheek—and here she was still thinking about it the next morning—she might have to tell him no kissing her cheek, either. The man was too irresistible for her good.

She stroked her paintbrush across the canvas covered in varying shades of gray, highlighting the dips and crannies of Mountain Peak Rock, the biggest monolith near Basalt Bay. She blended Titanium White into the glob of gray she already mixed to lighten the hues along the eastern side of the rock where morning sunlight hit. Pleased with how the painting was coming along, she swished the brush counter-clockwise in her paint-speckled Mason jar of water just like her mother used to do.

She loved the memories she had of her mom while she painted. The way they used to work on easels side by side had been so much fun. She missed Mom. Would like the chance to tell her about Forest. About their second marriage. Although, her mother probably wouldn't have approved of her reckless decision to marry him three years ago, or yesterday.

Still, Paige felt justified in marrying Forest without telling anyone. They were adults. They could live how they pleased. Yet, she couldn't deny the twinge of misgiving she had about not telling her family. She wanted to be close with Dad, Paisley, and Aunt Callie. She hated to have another secret coming between them, especially one concerning her fake marriage.

Groan.

Was their marriage truly fake? She cared for Forest. Was insanely attracted to him. She feared she'd never gotten him out of her system since their first marriage. So her willingness to marry him quickly, this time, even if their excuses centered on protection and keeping gossiping neighbors pacified, had legitimate reasons, too.

Plus, Forest was Piper's dad. He deserved the chance to get to know his daughter. What better way for that to happen than for the three of them to live together under the same roof? Even if sharing space was awkward?

Sigh. Even then.

For the last few days, she'd been painting a series of, what she hoped would be, tourist favorites during her early-morning sessions. Yesterday, she finished one of Lookout Point Lighthouse where she hiked two weeks ago and took photographs. Another day, she planned to paint Basalt Bay Peninsula which would soon be getting a facelift. Maybe she'd do a before and after painting of the coastal centerpiece. Now, she must focus on this painting. What did the rock need? More shadowing? More—

A sound. What was that? Oh. The bathroom door closed. Nothing strange or fear-inducing about that. Only a man using her bathroom at six a.m.? Peculiar, indeed. And something else she had to get used to.

Today she planned to switch up the bedrooms. That way Forest didn't have to sleep on the couch—right in the next room from her painting area. She'd haul her stuff into Piper's room and use the uncomfortable futon for a bed. Forest could have her bedroom. Then they'd be more settled.

One happy family.

Right.

How long would this situation last, being almost married but not quite? Or how long would it take for her to cave and want to share her whole life, every part of her life, not just bits and pieces, with her husband?

She dipped a brush into Phthalo Blue and mixed it with white. Smoothed the bristles across the sky beyond the monolith.

Cool lips brushed against the back of her neck. She jerked forward. "Forest!" Goosebumps frolicked up her spine at the same time a splattering of paint flicked off the brush and speckled the canvas. "Oh, no!"

"Sorry. I didn't mean—"

"It's okay." Wetting the edge of a paper towel, she quickly dabbed at the paint smear.

"Can you fix it?" His throaty voice rumbled over her.

"Yeah, I can. This needed more shading anyway." She wet another paintbrush and dipped it into darker gray, blending the colors where the paint smudged.

Forest's fingertips swept back wisps of her hair that came loose from her ponytail holder. Ticklish sensations. More distractions.

"Something smells good in here."

"Coffee?" She didn't assume he meant she smelled good.

She stole a peek at him in his dark lounge pants and a white V-neck T-shirt. Blondish hair peeked out from the point of the V. Ugh. Why was she staring at the man's chest hairs like she wanted to run her fingers through them?

"That too." He winked then strode to the coffee machine.

Focus on painting. Ignore him.

Easier said than done.

After fixing a cup of black coffee, Forest leaned against the counter, sipping his hot drink. His hair poked up in messy strands. His drowsy, lazy expression made her want to shuffle over and nestle beneath his arm. Maybe straighten his hair with her fingers. Silly infatuations. The stuff of dreams and make-believe.

If they were to succeed at living together without intimacy, controlling how they behaved around each other was essential. She had to tame her thoughts. Not think of kissing him. The opposite of how she felt whenever she met his warm, compelling gaze. Her mouth went dry at the sultry look in his eyes, the slight raising of his eyebrows as if he were asking, *May I kiss you?*

Ever since Forest moved in yesterday, she found herself staring at him, disbelieving he'd be staying in her house permanently. That she married this gorgeous man for a second time was crazy. And delightful. Also, unnerving.

A hazy remembrance of them being together during their first honeymoon crossed her mind—more forbidden thoughts. The loving way he treated her. The joy she felt waking up in his arms. But maybe all that had been as fake as what they were experiencing now. Or maybe, what they were experiencing now was as real as what they had back then.

So confusing.

"What were you thinking about with such a furrowed brow?" he asked.

"Nothing."

He cleared his throat as if challenging her to be honest.

"Okay, I was pondering something, but I'm not ready to share."

"Fair enough." He sighed. "Whenever you are ready to talk, I'm here. Will always be here for you, baby."

Baby. She loved the deep timbre of his voice. The way he called her sweet endearments. If they fell in love, really in love, what would she call him? Babe? Darling? Tiger? She snickered and met his gaze again. She'd better be careful, or he'd want to know what she was thinking just then, too.

Forest's beautiful gray-green gaze seemed to pull her to him. In her imagination, she danced in the street with him. Danced and sang over the love of such a handsome man being hers and her being his.

She could lose herself in his gray-green depths for eternity. That's what she had to be wary of ... falling for him too fast like she did before. This time, she wanted to know the real man before taking their relationship further. Before diving into sweet splendor that might blind her to the truth, she'd be smarter and guard her heart.

She dropped her brush into the water jar, beginning the process of cleaning up her paint supplies. Piper wouldn't wake up for a while, but Paige's muse had vanished. *Thanks a lot, Forest.* Hopefully, his presence wouldn't inhibit her creativity every day. She couldn't afford that. She needed to get a lot of painting accomplished before the gallery's grand opening.

"Any plans for today?" Forest rinsed his coffee mug and set it in the dishwasher.

"Bess and I are meeting to discuss the gallery remodel."

"Oh? Where are you meeting?"

She bristled. She was too independent for him to have to know where she was all the time. But then she remembered his concern for her safety. Isn't that partially why she married him?

"We're doing a walk-through at the building."

"As the third partner in this venture, were you planning to invite me?" He didn't sound offended, just inquisitive.

"Not really. Sorry." Wasn't he more of a silent partner? While he contributed generously to the gallery, she didn't want to feel beholden to him. How involved in her business did he expect to be? "You can be there if you want. It's an informal meeting."

"Okay. Count me in."

She sighed. His being around a lot was something else she had to get used to. Although, it wasn't all bad. She liked his chivalrous side, even if he was acting paranoid. What could go wrong at the gallery?

Oh, right. Edward kidnapped Paisley from there. Thankfully, he was behind bars. However, the person who sent the threats to her and Forest might still be in town. Might still be dangerous.

"I have a mid-morning interview." Forest stroked both hands down his scruffy cheeks. "I'll meet up with you ladies afterward."

"All right. Don't forget about the family dinner tonight." She tucked a couple of paintbrushes into her case. "Then we'll tell the gang our news. Be forewarned, Aunt Callie will go ballistic."

"My parents won't be happy they didn't get invited to the wedding, either." Forest clasped her hands. "You're not worried about telling your family about us, are you?"

"Sort of." She withdrew her hands and busied herself with picking up the wet canvas. "I just went through the whole ordeal of telling them about you being Piper's dad. Now, this."

"I'll be right there with you." He gave her a sidearm hug. "Sorry that I disturbed your art time. It looks great, by the way." He nodded toward the canvas. "I'm going to clean up. Then I'll fix you breakfast."

"You can cook?"

"You bet." He winked at her. "For the record, you married a great cook!"

Well, well, well. The man was full of surprises. And his chest hairs, cute smile, and sparkling eyes were still way too appealing.

Two

Forest sat across from Mia Till in the interrogation room at the jail, working hard not to scowl at her. Was she so ditzy? Or was she as much of a con as Edward?

"You are too cute, Detective." Mia smoothed her fingers over his wrist. "I wish I found you before Paige did."

Groaning, he pulled his arms out of her reach. "Were you at the North Bend hospital on the day Edward Grant dragged Paisley out of the facility?"

Mia twirled a curl of her hair around her index finger. "Why do you keep asking me the same droll questions? How about asking what I enjoy doing in my spare time? Or if I have a boyfriend." Inching to the edge of her chair, her purple-lined eyes glistened at him. "Why don't you tell me about your secret marriage to Paige Cedars? The town's abuzz with the news."

"What? How did you—"

"You didn't imagine it could stay a secret, did you? Word is spreading like wildfire."

Townspeople were already gossiping about their marriage? Here Paige thought her family would be surprised when she told them at dinner tonight. Did someone see them at the courthouse in Florence yesterday? But he was getting sidetracked. Mia's plan, probably.

"Were you at the hospital that day?" He forced himself to speak in a monotone and not reveal his level of irritation with her.

"How did you convince Paige to marry you?" Mia batted her eyes at him, grinning. "You are quite the catch, Detective. Got any single brothers?"

"I do not," he said through clenched teeth. "Were you at the hospital on the day in question?"

Mia sighed moodily.

The enhanced footage of the security video still hadn't arrived from the regional office. The technician who texted Forest said it might not show up until tomorrow due to technical problems. That meant Forest didn't have concrete proof of Mia's presence at the hospital. He should have waited to question her, but he'd been eager to be done with this part of the investigation. At least he had the still-life shot he printed to show her.

"You're talking about the North Bend Shoreline Hospital, right?" She shrugged as if she didn't have a clue. "I've been there before."

"On the day in question?"

"I'll have to check my calendar, but I volunteer there sometimes."

"You volunteer in the same hospital where Paisley was recuperating?" Why didn't he know this before? Why hadn't

Deputy Brian said anything about Mia volunteering at the hospital?

"Don't look so surprised." She chuckled and jangled her bronze bracelets. "People volunteer at hospitals all the time. I have some nurse's training."

"You do?"

With nurse's training, Mia would have known how to remove an IV. Not that it took a neurosurgeon. But Forest had wondered how Edward knew how to remove Paisley's IV.

"Want to know the truth?" Mia leaned forward as if she were going to tell him a secret.

"Yes. As long as it has something to do with the case."

She bit her shiny lower lip between her upper and lower front teeth. "I volunteer at hospitals because I'm on the lookout for a hot wealthy bachelor." She giggled. "Know the type? Handsome. Physically strong but with a broken arm or some minor ailment. A man in need of a pretty nurse to take care of his needs." She skidded the toe of her shoe up Forest's shin.

"Enough!" He lunged backward, nearly falling off his chair. Good grief! In ten years of investigative work, he'd never had anyone flirt with him so persistently.

"Detective, you've got to lighten up."

He'd like to toss Mia into a jail cell until she recognized he was serious about finding out the truth about this case. His job was to discover if she was as involved in Paisley's kidnapping as Edward. And if not her, then who?

"Did you know Edward planned to abduct Paisley?"

"Planned?" Mia stared at a fingernail. "If I've learned anything from TV police shows, it's that I can't answer certain questions without a lawyer present."

"Are you asking for a lawyer, Miss Till?

"Do I need one?" she asked in a breathy voice. "Maybe you could recommend a handsome lawyer with a delicious six-pack. I do appreciate an educated man with love handles."

"Miss Till, do you want a lawyer called in, yes or no?"

"Am I under arrest?" She gave him a petulant grin. "If so, lock me in a cell with Craig, will you?"

"Just answer the question." He'd had enough of this exasperating session.

"You're cute when you get all flustered. What lovely eyes you have."

"Your flirtations won't work with me."

"No? Because you're a happily married man?"

"That's right." He swallowed. "I am."

"If I had a dollar for every time a man told me that, I'd be a rich woman."

Unbelievable. Maybe he should postpone this interrogation until the evidence arrived—or until further notice. Except, he still had the photo. And Mia didn't exactly request a lawyer. He pulled a page-sized printout of the woman dressed like a nurse and wearing a medical mask from the file. Eyeing Mia, he slid the photo across the table. "Are you the woman in this picture?"

She glanced at the sheet of paper and her face blanched. "If that's me, it's the worst picture I've ever taken. This lady's eyebrows are in desperate need of tweezing." She shuddered and turned away from the photo.

Interesting reaction. Forest grabbed the page and examined the picture. The woman's eyebrows were thick, while Mia's were—he peered at her—sculpted thin lines. How had he missed that detail?

"Do you know her?"

"I can't say." Mia twiddled with her fingernail.

"Who is she?"

"By her outdated attire, I'd say a hospital worker."

"When you volunteered at the North Bend Shoreline Hospital, did you see her? Have you two met before?"

"Can I see Edward now?" she asked in a whiny voice.

"No, he's in lockdown." Her requesting to see Edward made Forest more suspicious of her. "What does he have to do with this woman?"

Mia rolled her eyes. "Give it a rest, Detective."

"I can't do that. However, I can subpoena you for the answer. Hold you in contempt."

"You mean throw me in a cell with Craig? Make my day!" She nodded toward the photo. "For the record, that isn't me. Now, can I go?"

Forest sighed. The woman's eyebrows in the photo and Mia's didn't match, meaning this case wasn't nearly as wrapped up as he'd hoped. But what if Mia's current eyebrows were as artificial as her eyelashes?

He'd try one more question. "Were you in the storage room watching Edward haul Paisley down the hospital hallway?"

Mia's deep red lips pressed together. "If I were, I wouldn't admit it to you."

Bingo! Although not an admission of guilt.

"Are we done here? I have things to do." She stood, tugging on her shorty skirt.

"Fine." He didn't have grounds to detain her, yet. "Don't leave town."

"Whatever."

Forest strode to the door. Hopefully, this was the last time he had to question Mia Till. But somehow, he doubted it.

Three

After dropping Piper off at Dad's house, Paige let herself into the dark, damp gallery where she was going to meet Bess and Forest. She reached for the light switch and flicked it on. Water-stained walls, swollen floorboards, and broken, peeling Sheetrock greeted her. As did the salty scent of sea air coming through a gash in the plastic sheeting covering the window. So much work. So many needed repairs. Talk about overwhelming.

Bess had offered to help with the remodel. So did Forest and Judah. But with the guys helping with finishing the project house, their participation here might be slim. Forest still had to work on Edward's case. By his muffled phone conversations, something secretive was going on. Not that she'd been eavesdropping.

The creaking sounds in the old building sent chills skittering up her neck. So did thoughts of Paisley lying in this room for hours, tied up, hurting, and no one hearing her attempted screams. How afraid she must have been. Did she lie here listening to the howling wind? Fearing Edward might return at any second?

The front door screeched open. Paige whirled around, clutching her hands to her chest.

"Why, Paige, you look white as a sheet."

Mia Till. What did she want?

Paige lowered her hands, forcing her fists to unclench.

The C-MER receptionist sauntered across the gallery, her vintage go-go boots clicking on the bare flooring. The last time Paige saw Mia was outside this building five days ago. The troublemaker, as Paisley liked to call her, had threatened Paige. That's why every step the woman took created tension across Paige's neck and shoulders.

"Hello, Mia." She forced a fake polite tone. "Did you need something?" She stepped to the side of the window where Mia couldn't accidentally bump her into the drink. Not that she would, but Paige's imagination leaped ahead to seeing herself falling into the sea, hitting her head on a rock, dying. "*The sea will take its own.*" Mom's warning flickered through her thoughts.

Where was Forest? He was supposed to be here.

"I thought I'd stop by and check on Edward's building." Mia pushed her hands deeper into a warm-looking coat with faux fur around the collar. "You know the business type. Always wanting to hear about his investments."

"You mean Bess's investment, don't you?"

"Minor detail." Mia smirked. "By the way, congrats on the nuptials."

A strangled sound squawked out of Paige's throat. How did Mia know about their marriage?

"Aren't you the lucky girl for snagging a hottie like Forest?"

A hottie—? Paige coughed.

"Shame on you for telling me you didn't have a claim on him. Not that I blame you. He is yummy. I love his eye color. Don't you?" Mia met her gaze boldly, one eyebrow quirked. "It's quite unique. Just like your little girl's, hmm?"

Heat flooded Paige's face. Did Forest have an appointment with Mia this morning? Is that how she heard about their marriage? Surely, he wouldn't have told her anything about their nuptials, or about Piper.

"Don't look so shocked." Mia strolled to the window, gazing down toward the surf. "His grayish eyes were a dead giveaway."

Tension churning in Paige's stomach, she strode into the coffee shop, putting distance between her and Mia.

The woman's noisy boots clattered across the floor after her. "I have something to tell you from Edward."

"No thanks. I don't want to hear anything from him!" Her irritation with Mia emboldened her. "If that's why you're here, you might as well leave now."

Mia's eyes widened like she was surprised to hear Paige speak so confidently. "If you know what's good for you, you'll get out of this business deal with Bess."

"Listen here. Don't bring me warnings from Edward." Paige glowered at her. "I mean it."

"Just a little friendly advice is all."

"No, it isn't friendly. Besides, how are you speaking with him? Last I heard, he couldn't have visitors."

Chuckling, Mia smoothed her fingers over the countertop. "If you can't guess how I might be communicating with Eddie, or those he communicates with, you lack any imagination."

"Please, just leave. I don't have time for this."

"You don't have to get all—"

"Paige?" Bess bustled through the doorway, her large purse clutched against her chest. "Mia? What are you doing here?" Bess's scowl mirrored Paige's internal reaction to Mia.

"She's just leaving."

"You ladies are in way over your heads. If I were you, I'd back out of this partnership now!" Mia shook her flighty blond hair, then clomped her go-go boots out the door. "Toodles!"

"Good riddance." Paige groaned. "I'm so glad you arrived when you did."

"Where's Forest?" Bess set her handbag on the counter. "I expected him to be standing guard outside."

"Yeah, me too."

"What did Mia say? Are you all right?"

"She irritates me to high heaven, but I'm okay." Still, Paige's hands trembled as she rolled out the drawings she'd made of the gallery.

"I don't understand her involvement in Edward's life." Bess stared toward the plastic sheeting over the window.

"Any chance there's more to it?" Paige hated mentioning it.

"You mean like an affair?" Bess pivoted back toward her, frowning.

"Yeah. Sorry."

"If so, it wouldn't be his first." Bess made a guttural moan. "Let's forget about Mia and Edward, shall we? How are your plans coming along?" She gazed at the drawings, her frown transforming into a soft smile. "My, my. These are lovely, Paige."

"Thanks. I've enjoyed—"

The door screeched open again. She held her breath.

"Paige?"

Forest. Oh, good. She exhaled.

"We're over here," she called.

He strode to the counter. "Sorry I'm late."

"Mia was just here."

"What? She was—" He clenched his lips together.

No doubt, Mia was his interviewee this morning. Somehow, she'd figured out Paige and Forest got married and that Piper was his daughter. She was a troublemaker—Paisley was right about that.

"What did she want?"

"She warned me to get out of the building. 'Just friendly advice,'" Paige imitated Mia's voice.

"I can't believe it." Forest thrust his hand through his hair.

"Any chance we can set that aside?" Bess tapped her wristwatch. "I have another appointment in a few minutes."

"Sure, we can." Taking a deep breath, Paige focused on the pencil drawings she'd made of the gallery and coffee shop. "Here's what I'm picturing ..." She explained the changes she wanted to incorporate into the new design. The dark walls painted a lighter color. New flooring. Soft lamplight with various artist's nooks. Imagining tables in front of the coffee bar, and patrons sipping hot drinks and admiring all the art, she felt the old thrill of being back in the role of business owner.

Yet, as much as she tried, Mia's words troubled her. If Paige proceeded with the plans to open the gallery, supposedly against Edward's wishes, was something bad going to happen?

Four

That afternoon, Forest drove to the North Shoreline Hospital in North Bend, an hour from Basalt, to make inquiries concerning the photo. Unsure whether to leave Paige and Piper, he insisted that they stay at Paige's dad's until he returned. Mia's visit to the gallery seemed more of a nuisance than anything, but he could tell Paige was bothered by it. He didn't like it, either.

He had half a mind to escort Mia to the Florence jail—not to the Basalt Bay jail where Craig was—but on what charge? Giving unsubstantiated threats? Being a nuisance? She was that, and more.

How in the world was she corresponding with Edward when all visitation to the jail had been suspended? Was Deputy Brian sneaking her in? Was he passing mail between Mia and Edward?

Forest hated that Mia came to the gallery when he wasn't there. What had it been, fifteen minutes, between the time she left the interrogation room and when he arrived? He had to be more careful. Stay closer to Paige. Yet here he was driving an hour out of town. He groaned.

Hopefully, this quick trip to speak with Doctor Clark yielded answers about who assisted Edward in kidnapping Paisley. He was frustrated that he hadn't solved the case yet. Frustrated, too, that he couldn't keep watch on Paige and Piper around the clock. He could have brought them on this drive, but hanging out in the hospital waiting room with a two-year-old wouldn't have worked well for Paige.

Besides, she had dinner preparations to complete for tonight. As a compromise, he helped her haul all the ingredients to her dad's house so she could work on the meal and bake pies there. He also left her with instructions not to answer the door, even if someone she trusted came to Paul's house.

She'd mockingly said, "Yes, Detective," to each of the things he told her.

He chuckled about that now. At the time, he didn't see anything funny about it.

When he reached the hospital, a helpful young nurse led him down a long hallway to an employees' lounge. Entering the space with small tables in the center and a comfortable-looking leather sofa along the back wall, she directed him to a dark-haired man seated at a table eating a sandwich.

"Doctor Clark," she said, "this is Detective Harper. He'd like to speak with you. Says he has an appointment."

"Mmm. Yes." The doctor gulped down water from a disposable cup, then shook Forest's hand. "Sorry. Please, have a seat."

"Thank you." Forest sat down, nodding his thanks to the nurse before she walked away. "I appreciate your taking the time to talk with me."

"You said Paisley Grant is your sister-in-law?" Doctor Clark wiped his mouth with a napkin.

"That's right." Forest didn't mention that he married Paige only yesterday. "I'm the detective on Edward Grant's case. I have a couple of questions to ask you."

"Sure. Didn't we speak before?"

"Yes, on the telephone."

"I have to warn you, I don't have long. I could be paged at any moment." The doctor swayed his hand toward his sandwich. "Do you mind?"

"Not at all. Finish your lunch. I'm sorry for this intrusion into your busy schedule."

"A couple of emergencies are keeping me hopping." Doctor Clark clutched his sandwich. "If I don't eat now, I'll miss my chance."

"I understand." Sometimes Forest had to eat on the run in between interrogations or chasing down leads, too. He pulled out the print he showed Mia earlier and pushed it across the table. "Do you recognize this woman?"

The physician chewed his food and eyed the photo.

"Sorry it's blurry."

"Is she involved in the case?"

"I can't say for certain. The time stamp on the hospital security video has her in the storage room at the same time Edward dragged Paisley out."

"She looks familiar." The doctor glanced up at the ceiling as if thinking. "We have quite a few nurses and volunteers rotating between various smaller hospitals along the coast. Keeping them all straight is challenging."

"I bet." Forest waited while the man dressed in a white lab coat ate his food in between glancing at the photo.

"I recognize her but can't place her name." The doctor tapped the table with his knuckles. "She's a volunteer. Reads mail or books to the residents, assists with walks, gets supplies from the gift shop, that sort of thing. Kind of like a candy striper, only older."

"Older?"

"Mid-fifties, I'd say."

"Huh." Forest picked up the photo and peered at the woman's face above the mask, trying to imagine her older than Mia. No wrinkles or age marks. No gray hair. There were those thicker eyebrows, something Mia didn't have. "Her name? Anything ring a bell?"

"No. I'm sorry."

Forest had a photocopy of Mia's driver's license photo too. Pulling it out, he pushed it across the table. "What about this woman? Do you recognize her?"

Doctor Clark burst out laughing. "That's Mia. Who wouldn't recognize her?"

"You know her?" Forest didn't try to cover his flabbergasted tone.

"Every man on staff probably knows her." Doctor Clark shook his head in mirth. "She's, how shall I say, someone who brightens our workday with wit and charm. Harmless flirtations, you understand."

"Uh-huh." Forest eyed the other man, who wore a wedding ring, skeptically.

"She volunteers here, once a month or so."

"Could these photos be of the same woman?"

"Not a chance." Doctor Clark wiped his mouth with his napkin. "I just remembered. The older woman's name is Evie. She's quiet but pleasant." He tapped Mia's photo. "Effervescent, late twenties, blond beauty." He sighed like his thoughts were transported to another time and place. "Huge difference between these two."

"Thanks. That helps a lot." Forest scooped up the photos.

"Doctor Clark is needed in Bay Four," a woman's voice boomed over the intercom.

"Duty calls." The doctor jumped up, quickly cleaning his eating area and tossing paper products into the garbage. "Go by the admin desk and inquire about Evie's last name. Tell them I sent you." He jogged out of the break room.

"Thanks, again!"

It took some maneuvering, but Forest found the receptionist's desk where he first entered the building and asked for directions to the administration area. Eventually, he stood in front of a dour-looking white-haired woman with the name "Glenda" on her nametag.

"Whom do you wish to see?" she asked in a tight clip.

"Can you tell me the last name of one of your volunteers?"

"We can't give out that private information."

Something about her stern features reminded him of his second-grade teacher.

"Sorry for not mentioning this sooner." Forest whipped out his badge. "I'm Detective Harper with Sheriff Morris's task force. I have investigative authority to pursue all leads in an ongoing case."

Glenda examined his badge as if it might be fake. "We'll see about that. Who sent you?"

"Doctor Clark."

"Wait right here." She pointed to the floor. "Don't move an inch."

"Yes, ma'am."

Huffily, she exited a door behind her. Forest stood in the spot the woman ordered him to, barely moving a muscle.

A few minutes later, Glenda returned, still eyeing him suspiciously. "Your story checks out, Detective. Who did you say you're looking for?"

He pulled out the photo. "This woman. I need her last name."

The receptionist stared at the sheet. "How am I supposed to tell who this is?"

"It is blurry, but Doctor Clark thought her name might be Evie."

"A lot of good that does." Glenda sat down, her fingers tapping across the keypad. "Hmm. We do have one volunteer named Evie."

"Okay." Forest gave her the date. "Can you check if she volunteered on this day?"

"Let me see." She tapped a few more keys.

Forest itched to get back on the road, back to Paige. At least this trip hadn't been a waste of time. He had confirmed proof that the woman in the photo wasn't Mia. However, Doctor Clark's validation of the photo being Evie, whoever she was, and not Mia, was a little disappointing. Even with the whole eyebrow difference, Forest hadn't been convinced that it wasn't her. Not that he wanted the C-MER receptionist to be guilty of accessory to kidnapping. But her suspicious behavior, innuendos and threats toward Judah and Paisley, even Paige, made her seem embroiled in the crime.

Glenda wrote down something, then aimed her gaze at Forest. "I'm giving you this woman's name only because you're an officer of the law."

"Yes, ma'am."

She clutched the edge of the paper between her fingers and thumb, not letting go when he tried taking it. "Don't you dare bring shame or disrespect to our facility."

"No, ma'am. I wouldn't think of it."

"Good day, then." She released the paper and clicked the mouse, closing the screen and abruptly ending their conversation.

Forest glanced down at the name on the paper—Evie Masters.

Masters? Was she any relation to Craig?

Five

Nervous about the evening's gathering, Paige set out the meal she'd prepared buffet style on the kitchen table. Too cold to eat outdoors, this was the easiest way to feed the family, although it would be close quarters.

It had been challenging to fix all the food at Dad's house, then when Forest picked her up, they had to maneuver a big pot of potatoes, a roasting pan, several side dishes, and two cherry pies into the car. Only one mishap took place when Forest spilled carrot juice all over the front of his clothes. A buttery, sticky mess. His shocked expression was priceless. If only she'd had her camera handy then.

At some point after everyone had their plates filled and were seated in the living room, she and Forest would explain about their impromptu wedding. Hopefully, no one would get upset or have their feelings hurt. Aunt Callie's possible reaction caused Paige the most concern. The woman could make a snake squirm into submission with one of her intense stares.

Fortunately, the slow-cooked roast, carrots, potatoes, and cherry pies turned out lovely. The brown gravy smelled divine. Maybe the wonderful scents wafting through the house would soften her aunt's outrage.

Paisley and Judah were the first to arrive. As soon as her sister crossed the threshold, Paisley grabbed Paige by the wrist and tugged her into the kitchen. Piper's squeals for "Unca Dzuda" nearly overrode Paisley's whispers.

"What's this I hear about you marrying Forest?" Her eyes bulged. "Is it true? Is that why you invited us over? Paige, did you marry the man again? Everyone at the diner's talking about it."

"Everyone?" Groan. Forest told her someone—and she could guess which someone—mentioned knowing about their marriage. Paige hated being the center of gossip. Here she married him hoping to avert such talk. Had Aunt Callie already heard the news too?

"Is it true?" Paisley asked again.

"I—" Paige blew out a breath. "Look, I'm sorry. Just give me a few minutes, okay? I'll explain everything to the whole family, I promise." She hugged her sister. "Don't be mad at me, please. Listen to what I have to say with an open heart and mind."

"I'll try." Paisley gave her a long look. "You still love him, don't you? I mean, that's what matters. You love each other, right?"

Paige almost agreed, then clenched her jaw. "I'll explain everything. Now, I have to greet the other guests." She rushed past her sister and went back into the living room. Would the whole family be asking questions as Paisley did? Would they

36

put her and Forest on the spot, demanding to know if they loved each other? Goodness. What was she supposed to say to that question?

She and Forest had made the decision to marry quickly. Whether they loved each other was their business, no one else's. Paige wanted her family's understanding and support. Surely, Paisley's question was born of curiosity and concern for her younger sister's welfare. But being cornered like that? No thanks.

Bess, Aunt Callie, and Kathleen entered the front door, and Paige's living room felt tiny. Hopefully, everyone would fit once they were seated.

"Aunt Callie!" She greeted her aunt, unsure if she should hug her or beg for her forgiveness.

"Paige." Aunt Callie slipped out of her coat and handed it to her. A narrowing of her eyes sent a warning. Had she heard the rumors? But then, she sniffed. "Something smells fantastic."

"Oh, good." Saved by the meaty scent of roast beef.

"It certainly does." Bess smiled. "Thank you for inviting us."

"Of course."

"I hope you don't mind my tagging along," Kathleen said in a soft melodic voice. "I'm the fifth wheel of the party."

"Nonsense." Bess patted her arm. "You're family now."

"That's right." Paige hugged the older woman who always seemed to have a kind word and a smile. "You're welcome to all our family dinners from here on out."

"Thank you, dear."

Forest helped take all the coats back to Piper's room. When he reentered the living room, he carried a couple of children's books. He must plan to distract their daughter with those. *Good job, Forest.* His sharing childcare tasks with her was a perk of their marriage. If only she could convince her family of that.

As everyone settled on the couch, recliner, and extra kitchen chairs Forest had placed around the room, they chatted and awaited Dad's arrival. Paige checked her phone. No calls or texts.

"What's keeping Dad?" Paisley whispered.

"I'm wondering the same thing." While Paige spent the afternoon with him, preparing the food, she'd kept quiet about tonight's announcement. Hopefully, since then, some neighbor hadn't yacked in his ear about her elopement. How did people even find out?

A knock sounded at the door, and she scurried across the room to answer.

Dad stood on the porch, arms crossed, a wary expression on his face. "Callie here?"

"Yes, she is. Come in, Dad."

He scowled and didn't budge. "Is this your idea of some lock-us-up-in-the-same-room-and-talk therapy session?" He whisked off his hat and wiped the back of his hand over his forehead. "Cause if it is, I'm heading back home."

"Oh, Dad." Paige hugged him. "Come in and eat with us, okay? This isn't a plot to get you and Aunt Callie to work out your differences. I have news to share with you and the family. That's why I invited you all over." She linked her arm with his. "Although Callie is your sister. I think you should sit down and talk with her."

"That'll be the day," he said grumpily with a John Wayne inflection. He shuffled into the crowded room and plopped down in a chair farthest from Aunt Callie's. Piper, sitting in her uncle's lap, leaned toward her grandpa, chattering something to him. His answering smile probably meant he'd stay a while.

Getting eight adults through the food line turned into a major production. Eventually, everyone had full plates in their hands. Paige and Forest worked together to fill drinks—tea, coffee, water, or soda. Again, she was thankful for his assistance.

They even got to sit down and take a few bites. Piper tried some finger foods from Paige's plate before settling in on Judah's lap again.

When a solemn quietness filled the room, and gazes were aimed toward her, Paige knew she couldn't put off her announcement another minute. Setting her partially empty plate on the coffee table, she stood. Forest jumped up beside her, taking her hand in his. The simple gesture had a calming effect on her.

They'd agreed not to tell the family about this being a fake marriage, since Forest insisted it wasn't. Someday they might look back and even chuckle at the idea of a marriage of convenience. Right now, it wasn't trite or funny to her. More like survival.

"Everyone, if we could have your attention," Forest said. "Paige and I have something to tell you."

"We're all ears." Aunt Callie glared at him as if questioning why he presumed to direct this meeting.

"Go ahead, baby." He let go of her hand and set his palm on the small of her back. "Tell them our happy news."

Was he grinning for her family's benefit? Or was he truly excited about having married her again?

"I want to thank all of you for standing by me these last few years while I've been a single mom. For being here when I needed help with Piper." Paige nodded toward her dad, remembering times when he watched her daughter on the spur of the moment, and toward Judah, the go-to brother-in-law who'd often come to her rescue. "As most of you know, I didn't contact Forest about Piper being born. I regret that now." She leaned into him a little. "I've explained and apologized to him, and to some of you." A wad of emotion clogged her throat.

Forest's hand smoothed across her back.

"With the threats recently made against me, and Forest too, we thought it might be best ... that is, right for us ... to, um, go ahead and ... just get married again." A nervous laugh burst out of her. "Why wait, right?"

"What?" Dad asked gruffly.

Aunt Callie made a howling noise. "Lord, have mercy on us all!"

"We chose to do it without fanfare," Paige spoke fast. "This way Forest can stay here in the house and protect Piper and me until whoever is doing the wrong stuff against us gets caught." She took a breath. "And he'll have the chance to know his daughter like he didn't get to before."

Everyone gaped at her, eyes wide.

"He's been a great help with Piper and stuff around the house. So, yeah, we're married. Surprise!" She held up her ring finger with her previous wedding ring on it.

No one clapped or cheered. A couple of hushed comments—"Wow." "Huh." "Didn't guess that"—reached her.

She met Forest's gaze. What now?

"Sounds more like a business arrangement." Aunt Callie harrumphed. "After all the uncertainty ends, are you going to split up again?"

"No, of course not!" Paige's face flamed hot. Although hadn't she contemplated that herself? Once the tension and worry over the possibility of criminal misbehavior passed, would Forest stick around? Might he even find the enticement of potential danger alluring? When their lives returned to dull and boring, would he stay with her?

Forest drew her against his side, his arm draped over her shoulder. "I can assure you, Callie, I love your niece. I'm going to be married to her for the rest of my life."

His tender tone and promise brought tears to Paige's eyes. She blinked fast to absorb them. Didn't want Aunt Callie seeing her being emotional.

"Then why didn't you have the decency to have a proper ceremony where your family could attend?" Aunt Callie's cheeks puffed out like a raccoon with its mouth filled. "Why go behind our backs, again?"

Paige tugged on Forest's hand before he tried going up against her aunt. "Auntie, we made a decision for us—me, Forest, and Piper. I'm sorry if you don't like it, but this is what we've chosen to do. We're legally married with all the 'I dos.' Like before, it happened quickly."

Forest gulped noisily.

"We invited all of you here to share in our good news." She forced a smile. "I understand your concerns, but please, just be happy for us."

"Maggie said she heard some nonsense about you two getting hitched. I told her she was dead wrong. My niece would not make such a dreadful choice again." Aunt Callie groaned. "Now, I'll have to apologize. Turns my stomach." She glared at Dad. "Aren't you going to say anything, Pauly? Or are you going to sit there like a lump on a log like usual?"

Why did Aunt Callie have to badger Dad like that?

"You happy w-with this d-decision?" He asked in a choking voice. "You and your sister seem to like doing things in secret."

"Dad—" Paisley objected.

"I'm sorry," Paige said. Although, he was right. She and Paisley did like doing things without an audience, and yes, secretively, sometimes. She'd married Forest privately, twice. However, Dad had walked Paisley down the beach for her vow renewal.

"I'm asking, and not because my sister can't keep her thoughts to herself, are you happy with this decision to marry him?" Dad eyed Forest disapprovingly. He pulled a hand-kerchief out of his jeans pocket and wiped his nose. "You and Piper being safe and happy are all I care about. The rest"—he eyed Forest again—"I'll adjust to."

Forest shuffled back and forth on his loafers.

Paige couldn't lie to her dad and tell him she and Forest were blissfully happy. But no one forced her into this arrangement. She took the marital plunge of her own free will. She was thankful Forest was here with her now. A great dad for Piper. A great husband to her, too, if she'd let him.

Was she stopping him from being a great husband? Keeping him at arm's length? Expecting him to apologize for something he might not even know he did?

She took a deep breath. "I'm happy, Dad. Being assured of Piper's safety is a huge burden off my shoulders. Forest being here at night makes me feel like no one can hurt us. His presence is comforting and safe." She didn't mention they were sleeping in separate rooms. Or that, with Forest preoccupied with his case, she had an unfortunate visit from Mia.

"Maybe we could have a reception and recite our vows so you all can be a part of that." Forest linked his fingers with hers. "I want you to meet my parents and my sister, Teal. They are eager to meet their granddaughter, too."

"Sounds nice," Dad said, stuffing his handkerchief back in his pocket.

"I, for one, don't appreciate being kept out of the loop." Aunt Callie's voice deepened. "I didn't get to attend Paisley and Judah's marriage or remarriage. Now, Paige has gotten married for a second time without letting me witness the happy event."

Bess patted her shoulder.

"I'm sorry, Auntie," Paige said. "I didn't mean to leave you out. It just happened."

Piper slid off Judah's lap and thudded onto the floor with a scream, then sobs. Paige moved toward her, but Forest scooped her up first.

Cuddling Piper, he took her out of the room and down the hallway. "There, there, princess. It's okay."

Piper's wailing lessened.

Paige sighed.

Murmurs of sympathy, and maybe a little admiration for him promptly taking care of her, spread across the room.

Paisley stood and gave Paige a hug. "I'm happy for you and Forest. Really, I am."

"Thank you."

Judah hugged Paige, too. "Sorry for letting Piper go too soon."

"That's okay. She has a mind of her own."

"Congrats on marrying Forest. He'll make a great husband for you."

She met his gaze. "Thank you, Judah. Your opinion means a lot to me."

The older ladies transitioned back to eating, although Aunt Callie kept casting mournful glances in Paige's direction.

Paige fixed Piper a bowl of finger foods and let her sit on the floor by the coffee table once Forest got her settled. Then, together, they served slices of cherry pie with whipped cream to their guests.

No other comments were made about their marriage announcement. Maybe the group was already accepting their explanation and, hopefully, accepting Forest as part of the family.

"Sorry that didn't go better," he said after everyone had left and he put Piper to bed.

"I figured Aunt Callie would be a pill." Paige deposited the last of the dirty silverware into the dishwasher. "I wasn't wrong."

"She's a formidable character."

Forest gently drew Paige into his arms. She should have pushed away or thought of something anti-romantic to say. Too tired to object, she fit in his arms just right.

He tipped up her chin, their gazes tangling. This wasn't supposed to be happening. What about her no-kissing rule? *Walk away. Don't kiss him.* Not heeding her advice, she gazed into his green eyes a little too long, getting lost in their sparkling dark hue.

"May I kiss you, baby?" His warm gaze begged her to look beyond the rules and the hurts of the past. To trust him. To let them have this moment of tenderness they both probably needed after that family ordeal.

Did she nod? She must have since his lips landed softly over hers, tasting of mint and coffee. She kissed him back much too fervently for her to have said, "No." Their passion heated up. His lips brushing over hers was intoxicating. Breathtaking.

Then, realizing how easy it would be for one thing to lead to another, and since she wasn't ready to take the next step with him, she shuffled backward. "I, um"—she cleared her throat—"need to finish cleaning the living room, putting the chairs back."

"Right. I can help with that." He seemed breathless too. "And … thank you."

"For—?"

"For kissing me back." Grinning, he winked at her.

Despite her fatigue and just having given into kissing him when she'd been so determined not to, she chuckled. She did kiss him back. And she liked it immensely.

Six

A loud crash like shattering glass awoke Paige from a deep sleep. Heart thundering in her ears, she sprang up, peering into the darkness, trying to get her bearings. What was that? Did someone break into the house?

"Stay put, Paige," Forest said gruffly from outside her closed door.

Stay put? Not likely. She slipped into her robe then held up her cell phone light to check on Piper. Her daughter was snoozing soundly in her toddler bed.

Paige stepped into her slippers, tightened her robe around her waist, and opened the door cautiously. Still shining her cell flashlight, she crept into the living room. Cold air pulsed over her.

"Forest?"

"Over here."

She pointed her cell light toward the curtains on the other side of the room. He flinched, caught in the beam.

"Sorry." She tipped the phone away from him. "What's going on?"

"Stay back."

His cell light came on, aimed at the carpet. He bent over and picked up a rock big enough to fill his hand.

"What happened?"

Still groggy from sleep, she tried to assimilate what happened. A loud crash. Forest told her to stay put. Now he clutched a six-inch stone. Someone must have hurled it through her window. How terrible!

"There's glass all over this side of the carpet," he said hoarsely, shining his cell light in a zig-zag pattern across the floor. "Window's busted."

"Who would do such a thing?" She stared at the glass-littered carpet, the drapes pulled back, then at him, bare-chested and wearing only pajama bottoms.

"This happened too." He lifted his right foot. Blood dripped from beneath his toes.

"Oh, Forest!" She started toward him.

"Don't come over here. I made the mistake of running into the room without checking the conditions." Taking a couple of hobbled steps, he grimaced. "I thought I'd catch someone in here in the dark."

"What can I do?" She wanted to ease the pained expression on his face.

"Got a first aid kit?"

"Uh-huh."

"I'll make my way across the room. Might take a minute."

"Okay. I'll grab the kit." She backed up. "How bad is the window?"

He pulled the long drape away from the glass, revealing a hand-sized hole where the rock went through. "The curtain kept the glass somewhat contained." He took a step and moaned.

"I'm sorry you got hurt." Paige switched on an overhead light. "That should help you see better. I'll grab a washcloth and meet you in the kitchen." She dashed into the bathroom.

By the time she returned with the first aid kit and a washcloth, Forest sat at the table, his leg crossed over his knee, his foot lifted. She ignored the sight of his bare chest and went straight to the sink and ran warm water over the cloth. Grasping a roll of paper towels, she rushed back to him. Then knelt and gently cleaned the blood around his toes.

He sucked in a sharp breath. "Wait. I—"

"Does it hurt?" She smoothed her hand over his wrist. "Of course, it hurts. Sorry, Forest."

"I think there's still glass shards in a cut or two."

"Oh, no." She lifted his foot a bit higher and bent lower to check the bottom of his foot. It was still bleeding, but not as badly as before. "Shall I pull out the glass? The cuts don't look deep enough to warrant stitches. Hard to tell for sure."

"Do what you can. I need to be able to walk. I'll grit my teeth. Just be fast."

Using tweezers from the first aid kit and shining her cell light at the bottom of his foot, she grabbed hold of the offending glass pieces—three slivers by her count—and pulled them out one by one. Each time, Forest gasped.

"Sorry. I'm so sorry," she said after each extraction. When she couldn't find any more shards, she sank back on her heels. "I hope I got them all. How does that feel?"

"Not great. But better." He wiped his arm across his sweaty forehead.

"I'm sorry this happened." She patted his pajama-clad knee. "What shall I do next?"

"Maybe put one of those wide bandages on it and wrap it a little."

"Okay." She pressed a few paper towels against the lower part of his foot. After applying antiseptic gel on the cuts, she placed a couple of square gauze pads against his skin and adhered it with paper tape. Each time she did something with his foot, he grimaced. "How's that?"

"Better. Thanks." He flexed his foot and made a face.

"Can I get you anything? Soda? Aspirin?" She picked up the paper towels and bandage wrappings and tossed them in the garbage. Then washed her hands.

"Maybe I'll take something before I go back to sleep." He tapped his finger against the rock on the table. "We should take a look at this note, also."

"Why would someone bust my window to send a message? Haven't they heard of the Post Office?" She dropped into the chair next to Forest's and found herself staring at his chest. This wasn't the time for her to be entertaining romantic ideas about her husband, even if she still felt a little gaga toward him after that kiss they shared a few hours ago.

"Maybe I'll take an aspirin now, if you don't mind." Forest winced.

"Oh, right." She jumped up, glad for a task, and rummaged around on the high shelf where she kept vitamins and over-the-counter medicines. Finding a small bottle of aspirin, she set it on the table. Then poured him a glass of water.

"Thanks." He opened the bottle and popped two pills into his mouth. Gulped the glass dry. "Thanks, baby. You make a cute nurse."

Hearing him call her an endearment, even during his own pain, struck a tender nerve. He was such a nice man. And she was so attracted to him. Sitting back down, she tugged the belt tighter around her robe.

Forest gazed at her as if watching her every move, then he peeled the duct tape off the rock. The paper stuck to the tape and tore. Groaning, he smoothed out the sheet. "I shouldn't have done that."

"What?"

"I'm not thinking straight. I manhandled the rock and the paper when there might have been fingerprints on them." He sighed. "Will you read it?"

"Sure. 'I watched your shindig tonight.' What?" Her jaw dropped. She met Forest's equally flabbergasted expression. "Someone stood outside my house watching us?"

"Apparently." A gray shadow crossed his face.

"My house" replayed in her mind. She should have said, "our house." Should probably correct her mistake.

Forest tapped the paper.

"Right. 'Nice family,'" she continued reading. "'Cute kid.'" Paige clutched the paper and shook it in front of Forest. "I can't believe whoever wrote this would comment on Piper. That's creepy and makes me mad!"

"Me too. He's just trying to scare us."

"You think it was a man?"

"I'm not sure." Forest stared at her intently.

What wasn't he telling her? "Who do you think it was?"

"I can't say. I mean, I don't know."

She focused on the page again. "'Watch what you're doing, Detective. Or all of Basalt Bay will hear about your mistakes.' What mistakes? Does he mean our elopement?"

"Who knows?" Forest leaned his forehead against his fists with his elbows resting against the table. "We should get some sleep. Deal with this tomorrow. I'm zonked."

"But the window is busted. Glass is—"

"I'll clean it up and report it in the morning."

"I think I'd better tape a chunk of cardboard over the hole." Thoughts of bugs flying inside the house creeped her out. Or what if the rock-thrower came back and tossed something else through the empty space? Dynamite, maybe?

"I can help with that." Forest pushed away from the table.

"Stay put and rest. I'll do it."

Sighing, he sat back down. "Let me clean up the glass in the morning, okay?"

"Fine."

"Be careful around the broken glass."

"Yes, Detective," she said in a teasing tone, trying to bring some lightness to the mood.

She grabbed duct tape from a pantry shelf and cardboard from the living room closet. Ten minutes later, she'd secured a square of cardboard over the hole to her satisfaction. No bugs, dynamite, or anything else was invading her house tonight.

When she reentered the kitchen, Forest stared at her with dull, tired-looking eyes. Maybe the aspirin was kicking in. Or he might be in shock.

"You should go to bed," she said.

"I doubt anyone will return tonight, but I'm going to sleep on the couch, just in case."

"Would you hear anything? You'll probably fall right to sleep." Should she keep watch in case he didn't hear something?

"If anyone does anything, believe me, I'll hear it."

"Okay." Still, she doubted his ability to respond quickly in his condition.

Forest stood, moaning as he put weight on his injured foot.

"Let me help." She got under his arm and wrapped her arm around his bare back.

After getting him settled on the couch, she ran to the master bedroom and grabbed a blanket off the bed. Spreading the fabric over his shoulders, she whispered, "Sleep well, Forest."

But he was already snoring.

Seven

Forest opened his eyes and squinted into the semi-lit room. Where was he? Oh, right. On Paige's couch. There she was, curled up in the recliner kitty-corner from him, her dark hair covering part of her face, looking sweet and beautiful. Was she watching over him through the night? The thought of her caring for him that much tugged on his heart. Even if she couldn't say "I love you" to him yet, this was her way of showing him she did, wasn't it?

He shifted his foot. Groaned. Thanks to tender toes he'd be hobbling today. But that wouldn't stop him from working on the case. He needed to figure out who did the vandalism with the rock and sent the note, too. Was Mia carrying out Edward's schemes? Or Evie Masters? Did she hear about him asking questions at the hospital? Was she retaliating by threatening him?

He had a job to do. But first, his sore foot needed relief.

Maybe a crutch. No, he'd get by with limping and some aspirin. And loads of coffee.

He pushed up from the cushions, stifling his moan, and shuffled into the bathroom. After washing his face with hot water, he retrieved his T-shirt from the bedroom and returned to the kitchen.

Something seemed odd. Too quiet. Oh. Didn't Paige usually paint every morning before Piper woke up?

He put the breakfast-blend pod into the coffee machine, eager for his morning brew.

"Hey."

He turned at Paige's soft voice. "Good morning."

"How'd you sleep?" She tightened her robe belt around her waist which only made it appear more form-fitting.

His mouth dry, he glanced away, focusing on his mostly-filled coffee cup. "Okay as can be expected."

Yawning, she sauntered across the room and stood next to him. He wanted to pull her into his arms and kiss her like he did last night. But staring into her dark gaze, her dressed in her robe, he'd wish for more than kisses, even with his injured foot. He stayed by the sink and took a couple sips of hot coffee. "You okay?"

She nodded and shrugged.

"I'm surprised you weren't in here painting this morning."

"Yeah." She glanced at the wall clock. "Rough night. I slept through my session."

"Want some coffee?"

"Yes, please."

He pulled down another cup and prepped it. Paige grabbed the creamer out of the fridge. He let her fix her cup, observing her preference—one overflowing tablespoon of creamer.

She sipped her drink and made purring sounds of contentment. "Thanks. I needed this."

"Me too."

"How's the wound?"

"Sore." He wouldn't lie, but he wouldn't play on her sympathy, either. "I'll rebandage it after my shower. It'll be fine." Well, sort of fine.

"I'll help with the bandage if you want." She glanced at him almost shyly. "I should check for glass particles in better lighting."

"I think it's all right. I can walk on it. Just tender."

"Okay. If you're sure."

They finished their coffees in silence. Although his thoughts were abuzz with worries about the vandalism, he liked them starting their day together like this, like a real couple.

"What now?" Paige asked. "Should we call the deputy about the rock and the warning?"

"When I go over to the station, I'll fill him in." He rinsed out his cup and set it in the dishwasher. "I'll clean up the glass and have a look in the living room, then take a shower." He cleared his throat, mentally framing how to best say what needed to be said. "The note still troubles me."

"Someone smashing my front window riles me. What did the note even mean?"

He couldn't tell her his suspicions about Mia or Evie.

"I'm not sure." Shuffling across the kitchen, he minimized his need to limp by walking on his heels. "However, I may have invited more trouble by moving in with you." He paused at the doorway. "Here I was wanting to protect you and keep you safe by marrying you and living with you."

"What are you saying?" She crossed her arms over her middle.

"I think I need to talk to some of my old coworkers. Get to the bottom of the insinuations."

"Your coworkers in Portland? You're going to leave?" Her voice swelled.

The argument they had before they split up three years ago, and Paige's strong reaction then, flared up in his thoughts. Maybe he should put a few more feet between them in case she started throwing things. But then, a sad look crossed her face. She was obviously distressed by the idea of his going.

"Hey, I didn't mean leaving, leaving." He sighed. "I'd never do that. Only, if it meant protecting you and Piper better, I might have to go away for a couple of days."

"I thought you were going to be here for us." She swallowed hard. "Someone threatens us, and you're just going to take off again?"

"Again" coursed a hot track from his brain to the pit of his stomach.

"Not like that. I'd ask Deputy Brian to watch the house. Or you could stay with Judah and Paisley." He pressed the back of his fist against his forehead. Why did he even mention leaving? "Edward might be trying to blackmail me. I must figure it out before anything else happens. Surely, you understand—"

"Of course." Her cool tone indicated she didn't see at all.

"I won't go if you hate the idea." He probably needed to take a couple more aspirin to stop the throbbing not only in his foot but behind his eyeballs.

"Do what you have to do." She lifted her chin. "I'll clean up the glass before Piper wakes up. I'll call a glass installer, too."

"I said I'd do it."

"Don't worry about it." She left the room, muttering, "It's better if I don't count on anyone else."

Of course, she meant him. His groan felt dredged from the bottom of his ribs.

Eight

Forest hobbled into the deputy's office. Man. He stuck his foot in his mouth back at the house. Going up to his office in Portland had seemed like the right thing to do for the case and his career, but it brought out such a strong reaction in his wife, he'd rethink that idea before bringing it up again.

Wife in name only, pulsed through his thoughts.

Not in name only! He loved Paige. Being with her for the rest of his life was his whole plan. No Plan B. He was one-hundred-percent committed to her and their marriage. Yes, he spoke about going away, which must have plunged her back into thinking the worst about him.

Lord, please help us through this mess. Help Paige to trust me. Help me to be more sensitive to her needs, too.

Limping, he went straight to the computer station he'd been using on the far side of the room. After plopping down on the chair and logging into the server, he checked his emails. Oh, good. Something had arrived from tech support, finally.

Before he got a chance to read the email, Deputy Brian entered the office from the door leading to the two jail cells.

"Detective. What brings you here so early?"

"Problems," Forest said grumpily. Yeah, he felt grouchy. His foot hurt. He had a bad night's sleep. And he left the house without working things out with Paige.

"Marital bliss not going well?" Brian guffawed and strode to the coffee pot. He poured a cup of the thick, nasty-looking black brew he usually made.

"It's not that."

"So, you and Paige tied the knot in secret, huh?"

Here was one more person who'd heard through the grapevine about his and Paige's marriage.

"Yeah, we did." No reason to hide it now.

Pushing up from his seat, Forest picked up the stone he brought in to show Brian. He hobbled over to his desk and set the rock on a pile of papers. "Someone sent this projectile with a note attached to it through Paige's, our"—he corrected, even though he still thought of it as her house—"front window."

"That's rotten. Who'd do such a thing?" Brian dropped onto his chair behind the desk, cup in hand. "What's with the limp? You and the wife have a lover's spat?"

Forest let the comment pass. "Here's the note." He handed the deputy the wrinkled paper.

Brian stared at him, then the sheet of paper, and took a slurp of his coffee. "Mistakes, huh?"

"I have no idea what it's referring to."

"Any suspects?"

"Only one." Forest jutted his chin toward the jail cell door.

"Edward or Craig?" Brian looked baffled. "No one's been in to talk with either of them in several days. Edward's as mad as all get-out about it, too."

If no one had been by, how was Mia receiving messages from him? Or was she just making up the stuff she told Paige?

"What happens when you go home in the evening?" Forest leaned against the edge of Brian's desk.

"What do you mean?"

"Who watches the prisoners?" Maybe someone was talking with Edward then.

"My replacement comes in from Florence each day at four. We have a rotating shift. Why?"

"Just wondering who else might be chatting with Edward."

"The guys know not to let anyone in or out of the jail." Brian squeezed his eyes nearly shut, perusing the note. "What's this part?" He held it up to the light. "I can barely make out something."

Forest snatched the paper from him.

"Hey!"

"Sorry." Did he miss something last night when he was so fatigued?

In tiny one-sixteenth-inch letters, a sentence stretched across the bottom edge of the sheet in light printing. He squinted at it. "Tell anyone about this and the whole world will know about you."

Was this Mia's or Evie's handwriting? Who would benefit by threatening him like this?

"Where's Paige?" Brian asked.

"Why?"

"Doesn't this concern her? I thought you were worried about her safety." Brian stood as if he were going to go check on her himself.

"I am. She's with Bess Grant at the gallery." Forest rocked his thumb at himself. "This threat seems aimed at me."

"Are you filing a report about the window? Or is she?" The deputy sure changed subjects fast.

"I'll do it."

Withdrawing a small notepad and pen from his shirt pocket, Brian asked, "How big of a hole did the rock make in the window?"

"Like this." Forest spread his hands, forming a saucer-sized shape.

"You and Paige probably handled the stone, the paper too, huh?"

"Yeah, we did."

"Not much value in dusting for prints then."

Forest sighed. If only he could start this day over.

He answered a few more questions, then went back to the computer station where his email list was displayed on the screen. He clicked on the letter from the regional office and adjusted his foot, trying to get comfortable.

"After taking the video through enhancement procedures," he read silently, "it's been devalued to inconclusive in proving the woman's identity. She doesn't match any person living or dead in the FBI database."

"What?" Forest grumbled.

"What's going on?" Brian asked from his side of the room.

"More dead ends."

So, the blurry video couldn't prove the woman was Evie because she was wearing a medical mask? What should he do now? Other than banging his head against the wall.

Forest had thought Mia was the most likely suspect as an accessory to Edward's crime. Now, finding Evie Masters was his top priority. Where did she live? Did Edward know where she was? How was she related to Craig? Him and Evie sharing the same last name couldn't be coincidental.

"I want to question Edward again. Then Craig."

"Aren't you off the case?"

"Not by a long shot. Who gave you that idea?"

"Sheriff Morris."

Forest groaned. A gnawing in his gut reminded him he left the house without eating breakfast. "He wants me to finish up ASAP. But there's more to the case. Why else would someone threaten me with public humiliation? Why would Edward send Mia to warn Paige about what he wants?" Forest was sick of the way the man ordered people around, almost like a mafia kingpin. Why did anyone even listen to him?

"Do what you've got to do." Brian shrugged. "Did you take pictures of the broken window?"

"Yes. I'll send them to you." Forest set up a text message and attached a couple of photos.

He wasn't thrilled with questioning Edward again. Or Craig. But if there was any hope of him and Paige beginning a normal married life, without suspicions or threats hanging over their heads, he had to keep pursuing the truth.

Nine

Sitting across from Edward in the interrogation room, Forest leaned forward in his chair that was bolted to the floor, eyeing the prisoner. "Who assisted you on the day you tried removing Paisley from the hospital?"

"So, you're back to that?" Edward snarled.

"That's right. Who unplugged the IV?" Forest persisted. "Did a nurse help you? A volunteer?"

"I told you, Paisley needs mental help. She's a liar. My son should never have gotten involved with that—"

"Uh-uh-uh," Forest said, stopping him from saying something derogatory. "Who helped you with the kidnapping?"

"Kidnapping," the ex-mayor spit out. "Why would I do such a thing?"

"The million-dollar question. Why would a wealthy, influential man kidnap his own daughter-in-law?" Forest clenched his fists beneath the table. The urge to grab Edward by his jailhouse orange jumpsuit and shake him until he owned up to his crimes shot through him so sharply, he didn't know how long he could sit here and do nothing. This interview may have been a bad idea.

"I have information on you." Edward smirked. "Data about your past mistakes."

Mistakes, huh? Was he alluding to the note on the rock? If so, how was he communicating with someone on the outside? With Mia? Or Evie?

"My information could break this case wide open." Edward dragged out the word "wide" and leaned back in his chair. His jail attire stretched taut across his abdomen, two buttons on his chest popping loose. It seemed Edward had been eating just fine in lock-up.

Forest mimicked the man's slouched position. "Go ahead. Shoot. What information do you have that's so vital to this case it could set you free?"

Edward's lips twitched. "Mia visited someone in Portland who has a beef against you. Someone you treated poorly."

"That so?" Forest's heart beat faster, leaving him as undone as the buttons on Edward's shirt. "Mia left town, did she?" After he told her not to? "Who'd she see?" Even if she went to Portland and talked to someone at his office, no one would tell her anything. They all signed confidentiality agreements. He trusted the other detectives like brothers. So, then, why was his heart racing like this?

"She's quite the little investigator." Edward grinned cockily as if he'd groomed her himself. "Maybe you should hire her."

Right. "What's her big scoop?" Forest feigned an interest he didn't feel.

"The name Elinore Radcliff ring a bell?"

Forest forced himself not to react to his ex-fiancé's name. "Elinore's a friend. So what?"

"A wealth of information, you mean." Edward guffawed. "You should have warned your ex-sugar-pie to keep her trap shut. She's lonely and bitter. Willing to tell all for a price."

They bribed Elinore? And she supposedly accepted? No way. She wouldn't tell Mia anything. If she did, Mia must have bamboozled her into saying something. What could she even know? He never talked about case details with her.

"Aren't you curious, Detective?" Edward's sleazy tone irritated Forest. "You jilted the wrong girl. She's out for revenge. Payback."

"I doubt that." Forest would call Elinore and ask her about this himself. The idea of her feeling jilted after three years was bizarre. "I am curious how you know anything about Mia's supposed visit to Portland. How are you corresponding with her?"

Edward roared with laughter. "It's baffling, isn't it? Our unseen communication must drive you crazy."

Yes, it did, but he wouldn't admit it out loud. "Back to my question, who assisted you at the hospital? Mia?"

"You're something. Digging. Always digging."

"That's my job. I'll keep digging until I unravel this case too. Now, did you pay someone to remove Paisley's IV?" Saying his sister-in-law's name without emotional inflection took nerves of steel.

"Why would I need to pay anyone to do my wishes?"

"It must help to have acquaintances within the hospital personnel. A volunteer, perhaps?" He wanted Edward to admit to Evie's involvement without him mentioning her name first.

Edward's eyes glinted, but his lips remained pressed together.

"If someone helped you, or if you paid her to assist you in removing Paisley from the hospital, tell me who it was, and we'll be done here."

A full minute passed.

"If I admit to such a thing"—Edward shuffled in his chair—"would you reinstate my visitation privileges?"

So, he wanted to barter?

"I'll see what I can do." Forest wouldn't agree, but he wouldn't say no, either.

Edward tilted his chin toward his handcuffs and scratched his rough face. "It wasn't Mia."

"Who, then?" Forest tried not to sound overly eager.

Maybe Edward would have a change of heart in prison. Perhaps become a kinder human being. Right now, he still seemed prideful and full of himself, even in his orange jumpsuit.

"Did someone assist you in your attempt to kidnap Paisley?"

"Sorry. Changed my mind." Edward chortled like it was a joke. "Figure it out yourself, if you're so smart."

Clenching his jaw, Forest jumped up and strode to the door. What a waste of time! If he hadn't injured his foot, and if he'd worn a heavy pair of work boots instead of his loose-fitting loafers, he'd be tempted to kick Edward into the next county.

"Don't forget what I said about your ex-girlfriend," Edward said in a throaty voice. "You might want to rethink your involvement in this case."

Yeah. Forest might want to rethink a lot of things. Like recommending to his supervisor that Edward be transferred to another facility. One where he would not only be deprived of communication with Mia Till, but he wouldn't have any interaction with the outside world.

Ten

Paisley snuggled into Judah's arms, prolonging their embrace before he left for work. His spicy, freshly-showered scent of soap and deodorant clung to his blue T-shirt and lingered in the air to remind her of the nights they shared over the last few days since their honeymoon started.

"I don't want you to leave," she whispered, nuzzling her cheek against his clean-shaven face.

"Me neither." Tipping up her chin, he lowered his mouth to hers.

Their kiss intensified. She ran her fingers through the back of his hair, still damp at the ends from his morning shampoo. "I love you."

"Love you too, Pais." He dropped another kiss on her lips. "Be safe today, okay?"

"Always. I'm in God's hands."

"I know. I'd like my gaze to be on you too." He winked.

Was he concerned about leaving her because he got a text from Forest this morning saying someone threw a rock into Paige's window last night? Even though their brother-in-law said a note taped to the rock had to do with him, not Paige or Paisley, Judah still seemed troubled.

"See you later, okay?"

"Okay." She sighed.

One more hug, another kiss, and he traipsed out the door.

Today would be Paisley's first normal work day at the diner since Mia and Craig said some things that put her, Judah, Paige, and Forest on pins and needles for several days, fearful something bad might happen. But when nothing unsuspecting or evil transpired, until last night, it seemed they'd all relaxed a little.

At breakfast, Judah asked her to text him every hour throughout the day to assure him she was okay. But Bert didn't like his servers using their phones during shiftwork. How could she follow her employer's wishes and still text her hubby? Besides, she was ready to put the fears about her kidnapping behind her. If only dusting her hands of the bad memories was as easy as dusting them of the flour she used to make pancakes this morning. Sigh.

She crossed the living room and trudged down the short hall. In the bathroom, she peered at herself in the mirror. Catching a glimpse of her cheek above Judah's flannel shirt she wore for a robe, she fingered the scar on the right side of her mouth. Would it ever disappear? She patted a thick layer of foundation over the mark, hiding it the best she could.

She didn't like people asking embarrassing questions— "What happened to your face?" "Did Mayor Grant do that when he kidnapped you?" "Are you going to sue him?" She disliked public attention of any kind.

After tugging on black pants and a white button-up shirt for her shift at Bert's Fish Shack, she did a few chores. Tossed a load of laundry in the washer, put Judah's and her coffee mugs in the dishwasher, and straightened the cushions on the couch—their only piece of furniture in the room. Thankfully, they had that after Hurricane Blaine destroyed almost everything else in the house. The plywood flooring with throw rugs tossed about was functional. But someday they'd fix up their little beach house just the way they wanted it.

A strong knock reverberated through the room. Every muscle in Paisley tensed up. Should she make a run for her bedroom and bolt the door? Or stand here and wait for the knocker to go away? Ever since the kidnapping, she'd been jumpy.

Finally, she drummed up enough bravery to peek around the edge of the curtain by the door. A woman with long red hair blowing in the breeze like a flag flying behind her stood on the porch, facing the sea. She appeared to be in her mid-thirties and wore a slight smile, perhaps a yearning that Paisley felt a kinship with, since she loved the ocean, too.

The redhead didn't appear dangerous. Yet how could someone know if another person was dangerous? Paisley wouldn't have imagined Edward could be as brutal as he turned out to be. Ugh. Why did she have to think of him?

She opened the door a few inches, keeping her foot wedged behind the door. "Can I help you?" Was the woman lost?

"Are you Paisley Grant?"

"I am." How did this woman know her name? What if Mia sent her to fulfill some diabolical wish of Edward's? Paisley started closing the door, pressing the wood with her black tennis shoe. Maybe she jumped the gun in answering a stranger's knock, even if the woman didn't appear dangerous.

"Wait." The redhead thrust out her hand. "Please. I'm Ruby Tate. Um, Cedars. Ruby Cedars." Her voice went soft on the surname.

"Cedars?" Paisley loosened her death grip on the handle. Was she a distant cousin? Ruby's hair was red, while Paisley's was dark brown. Their facial features didn't look anything alike, either. Still, it was a possibility.

"Yes. Ruby Cedars. May I come in?"

Any chance this was a trick? A pushy woman showing up at her door claiming to be a relative seemed suspicious. Was Paisley supposed to trust her and invite her in? What would Judah say about that? She peered beyond Ruby and checked to see if Mia or some unsavory person stood in the driveway.

"An Uber driver dropped me off." Ruby peered at Paisley with a questioning look. "He already left. I came alone."

"All right." She couldn't be too careful.

Ruby, dressed in blue jeans and a cardigan with a black knit hat pulled over long wavy hair, met her gaze with a smile. A bulging backpack hung off one shoulder like she might have been traveling or else was homeless. Not dangerous. Not following Edward's bidding.

"Who are you again?" Paisley didn't widen the gap in the door. Distrust mingled with the apprehension tightening her chest muscles. Her uniform felt claustrophobic. Her throat clogged like it was clamping shut. She focused on her inhalation and exhalation, tamping down panic. Would she ever fully trust anyone again?

"I need to talk with you." The woman swept her wind-tossed hair back over her shoulder in one swoop. "I'm Peter's wife. You and I are sisters-in-law."

"Peter's—"

"That's right. I've traveled from Ketchikan, Alaska, to talk with you and your dad."

She came all the way from Alaska? Ruby was married to Peter? Why wasn't Paisley aware of her brother's marriage before now? Did her father know?

"Is Peter okay?" She opened the door fully. "He's not—?" Her mind leaped to worst-case scenarios. A tragic accident at sea. His fishing boat capsizing. An earthquake.

"He's safe." Although a grimace crossed Ruby's face, wrinkling her smattering of freckles.

"Okay. Good." Something compelled Paisley to trust this woman who claimed to be her sister-in-law. "Please, come in."

"Thank you." Ruby crossed into the mostly vacant space and set down her backpack by the corner of the solitary piece of furniture. "This is nice. Homey."

"Thanks. A hurricane destroyed our furnishings. Please, have a seat."

Ruby sat on the edge of the gray couch cushion, then swept off her knit cap. "I'm so glad to finally meet you. Peter has told me a lot about you. The two of you running on the beaches when you were kids. Acting like pirates. Hooligans, he said."

Ruby wore a wedding band, but Paisley was relieved to hear her say something that confirmed her relationship with

Peter. She dropped onto the other side of the couch and faced the redhead. "Is Peter in Basalt with you?"

"No."

"Oh." A pause. "I didn't know he got married." Although she hadn't contacted him about her marriages to Judah, either. But she and Peter had been close before he left to work in Alaska.

"We've been married for five years." A pink flush washed over Ruby's cheeks. "We worked on the same fishing rig."

"My uncle's?"

"Yes."

What was Peter's wife doing here? They'd been married five years without telling the family? Aunt Callie would go nutso, especially after Paige's wedding announcement the other night.

"We had a quiet wedding in Ketchikan." Ruby's voice softened. "We were in love. Had similar goals. Things were perfect." She stared out the window as if lost in a memory.

Paisley was getting the picture. "And now?"

"Now, things aren't so lovely." Tears filled the woman's green eyes. She shook her head as if stopping herself from showing any emotional distress. "Thank you for letting me come in and talk with you."

"Sure. Where is my brother?"

A rueful smile crossed Ruby's mouth. "On his boat, the thing that matters most to him."

"His boat?"

"His troller. He said he needed to skipper his own boat like he needed air to breathe." Ruby ran her hands over her long strands of hair. "If only we continued as comrades, instead of captain and deckhand, things might have turned out differently. Maybe we'd still be in love. Still together."

"What happened?" Paisley asked since the woman seemed to need to talk.

"You have a marvelous view of the sea from here."

"Thanks. We love our cottage and beach." She breathed out some of the tension Ruby's arrival caused. Forgoing her previous question, she asked, "Would you like some coffee or tea?"

"Yes, thank you. Tea sounds perfect."

"You got it." Paisley hopped up and heated a cup of water in the microwave. Then prepped coffee for herself. She glanced at the clock. One hour until her shift started. She'd have to leave soon, since she planned to walk to town on the beach. "Sugar or cream?"

"One sugar, thanks," Ruby called from the other room.

As soon as the hot drinks were ready, Paisley carried them into the living room and handed the hot tea to Ruby.

"Thank you."

They sat quietly, sipping their drinks.

"You asked what happened between Peter and me."

"It's none of my business." Paisley patted Ruby's hand. "My husband and I have had our difficulties. I understand marital unhappiness more than you might think."

"You left him, right?"

A thorn twisted into Paisley's tender emotions. She sighed. No use being offended. She had left Judah. Peter probably told Ruby something he heard from Paige.

"I lived in Chicago by myself for three years."

Ruby sipped from her cup. "You know Brad Kiefer, right?"

"I do. He and Peter were friends. They used to fish together."

"They stayed in contact. That's how Peter hears tidbits about your family. The guys even fished together in Alaska for a time." Ruby stroked her knit cap lying on the couch arm. "I met both on the *Merry J.*"

"The *Merry J*?"

"Your uncle's boat."

"Oh, right." Paisley drank a few swallows of coffee. Why was Ruby in Basalt? Was she in trouble? Needing money? "Do you need a place to stay?"

"No, I—" Ruby shook her head. "I plan to stay at the inn. The Beachside Inn?"

"Sure. Maggie's place." Paisley kept any unkind sentiments about Maggie and her outdated inn to herself. "We have a guest room. It's not fancy, but you're more than welcome to stay with us."

"That seems like such an imposition on you."

"Not at all. We would be glad for you to stay here." Paisley reached out for Ruby's empty teacup. "I'm sorry to be abrupt, but I have to leave for work. I'm due at Bert's Fish Shack soon. I'm a server there. However, I want us to talk some more."

"I didn't mean to wedge my way into staying with you." Ruby glanced away. "I do want to visit more also. With you, Paige, and Paul. I came to Basalt Bay to get to the bottom of what's going on with Peter."

"Is something wrong?"

"He's been withdrawn. I don't know ... full of angst or regrets, or something." She inhaled a ragged breath. "No matter what I say, or try to do to bring us closer, doesn't work. We've become strangers." Ruby stared at the ceiling, blinking fast. "We lost what we had and haven't been able to find it again."

Her words sounded familiar. Like what Paisley and Judah went through three years ago.

"I'm so sorry. If there's anything I can do, please let me know."

"Thank you. I came here first because I thought you might understand."

"I do." Paisley stood. "Judah and I just got remarried two weeks ago."

"You did? Congratulations!" Ruby jumped up and hugged her.

"Thanks." Only slightly taken aback by the hug from someone she just met, she said, "Come this way and I'll show you the guest room. Be warned, it's sparse."

"I'm fine with minimalistic living." Ruby sounded more relaxed now. "Peter and I live on a fishing boat, so there's no room for collecting unneeded items."

Paisley showed her the guest room, the bathroom, and where the towels were kept. Then Ruby left, saying she'd check out of the Beachside Inn and come back later when Paisley returned.

All the way along the beach as she walked toward Bert's, Paisley prayed for Ruby and Peter, and for whatever had happened in their marriage to make Ruby come to Basalt alone.

Eleven

Judah wore his grubby jeans and a workworn jacket for his visit to C-MER to speak with C.L. However, eleven years ago, during his first interview with Mike Linfield, he wore a white shirt and tie, and had big dreams of a lifetime of coastal work. So many memories were wrapped up in this building and the work he'd done here. Too bad it ended so badly.

Why did C.L. ask him to drop by? And why did Mia previously inform him of the new C-MER manager looking into his file? Maybe the two were connected. Maybe not.

In the email Judah received, C.L. mentioned he had a question about the dike. Due to his remodeling schedule for the project house, Judah could have declined the request. He didn't work for this company anymore. But setting past grievances aside, and for the goodwill of the small community, he decided to show up and find out what was going on.

As he strode across the parking lot from his pickup to the front steps of C-MER, he wiped mud flecks off his coat and jeans. Before heading over here, he'd been surveying the roof project, taking a general overview of what fixing all the leaks might entail. Now that they were in November, that part of the renovation loomed over him.

C.L. met him at the front door, his hand outstretched. "Judah, it's good of you to join me. I'm C.L."

Judah shook the man's hand, noticing Mia's raised eyebrows from behind her receptionist's desk. "Nice to meet you."

"Let's get right to it." C.L. pivoted and marched across the room.

Judah followed him at a slower pace as nostalgia seeped into him. Even the scent of the dunes and ocean air wafting into the space was familiar.

In Mike Linfield's old office, C.L. dropped into the chair behind the desk. "Have a seat." Not a single stray paper lay out of place on the wooden surface, far different than his predecessor kept his office.

"What's this about?" Judah asked as soon as he sat down. "Is anyone else joining us?"

"Just a minute," C.L. said in a detached tone. "There." He turned the computer screen 180 degrees, facing Judah. "What do you see?"

He stared at the familiar schematic of the coastline. "Basalt Bay Cove. The peninsula. Mountain Peak Rock." He moved his finger along the beachfront of the drawing without touching the screen. "Baker's Point."

"Who monitored this area for the last ten years?" C.L. crossed his arms. "Who reported changes? Updated records?"

Nothing like being thrust under a microscope. Or was it the bus?

"Until three weeks ago, that would have been me."

"Exactly."

Why was C.L. staring at Judah like he'd done something wrong?

"Look here." The manager tapped the wheel on the mouse which caused the schematic to zoom out. He repositioned the map. "Check the peninsula. See anything amiss?"

Judah perused the screen without spotting anything unusual. Why was he called in here like a kid sent to the principal's office?

"These are the diagrams of the coastline we use to mark up and identify changes," C.L. explained.

"Yeah." Judah knew that.

"You've probably worked with these drawings a thousand times. Making notes. Submitting them to headquarters." The man's thick black eyebrows lifted.

"Sure, I have." Judah shuffled back in his seat, forcing stagnant air out of his lungs. "Is something wrong? Why have you called me in here?"

"Did you change these maps for Edward?" C.L. stared intensely at Judah.

"What? Of course not. I wouldn't alter them because of anything he said." His tie felt too tight. Oh, right. He wasn't wearing a tie. "Frankly, I don't like what you're implying." Getting up and walking out of the office burned hot in him. Who was C.L. to set up an inquisition for Judah? But then, his mantra of *grace and mercy* circled through his thoughts.

There must be a reason C.L. thought he'd do something so unconscionable. "Why do you ask?"

"Because the documents have been modified." C.L. stared at the screen. "Updates have been tweaked to reflect a better soil condition than exists currently on the peninsula. Better rock placement. Lack of damage. Some of it doesn't make sense. When I discovered such startling variances, I stopped work on the dike immediately."

"No wonder." Judah perused the map again. "Can we get a printout of this?" He didn't work here, but as a resident of Basalt Bay, he didn't want anyone getting hurt on the peninsula, either. Following the hurricanes, some things had shifted and altered along the coastline, but he reported every change he saw. Mike could vouch for him, if he were here.

"I'll get one." C.L. clicked his mouse a couple of times, grabbed the phone, then tapped "1"—Mia's extension. "Pick up the sheet I sent to the printer and bring it to me." After a pause, he barked, "No, I don't want donuts! Just the printout." He dropped the phone in the cradle as if it were too hot to handle. "That woman exasperates me."

Judah almost chuckled at his vehemence, but the tension in the room was too sharp.

"While we're waiting, can you tell me why you were fired, twice?" C.L. crossed his arms again, his hands tucked into his armpits.

"Haven't you read my file?" Judah's firings were still a sore spot for him. Not something he cared to discuss.

"I have. But I'd like to hear the story from you."

Sighing, Judah briefly explained about getting into a fight to stop an inebriated Craig Masters from stealing a skiff. Then he described the second time when he tried convincing the town council to accept the terms for the new dike and got the boot the next day.

C.L. stroked his chin. "Doesn't sound fair. Have you considered making an appeal?"

A rat-a-tat sounded at the door. Mia pranced into the office, grinning like they were all pals. "Judah, it's wonderful to see you back. Any chance you're returning to work with us?"

"Uh, no."

"What a pity. Here's the printout you requested, C.L." She nearly sang his name as she spread out the two-foot-by-three-foot print in front of C.L., her arm lingering near his on the desk. "Anything else I can get for you boys?"

"This is all." C.L. jerked his arm away from hers and stared at the document. "This is what I was telling you about."

Judah stood and leaned over the desk to get a better look at the large sheet. Mia's hand brushed down his arm and he pulled away, glaring at her.

"I'll tell Eddie I saw you, okay?"

"How is that possible?"

"Where there's a will—" Laughing, she exited.

He groaned.

"When job cuts start, she'll be the first to go," C.L. said in a harsh tone.

Job cuts, huh?

Focusing on the blueprint, Judah saw some added markings on the north side of the peninsula where Sample D toppled into the sea during Hurricane Blaine. He pointed at the spot. "What's going on here?"

"I noticed that irregularity too." C.L. tapped another section farther back toward land. "And here. Did you add these notations?"

"No, I did not. Who worked on these after I left?"

"Mike. Jeff. Craig. Who knows?" C.L. shook his head. "You're certain you didn't make changes to the peninsula based on the mayor's pressure tactics?"

"I would never do such a thing. Ask anyone here."

"Oh, I have." The new C-MER director eyed him. "Someone altering the notations of soil erosion, making it look better than it is, is dangerous. Not to mention it'll cost a wad of money redoing the project. The work had to cease until this could be analyzed."

"I understand." Judah dropped back into his chair. "But it wasn't me. I didn't change anything to suit my father's manipulations. In fact, for public safety I went up against him about the new dike. He was more concerned about—"

"Money?"

"Or power."

"Listen"—C.L. spoke quietly, glancing toward the door as if fearing someone might be listening—"headquarters sent me here because of inconsistencies within the company, possibly within this building. Whether it was Mike Linfield's fault or someone else's"—he sent a suspicious glint arcing in Judah's direction—"I have yet to discover."

Judah had told him the truth. What else could he say to prove his integrity? Maybe he should leave. But he still wanted to hear what C.L. planned to do about the dike. "What comes next?"

"Getting to the bottom of this." C.L. ran his index finger along the markings on the drawing. "Whether accidental or on purpose, someone altered these. We're professionals who double-check everything, how could this slip by our team undetected?"

Judah knew the C-MER engineers cross-checked every fact, crunching numbers, figuring weight loads, questioning every data source. This oversight didn't make sense. "You could follow the log-in data. Find out who made the last alterations."

"I already did that." C.L.'s lips puckered. "It was you."

"What? That's not possible."

"Upon further investigation, I discovered the log-in date coincided with the week after you were fired."

"Oh." Judah exhaled. "Okay."

"Did you give anyone your password?" The blaming tone returned to C.L.'s voice.

"Absolutely not."

"Did you want to get back at the company? Or Mike? Your firing sounds questionable. Maybe you wanted revenge."

"I did not! That's not who I am." Judah stood and zipped his coat. "Are we done here?"

C.L. nodded once. "Thanks for stopping by. I'd appreciate your discretion until I can catch the offending party."

"No problem."

"One other thing." C.L. rolled up the large print into a tube shape. "Are you aware of anyone else who'd want to retaliate against C-MER?"

Other than Edward or Craig? "Not really."

"Against you?"

The same names came to mind, but both men were in jail.

"If you think of anyone, let me know."

Judah left C-MER frustrated, but he also had a higher respect for C.L. While he wasn't the most pleasant person to talk with, the man seemed to care about the shoreline and public safety—things Judah cared about too.

Twelve

Forest sat in his rental car outside the C-MER building, observing as Judah hopped into his white pickup truck and zoomed out of the parking lot. What was his brother-in-law doing here? Visiting old coworkers? Didn't he have too much to do at the project house to waste time here?

Judah probably wished Forest was working his tail off at the project house right now and not wasting time watching people come and go from C-MER. But he was still on official business for Sheriff Morris. His primary focus for today was discovering how Mia was communicating with Edward, then stopping it.

He'd questioned Craig about Evie, but that man wasn't helpful at all. He wouldn't confirm or deny that she was his mom, sister, or aunt. He just smirked and refused to answer.

After his futile discussion with Edward and Craig, Forest searched through the databases he had access to. Any minute he expected to hear back from Oregon's Vital Records and

Certificates' office where he sent a request for Craig's birth certificate. Once that arrived, he'd know for certain whether Evie was the prisoner's mom. Would that solve the mystery about whether Edward was his father, too?

Forest scrunched lower in his seat, peering at the glass windows of the C-MER building. Hopefully, Mia would leave for a break soon. Deputy Brian told him she often went to Bert's for lunch. If all went well, she'd go there today, and he'd follow her.

At least sitting in his car kept him off his sore foot. Enjoying the warmth of the sunshine coming through the glass, he closed his eyes. A few seconds of rest and—

Someone pounded on his window. He jerked. Did he fall asleep?

Mia leaned down, grinning at him. "You okay in there, Detective?"

He lowered the window. "Mia."

"What are you doing here? Are you waiting to talk with C.L.? Judah already came by, but maybe you know that, huh?" She giggled. "Unless you're here to talk with me! Why, Detective, did you hear about my little excursion to Portland? Sorry if that caused you any trouble," she said in a sing-song voice. "You know I wouldn't do that for anything in the world, right?"

Right. Irritation rumbled through him, alongside his growling stomach.

"See you later, hon. I'm off to lunch." She finger waved and scurried over to her red sports car, her heels click-clacking against the pavement. How she scampered around in those spikes without falling on her face he had no idea.

Why had he gone to sleep? The combination of aspirin and lack of sleep last night must be the culprits. He started up his car. Now that Mia spotted him, his chances of following her undetected were zilch. Still, she was probably going to Bert's. A bacon burger sounded great to him.

Following her red car, he kept a block's distance between them. He hated her flippant attitude about her trip to Portland. He still had to call Elinore and inquire about that. Even if Mia wasn't the woman in the photo, it seemed she was causing trouble every which way. Did she throw that rock through Paige's window last night? Was she involved with Edward's criminal dealings?

Forest drove slowly through town, past City Hall. Mia pulled into the parking lot at Bert's, just like he hoped. Maybe, after she went inside the diner, he'd saunter in and order lunch. Then watch to see who she talked with. Who else might be involved in getting messages to and from Edward?

So Mia didn't assume he was following her, he continued down the road toward the Beachside Inn. Before he got to the curve, he glanced into his rearview mirror. Wait. Mia didn't enter Bert's. She was crossing the street. He pictured the buildings on the other side of the street—the library, a gas station, a chocolate confectionary. Where was she going?

He did a U-turn and made another slow pass through downtown. He didn't see her anywhere. After turning around again, he pulled into a parking space at Bert's. Mia's car was still here. Eventually, she'd come back. The scent of burgers and fries reached Forest's olfactory senses. His stomach growled loudly.

Across from his position, Mia exited the library's front door with two books in her hands. Was she just picking up books? Not doing any mischief? He groaned. More time wasted when he could have been doing research on Evie.

A few minutes later, Mia's sports car revved past him and out of the parking lot. She wasn't even going to eat lunch? Groaning, he started up his engine and followed her car. Behind City Hall, next to Deputy Brian's office, she parallel parked. What was she doing here when she couldn't see Edward?

Tempted to pull in behind her and ask, Forest drove around the block and parked his rental. Exiting the vehicle, he limped down the sidewalk, waiting for a clear view of Mia's car.

He peered around the edge of the City Planning office. Across the street, Mia nearly pranced down the sidewalk toward the deputy's office, still carrying the two books. Was she bringing those to the prisoners? To Edward? Aha! Were they passing messages in the library books?

Forcing his sore foot to move faster, he trailed her, not even caring if she saw him. At the deputy's office, he thrust open the door. "What's going on here?"

Mia and Deputy Brian turned and gaped at him.

"Detective, you startled me!" Mia flashed him a flirty smile. "Are you following me? I thought you said you were a happily married man."

"What are you doing here, Mia?"

She held up a white book with the word "War" in the title. "Volunteering. Bringing books for the prisoners."

"May I see it?" He thrust out his hand.

"What's this about?" Deputy Brian asked, still sitting at his desk.

"Is bringing library books to the boys in jail a crime?" Mia asked in a mocking tone.

"No. But there is such a thing as being an accomplice to a crime."

"I wouldn't do that." Mia put her hand to her chest like she was shocked by his suggestion. "I'm a law-abiding citizen."

Forest barely stopped himself from coughing in loud protest. "I need to see any books before they go to Edward."

"He already can't have visitors." Mia wrapped her arms around the book. "Deputy, are you going to let him boss me around like this in your office?" She made pouty lips.

"Well, I—"

"How long has this been going on?" Forest glanced between Mia and Brian.

"What are you talking about?" Brian stood slowly.

"How long have you been receiving messages from Edward via library books?" Forest glared at Mia. "Who concocted that scheme? You? Or Edward?"

"I don't know what you're implying." She huffed and reached for the second book. "I have to get back to work."

"Not yet." Forest scooped up the book before she did.

"Hey. That's private property!"

"No, it isn't." He pointed at the Public Library tag. "I'm going to confiscate these books and check them over." He held out his hand for the other book.

"Detective—"

"Is this necessary?" Brian glared at Forest.

"Indeed, it is. I'm going to find out how she's been passing messages." Would he discover a secret code inside the book's pages? Maybe words or letters circled or underlined throughout the text? "Mia, may I have the book?"

"Deputy, please, do something," she whined.

Brian shrugged. "Sorry, Mia."

She slammed the book down on the desk. "I've never been so humiliated in my life!" She stomped her high heels toward the door.

"Hold it right there!" Forest barked. "Stay put until I've had a chance to look these over."

"I'm not under arrest, am I?"

"No, but you might be." Forest tapped his fingers over the word "War." "You wouldn't want to be considered an accomplice in Paisley's kidnapping, would you?"

"Of course not." Her eyes flared.

"Then I recommend you have a seat while I check over these books. If I don't find anything, you'll be free to go." He glanced at Brian. "Where are the ones she's returning to the library?"

Deputy Brian pointed at a small stack of books on a chair in the corner.

If Forest had been a minute later, he might have missed this opportunity. How had he overlooked Mia's library service during the two weeks he'd been in Basalt? This must be the answer he was looking for.

Yet, an hour and a half later, despite his painstaking search through each of the library books, he didn't find a single irregularity in any of the pages. No notations or codes. No vowels or consonants circled. No dog-eared pages. He went from elation, certain he'd solved the mystery, to bitter disappointment. How could he have been so wrong?

"You're free to go," he mumbled to Mia.

"Finally!" The blond spitfire stomped to the office door. "If I get fired for being late, Detective Harper, you're going to have to pay my salary. In fact, I may sue you for defamation of character! You haven't heard the last of this."

Yeah, yeah. She was probably still guilty even if he hadn't found any evidence to the contrary.

"You went too far this time," Brian said.

"I don't think so. I didn't solve what she's doing. But she's doing something." Was Mia bringing library books to Edward and Craig out of the goodness of her heart? Or something else entirely? "I don't want her stepping foot in this office until after the trial is over."

"What? How am I supposed to enforce that?" Brian strode over to the coffee machine. "You've seen her. She pushes to get what she wants. Uses her feminine wiles."

"I don't care what she uses. Post a watch. Lock the door. Whatever it takes. I don't want any more messages getting passed from Edward to her."

Enough was enough. Forest was drawing a line in the sand.

Thirteen

It had been a long afternoon, and even though he was tired, frustrated, and still hungry, Forest needed to clear the air with Paige. However, when he pulled into the carport at her house, her car wasn't there. A chunk of cardboard was still adhered to the front window where the hole was. Obviously, the glass installer hadn't arrived yet.

Sighing, he shot her a text. *Where are you? I was hoping we could talk.*

No answer.

Maybe she didn't want to talk with him. Was letting him cool his heels.

He tapped his fingers against the steering wheel. "Come on. Come on." He needed to head out to the project house and work for a few hours. Judah was expecting him.

Finally, his phone vibrated.

Piper and I are at Aunt Callie's.

Okay. I'll be there in a sec.

Without waiting for another text from her, he drove the couple of blocks over to Callie's.

Paige was waiting for him on the sidewalk when he exited his car. "What's going on? Did something happen?"

"Not really." He couldn't explain the frustrating rabbit trail he'd followed with Mia today. "I needed to see you. I'm sorry about this morning." If this was the only right thing he did today, he was going to make sure he did that. "I didn't mean to say I'd be leaving in such an abrupt way. I apologize for being an insensitive clod. Causing more stress between us. Believe me, leaving you is the last thing I'd want to do."

"Thanks. I appreciate that." Paige gave him a soft smile. "I'm sorry for overreacting. It was silly of me."

Her gentle response, her lack of anger, and the lousy day he'd had so far, made him want to take her in his arms and just hold her.

But Callie trudged onto the porch, jostling Piper, and eyed Forest like she suspected him of being up to no good. "What's going on out here?"

"Nothing, Auntie," Paige said.

"Good afternoon, Mr. Harper."

"Forest, please. How are you, Callie?" His heart rate ramped up. Paige's aunt had that effect on him.

"Until I see a genuine marriage, and a man behaving like a real husband, it'll be Mr. Harper to me."

"Auntie." Paige huffed.

"And I'm fine, thank you for asking." Callie harrumphed.

What would Forest have to do to prove his sincerity as a husband to Paige's aunt? He wanted to be a true husband to her. A loving husband and dad for all his days.

93

"This girlie needs a daddy, too," Callie said in a softer tone.

"He is her daddy."

It was nice of Paige to stick up for him.

"Hey, princess!" He waved at Piper.

His daughter cackled and jabbered back at him.

Callie shuffled into the house but managed to throw a glare at him over her shoulder.

He sighed.

"Sorry about that." Paige scraped the edge of her shoe on the sidewalk. "I tried explaining about our marriage to her, but she isn't buying that we're working on it. Got all worked up."

"I thought you weren't going to disclose the way we chose to live."

He would have been fine courting Paige, winning her heart, no matter how long it took. Instead, they were living like married strangers. Of course, that was partly because he'd wanted to stay at her house to watch out for her and Piper. But married only two days, he already longed for his wife to think of him as more than a protector. He wanted their marriage to be authentic.

"She asked if I thought Piper would have siblings, and I blurted out that it was impossible with the way things were now." An anguished look crossed her face. "I'm sorry. I shouldn't have opened my big mouth."

Not liking the wall of emotions that quickly rose between them, he said, "You know I want to 'behave like a real husband' with you, right?"

"I just need—"

"More time. I know." He understood. Or he was trying to understand.

The curtains of Callie's house rustled. Was she spying on them? Watching to see if Forest would act like a genuine husband with Paige? Maybe he should give his wife's aunt a preview of how serious he felt about their marriage. What would he have to do to convince this matriarchal relative he was a real husband?

"I love you, Paige." He smoothed his palm over her shoulder. "I have an idea. Just go along with it, okay?" He lowered his mouth almost to hers. Two inches away from kissing her, her sharp intake of breath stopped him from meeting her lips uninvited.

"What are you doing?"

"Your aunt's watching us. Let's show her we do care for each other. That it's not all fake."

"Forest—" She glanced toward the house, then met his gaze. "Okay. You're right. She is watching us."

"You have such beautiful eyes." He stroked hair off her cheek. He spanned the gap between them and kissed her soft, pliable lips, hugging her waist closer to him. The way she came to him easily, wrapping her arms over his shoulders and kissing him back, sent chills over his body. Man, he wished she wasn't just going along with this smooching to prove something to her aunt.

He lingered longer than he probably should have, holding her, kissing her again. Eventually, he glanced at Callie's front window. The curtains were closed. No more rustling fabric. He took a step back, catching his breath.

Paige cleared her throat. Chuckling with a self-conscious-sounding laugh, she wiped the back of her hand over her mouth. "If that didn't convince her, nothing will."

"I hope it did." He stroked her arm, his fingers encircling her wrist. "Be on guard, okay? With that rock-throwing business, I'm wary. If you see or hear anything unusual, call me immediately. I'll be at the project house for the next couple of hours."

"Okay. I'm sure everything is fine." Paige nodded toward the house. "Aunt Callie's a battle-ax. Being with her is probably the safest place in Basalt Bay."

"True." He chuckled.

He was glad he followed his impulse to drive over here and clear the air. The kiss was a bonus, even if it had been partially for show.

Fourteen

Ruby stood on the porch of the address she'd copied from the advertisement on the community bulletin board where Paisley worked. Lifting her fist, she knocked firmly on the door. Inside, a hammer pounded a steady rhythm and an electric saw buzzed. She could use a job, not only for the money, but to give her a sense of purpose and a distraction to keep her from worrying about her failed marriage.

From beyond the old house in need of a lot of remodeling by the looks of the bare roof, broken windows, and damaged siding, the surf rumbling from somewhere below created an earthy call to her. As if the waves whispered, *Ruby, Ruby,* over and over. If the project manager didn't hire her, maybe she'd hike down and walk on the beach. Get lost in the musical tones and rhythms of the sea.

She felt her phone vibrate but ignored it. Peter had already left her five voice messages and several texts. Other than the one where he demanded, *WHERE ARE YOU?* in giant letters, she didn't read any of them or listen to the voicemails. A week ago, she texted him that she was safe. When she was ready, she'd call him. Not until.

When no one answered her knock, probably didn't hear her with all the ruckus going on inside, she pried open the door a couple of inches. "Hello?" Still nothing. She stepped into the dust-filled entryway. "Hello? I'm Ruby. I'm here to talk to the project manager."

She sauntered into the empty kitchen, perusing the newly installed wood-patterned vinyl. Small chunks of the floor covering were piled in front of the open window, probably ready to be thrown out. She followed the hammering sounds into a larger room. "Hello. I'm Ruby Tate."

Two men stumbled into the space from separate doors. An older man had white dust covering him like he'd been spraying ceiling texture and most of it fell on him. The other guy, closer to her age, appeared semi-dusty with messy dark hair.

"I'm Ruby Tate," she said again, using her maiden name. "I'm here about the ad for work. Are you still hiring?"

The younger of the two came closer. "You're here for the laborer position?"

"That's right. Do you still need help?"

"We sure do." He wiped his hands on his dust-laden jeans, then thrust out his right hand. "I'm Judah Grant, project manager."

"Grant?" Something tight twisted in her stomach, but she still shook his hand. "Any relation to Paisley?"

"She's my wife." He smiled broadly. "You've met her?"

"I have." Ruby covered her face with her hands for a moment. "I may have made a mistake in coming here." She backed up into the kitchen. Then rushed out onto the porch. Did she want to be so entangled in Paisley's and Judah's lives? She hadn't seen a name in the advertisement. Had no idea who the boss might be until now.

"Wait." Judah followed her, as did the older man, both staring at her intensely.

Standing by a wobbly railing, she peered through the trees and caught a glimpse of the gray-blue water she only heard before. She came here hoping for a job, but working for her brother-in-law? How weird would that be? She'd had enough troubles working for her husband. Paisley invited her to stay at their house. If Judah hired her, he'd probably do so because he felt sorry for her. She bristled. She was a hard worker. Would prove it if they let her.

"You acted taken back by my name. Why?"

Judah was a handsome man with his amazingly blue eyes and wide smile. She could see why Paisley was attracted to him. Why she took a chance on him for a second time.

"I told you my maiden name." She inhaled deeply of the moist sea air. "My legal name is Ruby Cedars."

"Cedars?"

"I'm Peter's wife. Correction, estranged wife."

"Oh. I'm sorry to hear that." Judah swayed his hand toward her. "Not about your being my sister-in-law, but things not going well with you and Peter. Paisley sent me a text that you arrived today. And you'll be staying with us?"

"Yeah. Thanks. She invited me to bunk in your guest room, if that's okay."

"Of course." Judah nodded toward the house behind them. "Why don't you come back inside? I'll give you the grand tour. Then you can decide if you want to hang out with our motley crew."

"Hey, now," the older gentleman grumbled.

"We have one other worker who's here on a part-time basis," Judah said. "Forest is Paige's husband."

"Oh."

The older man held up his hands as if not wanting to share his dust and grime with her. "I'm James Weston, neighbor to Peter's father, Paul. We've been friends since elementary school."

"Nice to meet you."

Judah led her through the kitchen, explaining the wall dressing he planned to use—white painted shiplap, which she imagined would be beautiful. She followed him into the large living room, and he pointed out the damaged flooring that needed to be extricated and what had to be done with the walls—Sheetrock repair and painting.

Finally, James showed her the work he'd accomplished in the downstairs bathroom. "I'm helping the ladies out of the goodness of my heart."

"And because"—Judah nudged James's shoulder—"he's sweet on Callie."

"Now, now. We're only friends."

Judah winked at Ruby as if sharing the joke with her.

She enjoyed the camaraderie. Having lived in the world of fishermen, working around guys in an outdoor environment, their joking and teasing was nothing new to her.

"Do you have experience with carpentry?" Judah brought the conversation back to why she'd landed on their doorstep.

"I do. My father was a carpenter in Alaska. I helped him for years."

"Past tense?"

"Yeah. He passed away ten years ago." She clenched her jaw, putting the kibosh on any sneaky emotions. "I've worked on fishing boats ever since. Until now."

"I'm sorry for your loss."

"Thank you."

After a pause, Judah asked, "Fishing, huh? Sounds strenuous."

A nerve twitched in her jaw. "You mean since I'm a woman?"

He lifted his hands, palms out. "Not at all. For a man, also."

"Sorry. It's an automatic reflex." She shouldn't get so defensive, but she'd had a gut full of put-downs from men who thought a woman shouldn't be a carpenter, a fisherman, or a boat owner.

"If you've worked hard like that, the work we're doing here won't come as any surprise." Judah held out his hand to shake hers again and smiled. "Still interested in the job?"

"Absolutely. Thank you for the opportunity." Even if he was her brother-in-law, she needed the work.

"Now, can we get back to it?" James tapped his watch. "We've wasted fifteen minutes, and it isn't even our coffee break yet."

"Where do you want me to start?" Ruby asked.

Judah pointed toward the living room flooring. "Our next phase. You can begin by removing the damaged plywood."

"Okay. Great." She peeled off her raincoat. "Would you have a spare pair of gloves?" If she'd thought to do so, she would have picked some up at the hardware store.

"Let me check. I'll grab a few tools for you also." He strode out of the room.

Ruby took in the large room, noticing the swollen condition of the floorboards. It looked like a lot of work. However, helping Judah's crew get the house in shape, providing for herself, and keeping her mind off Peter and their broken marriage sounded like a perfect plan.

Fifteen

At the gallery the next day, Paige stood on a stepladder and tried to measure the plastic-covered window facing the ocean. Wind gusts blasting through the large tear in the plastic momentarily took her breath away. In her haste to clutch the top wrung and not slip off, she almost toppled backward. Groan. Centering herself, she extended the tape measure again. She needed an accurate measurement to send the glass company.

Thanks to Bess's and Forest's generous financial assistance, she'd be able to get the needed improvements done to the building, including buying new glass for this window and having it installed by a professional. She'd called the same company to fix her window at the house also.

Too bad Judah wasn't available to oversee this project. Forest said he'd pitch in during off-hours. Then he winked and said they could work on it together on the weekends. Funny guy. As if rebuilding the gallery was something romantic.

Hmm. Perhaps it could be. She enjoyed other things Forest did to be romantic with her. Like winking at her, kissing her cheek, and gazing warmly into her eyes as if making silent promises to her. Sharing coffee times in the mornings was a nice surprise, too. Sometimes it seemed as if they'd been doing that forever, not just a few days.

But she couldn't ignore the slight awkwardness between them, either. It was a chasm she had no idea how to cross, or if she wanted to yet, especially since he mentioned leaving to go back to Portland. But then he apologized, which was sweet.

Why had she reacted so strongly to his news? He had to go away for work. Big deal. It wasn't like he said he was leaving her forever. Just past angst rearing its ugly head. Worry over current threats, too.

Sighing, she descended the ladder to jot down the width of the window on her notepad. The front door screeched open. She turned, expecting to see Bess or Forest.

Mia sashayed into the room. Not again.

"I see you're determined to do something with this dump."

Hadn't Forest warned her to beware of Mia?

"It's in the town's best interest for the building to be restored and opened for business." Paige collapsed the ladder and leaned it against the wall to the side of the window, glad for a task to keep her hands busy. Better than clenching them into fists.

"Such a lovely view you have." Mia's heels tap-danced against the plywood floor, her blond curls bouncing as she approached the torn window covering. "Wouldn't a resort be perfect here? It's a shame for you to waste a bunch of work and money only for the building to be demolished when Edward's exonerated."

Exonerated? Demolished?

"He planned to tear down this building? A resort sounds far-fetched in Basalt."

"Why? It's a destination town near the sea." Mia smiled like she knew better than Paige, maybe better than anyone. "Even you have to adapt to modern times."

"Modern, sure. We're not a big city. No one wants a resort here."

"Eddie does. He said it would boost the local economy."

Yeah, his, no doubt.

"Fortunately for me, he didn't finish the loan process before he was incarcerated." Paige didn't mean to sound smug. Just stating facts. "So this building won't be a resort."

"What are you talking about?" Mia asked. "I turned his documents into the bank myself. I made sure everything was finalized properly."

"Not well enough, apparently." As soon as the words crossed her mouth, Paige wished she hadn't said them.

"We'll see about that!" Mia marched across the empty space. At the door, she paused. "Congrats again on marrying the detective. I think he's ravishingly handsome too." Tossing her hair over her shoulder, she strode out of the building.

Paige felt like hurling the tape measure at the wall. Or into the sea! Instead, she clenched her jaw and put her energy into setting up the ladder again. Thanks to Mia she'd already forgotten the measurements.

Bess strode into the gallery, frowning. "Good morning. Was that Mia?"

"Yep."

"What did the agitator have to say this time?" Bess dropped her purse on the counter and hurried over to Paige.

"She says Edward planned to demolish this building and make it into a resort." She smoothed her fingers over the metal measuring-tape shell. "Did you know anything about that?"

"No, but he had grandiose ideas."

"And Mia? What's she after?"

"Who knows? If she had an affair with him, she might think she has a vested interest. But she's just one in a line of—" Bess cupped her hand over her mouth. "I didn't mean to say that." She shuddered as if chilled. "What can I do while I'm here? Could you use another hand with measuring?"

"Actually, yes." Paige handed her one end of the retractable tape. "There is one other thing. Mia wasn't happy about the loan process not going in Edward's favor."

"Too bad. It's done now."

Hopefully, that's what Mia would find out at the bank and then keep her distance from the gallery.

Paige and Bess took measurements of the room and Paige wrote down all the figures.

"Have you decided who you're going to call to manage the job?" Bess asked when they finished calculating the flooring of the small bathroom.

"My dad gave me a couple of suggestions when I dropped off Piper." Paige glanced over the numbers on her notepad. "I'll call two or three and get bids."

"I hope you can find someone. Since it's been only seven weeks since Hurricane Blaine, most of the carpenters are probably still up to their ears in work." Bess strode to the counter and picked up her purse. "We might have to call in the troops."

"Meaning?"

"Friends. Citizens of Basalt Bay." A thoughtful expression crossed her face. "It's a benefit for our town to get the retail district up and running quickly, right?"

"That's what I told Mia."

"Good. Remember how our brigades helped residents with hauling garbage and fixing things after the storm?"

"Sure. But that was Mia's brainchild." Paige didn't try to hide her grumpy tone when she said the woman's name.

"Hmm." Bess pressed her fist against her chin, her brows furrowed. "What if the townspeople rallied together to rebuild your art gallery and the other businesses, too?"

"Sounds fabulous. Our stores would get opened faster."

"Exactly. I'll see what I can pull together." Bess dug into her purse and withdrew a manila folder. "Here's your copy of the legal documents for the building, should Mia or anyone else come snooping around again."

"Thank you." Paige gripped the papers. "Your support means so much to me."

"Glad to help. Now, I'm going to stir up our neighbors to do something good for our town again." Bess waved and exited through the broken doorway.

Paige's dream was to have the art gallery operational by Christmas. If people pitched in like Bess thought they would, her wish might come true.

Sixteen

Elinore's name was still in Forest's contact list, so while he was alone in the deputy's office, he ran his finger over the screen and tapped her name. Dreading this phone call, he'd put it off for two days.

"Forest?" Elinore answered.

"Hey, Elinore."

"Are you in town?" Was that hopefulness in her voice?

"Nah, I live in Basalt Bay now."

"Oh, right. I heard you and Paige got back together."

"Yeah, we got married again."

"Were you calling to tell me, finally?" Her voice took on a hard edge.

"Uh, not really."

"You know, the news hit me hard." She sniffed.

"Oh?"

"I guess I was still hoping—" She drew in a long breath. "This is embarrassing to admit. I don't think I ever got over you, Forest." She whimpered like she was fighting tears.

"Oh, uh, I'm sorry to hear that." Three years and she hadn't gotten over him? Now he felt like a louse. "I never meant to hurt you."

She sniffed a few more times.

Glancing at the wall clock, he waited for her to get herself under control. He shuffled his weight back and forth. Soon, Deputy Brian would be returning, and Forest didn't want him overhearing this conversation. He'd better get on with it.

"Elinore, I need to ask you something. Did you speak with a woman from Basalt Bay named Mia Till?"

"Yes," she said quietly.

"I'm sorry if she said anything that might have troubled you or made you feel bad." Forest leaned his backside against the desk, waiting.

"It's okay. She was nice. Sympathetic."

I bet. "What did she ask you about?"

"It was a private conversation, Forest."

Her sharp tone set off warning signals in him.

"Someone may have put her up to that visit." Although he couldn't give her any details. "Can you tell me what she asked you? What you said to her?"

"Why would I do that? I don't care to be treated like a child." Elinore huffed. "Asking me what I said or didn't say, what she said or didn't say, is juvenile and disrespectful."

"I'm not trying to treat you like a child. I'm sorry if it sounded that way." He took a breath. "As a detective, I ask lots of questions."

"A dishonorable detective, or so I've heard."

"Who said that?" He pushed away from the desk.

"Mia."

"Look, I'm pursuing the truth." Agitation seeped into his tone. "What did you talk about with her?"

"We had coffee and chatted. No national secret about that!" Elinore made a teeth-grinding sound.

"About?"

"About your breaking off our engagement so you could be with another woman!"

Forest inhaled slowly. "I didn't realize you were still so upset about our break-up."

"How could you know anything about it since you dropped me like a hot rock?" She hiccupped. "I'm in counseling over it."

Oh, man. "I'm sorry. Really, I am."

Three years ago, after her accident, when he left Paige and returned to Portland, he and Elinore had talked for hours. He thought they worked through her disappointment and hurts over their broken engagement. Apparently, not good enough.

"Mia told me about you getting Paige pregnant while we were still together."

"That's not true!" This time his emotions barreled into his words. "I called you before my wedding. In fact, before I asked Paige to marry me, I told you we were finished."

"You expect me to believe you didn't get together while we were engaged?" Elinore's voice skyrocketed. "Mia implied that wasn't the case."

"How would she know anything about it?" Forest groaned. His and Paige's personal affairs were their private business. He wouldn't discuss them with Elinore, but he felt the urge to lay this gossip to rest, too. "Remember when you asked me not to break up with you because of your father's condition? I went along with it because we were friends. I honored your wishes for your father's peace of mind." He paused. "I met Paige after that."

"See there."

"You and I weren't together as a couple." He wanted to howl in frustration. "Paige wouldn't even agree to marry me until I explained everything to you."

"Still doesn't justify having a child with her."

"I'm not going to explain the details of my time in Vegas. Other than to say I loved Paige and married her. And, yes, I have a daughter who I'm very proud to say is mine."

The front door opened, and Deputy Brian entered carrying a Lewis's Super bag. "I got snacks."

Forest lifted his chin in greeting then turned his back toward the officer.

"Is that all you and Mia talked about?" he asked in a quieter tone of voice.

"The rest of what she said is too painful to repeat."

"Please. Just tell me, okay?"

Why was Mia stirring up emotional stuff between him and Elinore?

"She says you were with someone else while we were engaged too."

"What?"

"Bridget Moore. How could you cheat on me like that, twice?"

Bridget, his previous coworker? He gripped the phone tightly. "What are you talking about?"

Deputy Brian leaned toward him. "Everything okay?"

Forest shook his head at him.

"Mia talked to a guy from your office." Elinore chuckled. "She has a way of getting people to open up and talk. Must be a gift."

"It's all an act."

"That's belittling of you, Forest."

Yeah, it probably was. But he was sick and tired of Mia's and Edward's underhanded schemes.

"What else did she say? Whatever it is, it'll be news to me, because I never went on a date with Bridget."

"The guy told Mia he saw you coming out of a club with her." She swallowed noisily. "That she was dressed like one of those dancers—you know the type—at some posh place."

A memory hit him between the eyes. There had been one undercover gig with Bridget at a nightclub. Not a real date. But he couldn't defend himself or discuss it with Elinore.

"I have nothing to say about that."

Deputy Brian made noisy rustling sounds as he set the packages of food on the counter by the coffeepot.

Forest missed something Elinore said.

"—for a fake marriage?"

"Who called my marriage fake?" Forest nearly shouted.

Brian's eyebrows shot up.

"Mia," Elinore said.

"She doesn't know what she's talking about. Paige and I are working on a real marriage that will last for the rest of our lives."

Brian cleared his throat and shook his head as if Forest had said something wrong. What?

"Working on it?" Elinore shrieked. "Who has to work on a marriage being real when they're newlyweds?"

He hadn't meant to say it like that.

"I have to go, but I wish you all the best, Elinore."

He was sorry for having hurt her. Sorry Mia was digging up the past. Sorrier still that he'd have to explain to Paige about calling his ex-fiancé.

Seventeen

After eating a late lunch, Forest loaded the dishwasher while Paige settled Piper down for a nap. His family's voices floated toward him from Piper's bedroom with Paige reading a book and Piper babbling in her cute voice. The best sounds in the world! He was blessed to be married to Paige. No matter their wobbly past or slightly uncertain present, their future together held so much promise of good things.

Earlier, when he told Elinore that he and Paige were working on a real marriage that would last for the rest of their lives, he meant it. He loved Paige and wanted their marriage to be whole and strong. Prayed about it every day. Several times a day.

Lord, thank You for giving me a family. It's a blessing beyond anything I could have imagined.

He set his hands on the countertop. Sighing, he thought over his morning's work. Craig's birth certificate hadn't been available from the Oregon Office of Vital Statistics, which meant he must have been born in another state. He ran Evie Masters' name through several databases and came up empty on a current address. Her last known place of residence was an apartment in Nevada. He called the business manager of the building, but the guy said he didn't have a forwarding address. He even called Glenda at the hospital, and the address Evie had submitted there was bogus.

If Evie assisted Edward in kidnapping Paisley, based on the video placing her at the hospital at the same time, how much did Craig know about it? Was he just as involved? Considering he helped rescue Paisley from Edward, that didn't seem likely. But what if he had a change of heart? Perhaps, plotted the kidnapping with Edward and Evie—co-conspirators—then changed his mind at the last minute?

Forest dropped a detergent pod in the dishwasher door, then pushed the start button. He heard the bathroom door close. Paige would probably be coming into the kitchen in a few minutes. It was time to tell her about his phone call to Elinore. With him unable to fully explain, how would she react? Would she think he was trying to keep things from her? After her reaction about him going to Portland, he dreaded the conversation to come.

He bowed his head. *Lord, could You help Paige and me face our past and work together as a married couple? Please heal the broken parts between us.*

Every time Forest looked into Paige's eyes, hoping she was softening toward him, he saw the shadows of hurt still in her gaze. How could he apologize enough times, or sincerely enough, for her to accept he'd never again treat her as carelessly as he had in the past? Now that he had to explain about

Elinore, without being completely forthcoming, would it make matters worse?

Moaning, he dropped onto the chair at the kitchen table and covered his face with his hands.

"Is something wrong?"

He lowered his hands and met Paige's gaze.

"What is it?" She sat in the chair next to him.

"I need to tell you something." He took her hand in his and imagined them doing this often in their marriage, telling each other they needed to say something or explain something. "I had to call Elinore today."

"Why?" She pulled her hand free.

"Because Mia went to see her."

"What? Why would that—" Paige squinted at him. "Is this what the note on the rock was about?"

"Possibly. I don't know for sure."

"How can I help?" She clasped his hand between both of hers this time. "We can't let Mia get away with this garbage. Her butting into our business. I've had my fill of her telling us what Edward says or wants. In fact, I'm downright sick of it! Someone needs to put her in her place. I have a mind to do that myself!"

He chuckled, immensely attracted to Paige being all worked up like this, like she'd go to bat for him, or join forces with him against the world. He kissed her cheek. "Thank you, baby."

"For what?"

"Being you. Understanding my predicament."

She gave him a small smile. "I overreacted about Portland. Sorry about that. Now, what did Mia want with Elinore?"

"I can't explain everything you deserve to hear. I'm conflicted about what I can say because it pertains to the case or has to do with secrecy in my department." He sighed. "But I want you to know the only reason I called her was to follow up on a lead about Mia talking to her. Can you trust me about this?"

"All right. I get that you can't talk about some things. I might not like it, but I get it." After a pause, she asked, "How did you feel talking with her? Can you tell me that much?"

"Yeah, I can do that." He tried thinking beyond her question to what she was really asking. Was she concerned he might still have feelings for Elinore? "It was partly a friendship call, and partly an investigative one. I'm concerned that a previous friend is being pestered by Mia, or Edward. Although annoying, asking questions isn't illegal." There was one other thing he should mention. "Elinore expressed sadness over our break-up. Says she's going to counseling about it."

"You mean like she still has feelings for you?" Paige crossed her arms over the table.

"Yeah. I'm not sure what was real or just stirred up by Mia's visit."

"Hmm. Anything else you can tell me?"

What could he share with her that wasn't against company policy and would show her that he was trying to be vulnerable with her? "I have done some undercover assignments in the past."

"Yeah, I know. Like when you watched my house. And the sting with Craig."

"Right. Also, I've pretended to be on a date with someone." He was being purposefully vague. But if this came up

117

somewhere down the road, he wanted to have been the one who told her about this part of his life.

"Wait. You've pretended to date someone?"

"Just job related stuff."

She rolled her eyes. "Something else you can't tell me about?"

"Sorry."

She sighed. "You being a detective means there will always be secrets between us, doesn't it?"

He wished he could disagree, but he couldn't.

After a silence, Paige got up and left the room. Was she offended? Annoyed with his lack of details? Should he follow her? Maybe they could talk some more. Although, it probably felt to her like he hadn't confided anything of substance.

A few minutes later, she returned and spread out the gallery blueprints and her pencil sketches across the table. "Want to see more of what I've been working on?"

"Absolutely." He'd do anything to be near her and not have to discuss Mia or Elinore or any potential problems between Paige and him. The case and all the unknowns still hung over his head, but he compartmentalized them and smiled at his wife.

For the next half hour, they discussed flooring ideas, laughed over the names of odd paint colors, both working with their cell phones, bringing up pictures of vinyl and linoleum options, cool ceramic tile patterns, then comparing their favorites. Being with Paige, getting to know her better as a friend and as a business partner was a wonderful respite after his worry over their previous discussion—or how it could have ended.

He spent the remainder of the afternoon working at the project house, then planned to attend a community meeting, but he couldn't let go of what Paige had said. Would his job requirements force them to always have secrets between them?

Eighteen

Judah dropped into the chair next to Paisley in the community hall for the town meeting. He met the gazes of a few attendees—Brad Kiefer, who helped him get back to Basalt Bay after the hurricane; Sue Taylor, the city council member who tried getting him to become interim mayor; Mia Till; and Mom, sitting on the opposite side of the aisle next to Callie and Kathleen.

These get-togethers usually made him itch to run out of the building. He hated the disunity and arguments that often ensued. Where was Maggie Thomas, innkeeper and town hothead? There she was, sitting on the front seat, frowning, looking like she was already chewing on nails.

Should be an interesting meeting.

Mia strode to the front of the room and tweaked the microphone. A shrill sound pierced the air. She waved at a few people like a queen acknowledging her citizens. "Welcome, Basalt Bay residents."

Why was she taking charge? Had the council given Mia authority? It seemed one of the town leaders should be directing this gathering, not her.

Not that Judah would say anything about it. He didn't want any attention on himself, especially in a meeting like this.

Glancing toward the back of the community room, he saw Forest standing by the door, arms crossed, glaring toward the front of the building as if he were perturbed with the speaker. It seemed fire darts of animosity were zinging between those two. Was it because of something Forest knew about Mia? Or because of her flirty behavior?

"We're all saddened by the events that forced our beloved mayor into exile." Mia's lower lip protruded in an expression of sorrow that didn't reach her eyes. "While we might not agree with his actions, let's honor the man who led our town through years of service with a moment of silence."

"Hear, hear." Deputy Brian pulsed his hand in the air.

Judah winced. Sometimes he doubted the lawman's loyalties. While he was the one who had arrested Edward— Judah witnessed that himself—was he doing all he could to ensure justice for Paisley? Why did he act like he was still loyal to the mayor when Edward was in jail?

After ten seconds of silence, Mia spoke again, "Tonight, the city council and I have decided—"

"Decided?" Maggie bellowed. "Why should you be deciding anything?"

"What I meant to say was, we need to bring a couple of matters before the residents." Mia smiled at the audience, then frowned toward Maggie. "We've already had debates about who should temporarily replace the mayor."

"Why temporarily?" Maggie lunged to her feet and faced the crowd from the front row. "Mayor Grant's going to prison for a long time. Why not vote in a new mayor? Let's elect an honest person who has a heart for service like we never saw in Edward Grant."

"Mrs. Thomas!" Mia said in a scolding tone.

Clapping and cheers followed. A few boos, too.

Mia pounded the gavel against the podium. "People! Order in the room."

Paisley ran her hand over Judah's arm. He met her gaze and shrugged. Things could get out of hand quickly if Mia or one of the council members didn't take control of the meeting.

The cacophony of applause, naysayers' shouting, and Mia pounding the gavel, finally quieted.

"Let's get down to business," Mia said with a huff.

"Why are you leading this meeting?" Maggie demanded.

Good question!

"I've moderated town meetings under Mayor Grant's leadership. Now, why don't you take your seat, Mrs. Thomas? Then the good people of Basalt Bay can get back to their homes quicker."

"That's telling her," someone in the back yelled.

Maggie dropped to the edge of her seat as if ready to pop up again.

Mia's bright red lips spread. "We all agree we need a leader, right? Someone who understands our town. Someone who'll take up the mayor's banner until these unfounded accusations against him are settled."

"Unfounded?" Judah muttered.

"Just ignore her," Paisley whispered.

Sue Taylor jumped up. "I nominate Judah Grant to take the position of interim mayor."

Not that again.

A few people in the rows ahead of Judah swiveled around and stared at him. He squirmed as others shouted agreements. "I second that!" "Let's keep a Grant in the house." "Judah's the best choice for the job."

Why did he even come to this fiasco?

Mia pounded the gavel and shouted, "Order!"

"Maybe you should say something." Paisley nudged his arm. "Even if you don't like what they're asking, Sue and the others are honoring you by recommending you for mayor."

"Yeah, okay. You're right." He stood slowly, palming the air to get people to stop talking. "Thank you, Sue, for your kindness in nominating me. I'm honored. But as I've previously said, I'm not interested in the position."

"Come on, man, you're our best bet," Brad spoke.

"Thanks, but no thanks." Judah wouldn't do anything that wasn't right for him and Paisley. He wouldn't take on such a huge task without knowing it was God's will for his life, either. Besides, he had enough on his plate with watching out for Paisley and all the remodeling work for Mom. When would he squeeze in time for mayoral duties?

"Judah, we still need funding for the shoreline restoration and cleanup," Brad said. "You're passionate about that too."

"Sure I am. I'd be glad to assist you and a private group. Just not as mayor." He nodded toward Brad and sat down.

Callie stood. "I nominate Bess Grant!"

What? Judah met his mother's gaze. She gave a slight shrug, not acting surprised by Callie's announcement. What was that about?

Fred jumped up. "I'm against it. We need a strong leader. Someone like Mayor Grant. No disrespect to Mrs. Grant, but I say we run a short campaign with two men expressing their views. Then the council can choose who will run the town until next year's elections."

"I must object, Fred." Mia set her hands on her hips. "A woman could be mayor just as well as any man here."

"That's right!" "I agree." Comments erupted around the room.

"I can't believe this," Judah whispered to Paisley.

She clutched his hand, but the way she didn't seem surprised over the nomination, either, made him wonder if she was privy to Callie's idea. Was this what the ladies' secrets meetings were about? Electing Mom?

He groaned.

"You mean to say, Fred Buckley"—Callie said his name with a fighting tone—"in the twenty-first century, Basalt Bay can't vote for a woman to lead our community with strength and compassion?"

"Yeah, Fred! Is that what you're saying?" Maggie stood and flung her arms out toward the group. "Do the rest of you agree with his antiquated 1950's sentiment?"

"No!" "Vote for Bess Grant!" People yelled, stomped their feet, and made loud whistles.

Mia pounded her gavel on the podium. "Order! Order!"

Fred's face creased into a deep scowl, aging him by ten years. "What I'm saying is women can be on the council. They can have their say about town matters. But when it comes to strong leadership, we need a male role model."

"A male role model?" Callie hooted and shuffled into the aisle. "Was Edward a good role model? How many of you agree with Fred's archaic ideas?"

No one raised their hands. Who would dare cross her?

"What this town needs is someone who has courage." Callie's voice took on a dogmatic edge. "Bess Grant has proven herself to be a reliable citizen of our town who's stood up under fire. She's survived and thrived. She's even initiated a new venture that will meet the needs of our retail community."

Judah agreed with many of Callie's points, but his mom taking over his dad's old post? Hadn't their family been involved in the running of Basalt Bay long enough? Let someone else step up.

"I say we hold a revote as Fred recommended"—Callie's wide eyes perused attendees—"and the first person on the ballot should be Bess Grant."

About half the people jumped to their feet, clapping and yelling out affirmations.

When the clamor died down, Mia said, "If you'll take your seat, Miss Cedars, we can continue."

Callie glared at the younger woman like she'd stand where she was all day if necessary.

Maggie leaped up again. "I second Callie's motion."

"I third it," came Kathleen Baker's much softer voice.

"Now, see here." Fred stomped to the front of the community hall, opposite Maggie. "You are not on the city council. We're not here to make nominations or to vote. That's not your place!"

"You mean because I'm a woman?" Maggie howled. "All of us are residents of Basalt Bay. We care about our town." She marched toward him. "I say we replace the city council too!"

"How dare you!" Fred punched the air with his index finger. "We are the backbone of this community."

"If you are the backbone, you're a spineless one with outdated, biased opinions."

Fred and Maggie continued shouting insults at each other.

Deputy Brian rushed to the front of the room and braced his hands between them. "Enough! Both of you return to your seats or I'll haul you to jail for disorderly conduct."

"It's her fault!"

"He should never have been elected to the city council!"

"Sit down, both of you!" Deputy Brian shouted, his face redder than Judah had ever seen it.

Casting dark sneers at each other, the duo stomped back to their seats.

A collective sigh crossed the meeting hall. Callie finally sat down too.

"Just so you know"—Mia waved her hands—"I've offered my services in Mayor Grant's absence. Judah doesn't want to fill his father's shoes, but I'm more than happy to oblige."

Judah groaned.

Forest marched down the center aisle like he was going to object to her comment publicly, but then he backed up, shaking his head.

Callie lunged to her feet again, panting like it took all her strength. "Miss Till, are you going to entertain our nomination for Bess Grant or not?"

"If you know how meetings are supposed to be run, then do your duty!" Maggie yelled.

Mia gawked at the innkeeper, then at Callie.

A few others shouted opinions. "Bess Grant for mayor!" "Get on with it." "Accept the nomination."

Did Mia even have the power to "accept the nomination?"

"Okay, fine. If that's what the majority wants, let's entertain nominations for an interim mayor. The town can vote in a special election sometime next week, right, Sue?"

"Yes," Sue said cautiously.

"Oh, Deputy?" Mia called in a sing-song voice.

"Yes, ma'am?"

"Do you have a candidate in mind to be your mayor?" She winked at him a few times.

Ah, man. Judah might be sick.

"Oh, right." Deputy Brian cleared his throat. "I nominate Mia Till as acting mayor."

"Deputy Brian!" Forest thundered.

The room exploded with yells and jeers.

Judah couldn't believe this. Mom and Mia were going to run against each other for mayor? He swallowed a bitter taste in his mouth. Just like he'd thought, another town meeting was ending in turmoil and chaos.

Nineteen

Disgusted after last night's disastrous meeting where Mia wormed her way into a mayoral nomination—Forest still couldn't believe the deputy did that—he spent the morning chasing down leads on Evie Masters. He'd discovered a trail of places she lived for the last thirty-six years—Basalt Bay, southern California, several states on the East Coast, and finally, Nevada. She'd moved ten times in 1985, the year she left the Oregon Coast. The same year Craig was born, according to his driver's license.

Forest crossed out Washington and Montana from his list of possible western states.

He was so close to finding the county of Craig's birth, he could almost smell success. But each lead took him off-balance, almost like someone had maneuvered hindrances to trip him up. Had Edward kept his ex-mistress, if that's who Evie was, moving like a chess piece, so no one could find her?

How would that have looked for a secret son to be exposed during one of Edward's mayoral races? As the eventuality of his past came close to catching up with the public eye, did Edward come unhinged? Is that why he pushed so hard for Judah to step up? Including his attempts to do away with Paisley?

Another possibility came to mind. What if Evie had been on the run to get away from Edward? He was violent with Bess. With Paisley. Had he been that way with Evie?

Forest needed more information to fill in the gap years. There was someone he could call and ask. Now that he and Bess were partners in the gallery, he had her number in his contact list. Although he hated putting her on the spot about Edward, he tapped the connection.

"Hello?" Bess answered.

"Forest, here. I need to ask you a question having to do with Craig's mom."

"All right," she said tentatively.

"Do you know where she went after she and Edward were … uh—" He didn't know how to end the question delicately.

"After the affair ended? If it ended."

"Right. Sorry, I didn't know how to mention it without being offensive."

She sighed. "I never knew where the woman lived. Edward made several trips to southern California that year. Business related, supposedly. I always wondered."

"Do you know which city that was?"

"He flew into LA, if that helps."

"Okay. Thanks."

"Forest?"

"Yeah?"

He hated putting Judah's mom through any more heartache than she'd already experienced in her marriage with Edward, which Forest could only guess had been rough.

"I'm going through divorce proceedings." She inhaled slowly. "Do you think it's possible he lived a duplicitous life? Not around Craig, because I've spoken with him, and he didn't seem to know if Edward was his father." She took a long draw of breath. "But with her? With … others?"

"Hard to say. Anything's possible." Forest circled California on his list. "I don't have evidence of that." Other than all the moves Evie made in one year was suspicious. "Thanks for your help, Bess."

"Not much help, I'm afraid."

Forest ended the call and tapped Paige's number. Asking for information from his wife felt like a conflict of interest. But since she and Craig had been friends, she might know something about his past.

"Hey, Forest."

"Hi, beautiful."

She sighed softly. "What's going on?"

"I have a question concerning Craig."

"Forest—"

"I know. Sorry. It's a simple question." He paused. "Can I ask you? If you feel too uncomfortable with this, I'll figure it out some other way."

Another sigh. "Okay. Go ahead."

"Where did Craig say he grew up?"

"Oh, um, I don't think he ever told me where his hometown was."

"You're sure?"

It seemed weird that Craig wouldn't have told his girlfriend where he grew up. Was she covering for him? He hated to think that of her, but she had defended the man before.

"Wait a sec," Paige said. "He mentioned a beach in southern California. Something about it being warmer than the beaches in Basalt Bay."

"That helps. Which one?"

"I don't remember."

"Santa Monica, Newport, Huntington," he threw out a few beach names in the LA vicinity.

"Huntington sounds familiar, maybe. Still not sure."

"No problem. Thanks, baby."

"Forest? Treat him nice, okay? I don't like that he's in jail. He's not a bad person. Just got caught up—"

"I know. I'll do my best."

Ending the call, trying not to be irritated with her defense of her old boyfriend, he pulled up a map and compared the ten addresses he'd located for Evie against beach towns near Los Angeles. Seaside City was a match!

Two hours later, after contacting several agencies by phone, and providing legal documentation for his official search, he spoke with the County Clerk in Orange County. While the website said it would take ten to twelve weeks to get a birth certificate, Forest asked for Sheriff Morris's help in expediting the process. An Informational Certified Copy of Craig's birth certificate should arrive in Basalt Bay via Fed Ex in two days.

It was just one piece of the puzzle, but it should confirm whether Evie was Craig's mom—since Craig and Edward remained mute on the matter and the DNA results still hadn't arrived. If Evie was his mom, how involved with Edward had she been in the last month?

Close enough to be his accomplice?

Deputy Brian ambled into the office from the jail cells. "Keeping Edward and Craig from yelling at each other is a full-time job."

"No doubt." Forest linked his fingers together. "Quieter since the library deliveries stopped, huh?"

"No kidding."

"One thing still bothers me." He eyed the deputy sternly. "How were Mia and Edward passing messages?"

"Beats me." Brian tossed out his hands. "What? You think I was involved?"

"It crossed my mind. Last night you nominated Mia as mayor."

"Yeah. But that was a joke." Brian dropped into his chair behind his desk.

"Nothing humorous about it." Forest set his elbows on his knees, leaning forward. "You announced to the town that you were on her side, no matter what she's done."

"Aww, man. It's not like that. Mia's a big flirt. What's the harm in letting her be mayor until a real one gets voted in?"

"A lot of harm. It seems she's passed threats from Edward to citizens of Basalt Bay." Forest jumped to his feet, not mentioning his own beef with Mia talking to Elinore. "If she was involved in painting a threat on my rental car or vandalizing Paige's window, those are serious offenses."

"I know." Brian ran his hand over his hair. "I didn't think it through."

"What are you going to do about it?"

"What do you mean?"

"You're a hometown boy who grew up to be the deputy, right?"

"Yeah. So?"

"Step up. Be good at what you do." Forest didn't mean to lecture Brian, but annoyance over last night's meeting still burned through him. "Be a man of integrity. The town's looking up to you for guidance, especially in the absence of Mayor Grant."

"Never thought about it that way."

"This stuff with Mia has to stop. We must find out what she's been up to." Forest took a breath. "Their transfer of information might have happened right under your nose."

"That sounds bad." The deputy's face went pale.

"Sure does. Especially if Sheriff Morris looks into it."

"I'll double down. Keep my ears open."

"Glad to hear it." Forest would be keeping a close watch, too.

Twenty

Ruby lowered the last chunk of plywood into place for the subflooring and picked up the nail gun. Thwack. Thwack. The noise echoed in the empty room. The task of pulling up the swollen floorboards in the living room and replacing them with new plywood kept her busy over the last couple of days. Sometimes, she worked alone. Other times, Forest and James pitched in.

Earlier, Judah mentioned that Callie Cedars, the matriarchal aunt of the family, was coming over to meet her. Forest cautioned her not to be overwhelmed by the woman's blustering and bossiness. She had a heart of gold, or so Paige had assured him. Then he chuckled in a way that left Ruby more nervous about the upcoming meet-and-greet.

She enjoyed the camaraderie between the workers at the project house. Even Bess laughed and bantered with the guys. James's wit and charm was fun, too. His eyes lighting up whenever he mentioned Callie's name made Ruby smile. The older gentleman had acted surprised by how much work she accomplished. He said she had "pluck," which made her feel like a character in some old movie.

Too bad Peter didn't appreciate her work ethic aboard the *Lily Forever*. Instead, he became lord of his domain, chief bellower, acting like a lion with a nail in his paw.

If it had been up to her, she would have continued working on the *Merry J*. But Peter got riled up about a dispute with his uncle and stormed off. Said he was finished working for other people, particularly relatives. Even when she disagreed, he pursued the purchase of his fishing boat. Didn't seem to care what she thought. In the end, she signed the bank papers to keep marital peace. A lot of good that did.

She would have been more willing to let the hard feelings go between her and Peter if he'd been willing to go along with something she wanted. Like having a house on land. It didn't have to be big. Even one bedroom. At the end of the day, she wanted a place to get away from their business. Away from the *Lily Forever*. Away from the pressure of a never-ending to-do list. Somewhere she could bring home a baby ... if such a time ever came.

However, the way Peter came unglued whenever she mentioned starting a family, she doubted he even wanted one. She wasn't getting younger. If she was going to have a child, they needed to consider it soon. But here they were separated. She was alone with no intentions of heading north.

"Looks great!" Judah smiled from the entryway between the living room and kitchen. "You're a great asset to our team, Ruby. A natural at carpentry work."

"Thanks." She held up the nail gun. "This tool speeds up the process."

"You bet it does." He held up his cell phone. "Got a text from Paisley. Callie is on her way."

"Thanks for the heads-up." Inwardly, she groaned. What would the older woman be like? What would she say about Ruby having left Peter?

Whistling, Judah strode back into the kitchen where he and Forest were installing cupboards.

So far, everyone she met in Basalt Bay had been kind to her. She'd spent two nights at Paisley and Judah's house, crashing into bed each night exhausted after a full day's work. Last evening they invited Paul over for dinner so she could meet her father-in-law, a soft-spoken man who shook her hand and asked about Peter. His eyes filled with tears, and he said he was happy to meet his son's wife, even if he hadn't known he had a daughter-in-law before.

If Peter were to return and make amends with his family, could he finally live at peace? Not that she could force that to happen. Her coming to his hometown, meeting his family, and seeing where he grew up were for her clarity. Her husband had become so brooding and unpredictable, she wanted to discover the reasons he might be that way before she took steps to separate from him permanently.

She hated the thought of divorce. But as things stood, she couldn't go back to living and working on the boat. They'd come to an impasse. So, here she was.

Ruby slipped into the small bathroom that smelled of fresh paint and closed the door. She washed her hands and rubbed dirt smudges off her face, hoping to make a good impression on Peter's aunt.

"Where is she?" a loud female voice boomed.

That must be her. Taking a deep breath, Ruby rushed out of the bathroom. "Hello! I'm Ruby."

"So, we finally meet." Callie stood inside the living room entrance, hands on her wide hips, breathing heavily like she'd exerted a wheelbarrow load of energy getting here.

"It's great to meet you." Ruby crossed the room and thrust out her hand.

Callie gave her a once over before shaking her hand. "You're Peter's wife, hm?"

"I am."

"Where's the boy?"

Ruby clenched her lips to stop a chuckle. With Peter's six-foot-three-inches height, two-hundred-twenty-pound girth, scruffy man-face, and work-roughened hands, he could hardly be called a boy.

Callie tapped her foot impatiently.

"He's in Alaska on his fishing boat," Ruby said quickly. "I'm here by myself."

"One of our builders, I see." Callie perused the room with a grim expression.

"That's right." Ruby spread out her hands toward the flooring. "I finished replacing the wood. The next phase will be laying vinyl."

"Seems you know what you're doing."

"She sure does." Judah strode into the room and gave Callie a sidearm hug. He winked at Ruby. "Everything going okay in here?"

He was probably looking out for her, silently letting her know if anything got weird between her and Callie, he'd step in.

"Everything's fine." So far.

"Okay, then. I'll just—" He nodded toward the kitchen and headed that way.

"Is this flooring stable?" Callie tapped her foot against the plywood. "One can't be too careful in a construction zone."

"This should all be safe."

James exited the downstairs bedroom and came to a stop. "Callie."

"I didn't know you were here."

"Still here. Part of the work crew."

"And you were in … my bedroom?" Callie gaped at him, clenching her hands to her chest.

His face turned ruddy. "Well … no … I—"

"Someone has to paint the room before you can move in," Ruby said, trying to ease the awkwardness between them.

"But in my—?"

"Would you rather I leave?" James jutted out his chin.

"No!" Ruby patted his shoulder. "We need you here, James."

"Who's leaving?" Judah popped back into the room.

Ruby nodded toward Callie and mouthed, "Help."

"What's wrong?" He rushed over to the older woman. "Anything I can do?"

"Sorry, Cal." James coughed. "What's the big deal? Judah assigned each of us a workspace. I helped with the bathroom. Then on to the first bedroom. If that's your room, too bad. I didn't ask for it," he said indignantly.

"As if I'd accuse you of that!" Callie nailed Judah with a glare. "Is this your doing?"

"Let's settle down." Judah rubbed her shoulder. "Do you need a chair?"

Ruby ran into the kitchen and grabbed one of the folding chairs. Snatching a water bottle from the stack, she brought both to Callie. She unfolded the metal chair and twisted the cap off the bottle. "Here you go. Why don't you have a drink?"

Callie plopped down on the seat and slurped some water.

"Better now?" James asked.

She gave him an evil-eyed glare.

He shrugged at Judah. "I don't see what's wrong. I worked where you asked me to."

"It's okay. Don't worry about it." Judah squatted beside Callie. "This is your house as much as my mom's, but I have the final say about who works where, okay?" His voice took on a deeper tone. "James has been a godsend. He's helping for free. If he's painting in your future room, get used to it. Or stay away until we're finished."

Callie scowled, lines deepening around her mouth. In stages, her face turned a deep maroon. She glanced shyly at James.

This was interesting. Ruby remembered Judah mentioning something about James being sweet on Callie. Did these two have feelings for each other? Is that why Callie was so upset over him being in her bedroom? An old-fashioned sense of propriety? Ruby smiled and caught Judah hiding a grin too.

"Let's get back to work, shall we?" Standing, he spoke in his boss's voice, "Good job on the flooring, Ruby. Vacuum it down and paint it. Vinyl pallet arrives tomorrow."

"Will do."

His shoulders slumped, James followed Judah out of the room.

"I'm embarrassed you heard all that during our first meeting." Callie looked up at Ruby, her eyes shimmering. "I overreacted. Behaved foolishly."

"We're all fools in love," Ruby dared to say with a chuckle.

"Watch your tongue, missy."

Ruby snickered. "How long have you been enamored with James Weston?"

"Enamored?" Callie glanced over her shoulder. "Fifty years long enough?"

"I'll say." Ruby dropped to the floor in front of Callie, crossing her legs. "You've liked this guy since you were kids?"

"He was my brother's best friend. I was the sister no one paid attention to. A nuisance if they did."

Boy, that sounded familiar. James didn't see Callie. Peter didn't see Ruby. It was as if her husband wore blinders where she was concerned. Maybe she and Callie had more in common than she would have even imagined.

Twenty-one

For the last two days, Forest had been putting in long hours. The first half of each day was spent working on the case. Then he helped the crew at the project house as they made a push to finish the living spaces for the three ladies. Exhausted, he returned to Paige's late each night, then crashed in the master bedroom.

Last night, when he strolled by her closed bedroom door, the one she shared with Piper, he paused and prayed for her. He couldn't help wishing she'd come out and say hi or tell him goodnight. Maybe join him in the master bedroom. Even if all they did was talk, he wanted to fall asleep with his wife beside him, maybe holding hands, knowing they were on this journey together.

How long must he wait until she trusted him enough to let him into her heart again? How long would they continue this fake-marriage business? Months? Years? Groaning, he adjusted the lighting he'd installed over the mirror in the first-floor bathroom.

As he worked, he pictured the way Paige sometimes gazed deeply into his eyes. Like just before they kissed. In those moments, he hoped things were improving between them, that she was getting closer to accepting him. But when she told him there was to be no more kissing until further notice, his optimism flew right out the door. No kissing set them back too far. He wasn't willing to let that happen.

But didn't Paige also tell him she had abandonment issues after the way he left? Didn't that mean he needed to have patience and help her through whatever trust problems she had with him? His first reaction was to groan again, but then his thoughts went to prayer.

Lord, here I am dwelling on negatives. You are my joy and peace, no matter the storm. But between You and me, I want a real marriage with my wife. Could You work on that, please? I'll praise You for it every day.

Judah shuffled into the bathroom doorway, the tools in his toolbelt clinking with his movements. His puzzled expression transformed into a smile. "Hey, this looks great." He gazed around at the walls, up at the lights, down at the copper sink. "Mom and the other ladies will be pleased. Good work, Forest."

"Thanks." Forest stepped down from where he had one foot on the ladder and one knee on the vanity surface. "Attaching the fixture plates, and with a good wash down, this room will be finished."

"Awesome! Could you spare a minute and give me a hand with something?" Judah strode out of the room without waiting for his answer.

"Sure thing." Occasionally, they each required another worker's help. Forest crossed the living room where Ruby was installing vinyl flooring and entered the kitchen. "What's up?"

"Grab the other side of the stove, will you?" Judah had spread chunks of flattened cardboard in a trail from the front door to the empty space where the range would go.

"Okay."

Working companionably, they walked the new stove across the room, then the fridge, into their places, being extra careful with the recently installed flooring.

"Oh, my. These new appliances make me so happy." Bess rushed over, caressing the silver and black stove and fridge. "Thank you. You guys have blessed me so much. I mean it."

"You're welcome, Mom." Judah hugged her, then stood with his arm over her shoulder. "Is it all you hoped it would be?"

"Absolutely. I can't wait to cook in here. It's so beautiful."

While they chatted about how the shiplap turned out, Forest fixed himself a cup of coffee at the counter where snacks mysteriously showed up daily. He chomped down a sugar cookie. "As soon as I finish the bathroom, what's next?"

"The handrailing," Judah answered. "In fact, Mom, do you mind washing the surfaces in the bathroom, so Forest can start replacing the handrail now?"

"Of course. I'll do anything to help."

"Good. That okay with you, Forest?"

He'd taken a slurp of coffee. After gulping it down, he answered, "You bet."

Judah pointed out basic instructions about removing the old broken banister on the stairway leading to the second floor. "Try not to make a big mess on Ruby's vinyl installation."

"Will do." Forest grabbed a sledgehammer, screwdriver, and regular hammer before heading to the stairs. "Hey, this might be loud and messy," he warned Ruby who was hunched over a cutting board on the floor, small knife in hand.

"Do what you've got to do." Moments later, she stood at the foot of the stairs. "It seems sad to destroy someone's handiwork. Any way you can rebuild the railing instead of throwing it out?"

He smoothed his hand over the scratchy wooden surface and felt the aged roughness beneath his fingers. The intricate woodwork of the handrail looked custom made, a part of the history of this house. With a bit of TLC, he could probably return it to its original beauty. Would take some time, though. Judah might not go for that.

"Sometimes it's better to fix what's broken than to replace it and get something new, wouldn't you agree?" Ruby gulped as if her words thickened in her throat.

Was she contemplating her marriage like he was thinking of his? "I know just what you mean. Takes time and work."

"But worth it in the long run, huh?"

"For sure." Especially if they were still talking about their marriages.

Striding back into the kitchen, Forest discussed the option of restoring the handrail with Judah and Bess. They were under a time crunch, so he kept his points simple. Reconstructing a few parts would take time, but so would demolition and installing the entire piece. If he repaired the banister, it would make a great centerpiece for the house and keep the historical aspect intact.

Judah palmed his chin. "We're under the gun to get this done."

"Yeah, I know."

"I love the idea of restoring the banister," Bess said, her eyes shining. "I think we should give the stairway some special attention. Make it shine. What do you say, Judah?"

He chuckled. "You two are ganging up on me. Okay. Fine. But try to be fast about it, will you? If you get called away to your case, I don't have anyone else who can do it."

"I'll give it my best effort." Forest met Bess's gaze, then Judah's. "But I think Ruby could do it too."

"You're probably right about that." Judah nodded.

Eager to get started, Forest hurried back up the stairs.

A half hour later, Ruby stood near the base of the stairway again, gazing up at him as he sanded a rough section of wood. "I've been wondering about you and Paige."

"Oh?" He wiped sweat off his forehead with the arm of his shirt.

"I'm curious about how your second marriage happened." She shrugged as if uncertain whether she should ask. "If you don't want to talk about it, that's okay."

"It's not that I don't want to share." But his and Paige's relationship wasn't something he could talk openly about yet. "It's kind of private. We're still working on some things."

"I understand. You've probably guessed things aren't going well between me and Peter." She exhaled. "Why else would I be here alone doing carpentry work, right?"

"Sorry about that." He ran a cloth over the dust particles on the wood. "I can see you're going through a rough time of it."

"Yeah." Bending down, Ruby picked up a two-inch piece of detailing that had broken off one of the railings. She smoothed her thumb over it. "I keep pondering why marriages fail. Where did the fault line begin? Did he fall out of love with me? Was there something I could have done differently? Lots to ponder."

"Heavy topic." He stepped down to floor level to meet her gaze.

In the background, he heard James pounding a hammer in the bedroom. Sweeping sounds came from the bathroom. Judah's voice echoed from the kitchen where he was talking on the phone. Forest focused on Ruby.

"I've tried to reach him." She squinted at something outside the window. "But he's so distant. It's like we're strangers from different planets and we have zero methodologies for communicating. That's why I came here." She inhaled slowly. "Why did you come back to Basalt Bay? For Paige, right?"

His swallow turned into a cough.

"I don't mean to pry. Sorry." Her face color nearly matched her red hair.

"That's okay. It's not an easy subject." And he was used to keeping confidential matters private.

"I thought you might relate to what I'm going through."

"Sure, I do."

"There is one thing. Since you're a man, how would you suggest I find my husband's heart again ... if it can be found?"

A surge of emotion hit him. He imagined Paige asking this question about him. "If Peter's heart can be found by anyone, it will be by you, his wife. The most important person in the world to him. The woman he loves."

Ruby closed her eyes for a moment. "If only that were so."

How could Forest hope to offer any wisdom when he'd made a disaster of his relationship with Paige in the past? He couldn't tell Ruby anything about their present marital arrangement, but to say nothing, to give her no hope, would be heartless.

"I'm not the best one to ask advice about married life. I failed when I left Paige before. But I've regretted that decision for three years." He met Ruby's empathetic gaze.

"But you came back. You're here now, trying. You obviously love her. I'd give anything to have my husband doing the same thing. If Peter tried to work things out with me, it would be a gamechanger." She rotated her shoulders like she was relieving stress in her neck. "I shouldn't have dumped this on you. I can talk to Judah and Paisley, but their marriage seems so … idyllic."

"Yeah." He heaved a sigh.

"They're hardly the broken hearts I thought I'd find when I came to Basalt Bay. Now Paige and you—" She shrugged.

What? Did she imagine he and Paige were living together blissfully? If so, they were doing a much better job of pretending than he thought.

Twenty-two

Forest hand-sanded the railing, being careful of the parts he'd glued, while his mind hummed with ideas about Paige and him. They'd been married for five days. Five days of living together, but not really being together. What could he do to help his wife realize he was all in when it came to their relationship? Spend more time talking? Should he make more of an effort in the romance department? She seemed to like it when they kissed, yet she was reluctant about it too. Did she like flowers? Roses? He didn't even know her preferences. What about love notes?

"Mr. Harper!"

He jerked at Callie's loud voice.

"Yes, ma'am?" He stood on one of the stairs, wincing at the stiffness in his knees and the pain that flared beneath his toes from the broken glass injury. The hours he'd spent kneeling at an odd angle didn't help, either. "Did something happen?"

"I'll say it did." Her chest swelled up like a balloon ready to explode. "I chose pale blue for my bedroom walls. Not pea green! Who's making these decisions? You?" She glared at him.

"Not me. Did Judah know about your color choice?"

"Knew and approved." She let out a growl. "It was probably that rascal James. He makes me so mad. Acts like his ideas are better than a woman's. I've got news for him. I have my own mind, and I'll speak it."

"I'm sure this is just an accident."

"Mark my words, he's out to cause me trouble." She yelled as if hoping the man heard.

James sauntered into the room whistling, obviously unaware of the turbulence boiling in the room. Coat buttoned up, his gaze clashed with Callie's. His whistling lips froze.

"There you are! You, instigator. Troublemaker."

"Me?" James flung out his hands. "What did I do?"

Should Forest dash in front of James to protect him? Or slither back to his knees and disappear into the stairway repairs?

"Why did you paint my bedroom an atrocious swamp green?" Callie thundered. If looks could kill, the man would be writhing on the floor.

James blanched. "It's Sea-foam. You chose the color."

"I did not!"

"What's the commotion in here?" Judah scrambled down the stairs, his gaze zig-zagging between Callie, James, and Forest.

Forest shook his head, warning his brother-in-law to stay out of the squabble.

"Callie, why are you upset?" Judah stopped a few feet from her.

She stabbed her finger toward James. "This incompetent worker painted my room a color I detest."

"He did?" Judah glanced at James. "Did you follow the master plan?"

"I did. Double-checked, too." He thrust his fingers through his gray hair. "I'm sorry if there's been a mistake, Callie. It wasn't intentional."

"I'm almost ready to move in. What am I going to do?"

"We'll paint it again," Judah said calmly, "today." He eyed Forest.

"I'll make a run to the hardware store," he volunteered.

"Good."

"Another delay." Callie wagged her finger at James. "You could have asked me! But, no, you charged ahead erroneously. Stubborn as a mule."

"James is a good worker. We'll get this fixed." Judah glanced at James with a question in his gaze.

"Sure. Sure." James toed the new vinyl flooring.

"Is that okay with you, Callie? Mistakes happen. I even put the stove vent in cockeyed."

Forest chuckled at his brother-in-law's attempt to soothe the woman's ruffled feathers.

Callie cast an irked expression at James. Then let out a longsuffering sigh. "Fine."

"I am sorry. Let's look at the master list and find out where the mistake happened. Maybe the store sent the wrong color. But I thought for sure—" James scratched his scalp and strode into the kitchen where the blueprints and room plans were.

Callie followed slowly behind him.

Hoping they could work it out among themselves, Forest resumed sanding the handrail. His thoughts returned to pondering ideas of how to romance his wife. When he picked up the paint, what if he stopped by Lewis's Super and grabbed a bouquet of flowers?

Words he might pen in a love note to Paige danced across his mind. *You are the best thing that's happened to me. I can't wait to walk on the beach with you, holding your hand, dreaming of our future together. I love you, baby.*

What if she hated flowers and love notes? Only one way to find out.

An hour later, after Judah called ahead for three gallons of sky blue paint to be prepared, Forest picked up the supplies that might make peace between Callie and James. One more stop and he'd head to Paige's.

After using his key, he walked through the back door and into the kitchen, a fragrant bouquet of mixed purple and blue flowers in hand, a note tucked into his coat pocket.

"Oh, Forest, it's you." Paige rushed into the room and jerked to a stop.

Had she thought someone was breaking in? He should have called out a warning, especially after the rock incident.

"Yeah, it's me. I needed to pick up supplies for the project house, and I wanted to stop by and give you these." He held out the bouquet to her.

"What are they for?" Her brows puckered as she brought them to her nose. "They're lovely, but we didn't fight or anything."

"No, we didn't." Did he need a reason to give her something? "I wanted to buy you a small gift to show you I care about you. That I'm thinking of you while I'm working."

"That was nice of you."

"I have a lot more niceness where that came from." He winked at her.

She chuckled, her face hueing a delightful pink.

He fingered the note he'd written. Should he give it to her? A hastily scrawled love note might be silly. On the other hand, she might like the gesture. He wouldn't know unless he gave it to her. He should go for it. Or skip it. Or— Slipping the small scrap of paper into her free hand, he let his hands linger around hers a few extra seconds.

"What's this?"

"Just some of my thoughts."

She unfolded the paper. "Oh, Forest." She met his gaze, her eyes glistening. "Thank you. Your thoughts are very sweet."

"And true." Glad she seemed to like the flowers and the note, he took the bouquet out of her hands and laid them on the table.

"What are you doing?"

"Just this." He clasped both of her hands and stared into her dark eyes. "I want us to find our way back to each other as a loving couple. More romancing. More trusting. More togetherness like this. I want you to feel safe with me, knowing I want you to be my wife forever."

"Forest—" She glanced behind her, probably looking for Piper.

"I plan to wait as long as it takes for you to love me back. But here's the deal." Time for him to put his heart on the line, even though he already did that in the note. "I desire a real and honest marriage with you. Whatever you thought this was—

marriage of convenience, fake matrimony, or in name only—I'd like it to stop being that for both of us."

"You don't get to decide that for me."

"I know." He gulped. "But we have to try to keep the doors of communication open. I want you to hear my heart—that I long for a real marriage with you, whenever you're ready. I need to hear what you want, too."

She didn't say anything, just glanced between him and the note.

"What do you want?"

She blew out a breath. "If only I knew."

After such a vulnerable answer, he gently tugged her into his arms. She might not know her own heart, but she didn't resist. The way she glanced at his lips a couple of times was his undoing.

He leaned closer and brushed his mouth against hers, feeling a powerful jolt of love and desire. "Oh, baby." He sighed. "You're really something. I can't get enough of kissing you."

She giggled and smoothed her hands over his shoulders. "You say the sweetest things."

If only she knew how much he wanted to say to her.

He kissed her again.

Piper screamed, "Mommy!" in the other room.

Paige stumbled backward, pressing her fingers against her mouth. Then she scurried down the hall. "Pipe, you okay?"

Forest strummed his fingers through his hair. Took a half dozen breaths. Poured himself a glass of water and guzzled it dry. Even though their kissing had been interrupted, he was glad he stopped by, and that Paige was receptive to his attempts at romance. Maybe he'd write her a few more love notes.

She strode back into the room, her soft expression gone. "So, you think you get to decide?"

"About?" He set down the glass.

"Bring me flowers, kiss me like you did in Vegas, and I'm supposed to do what? Crumble at your feet? Succumb to your charms?" She hiccupped as if close to crying. "It's not going to be like that, Forest."

"Like what?" He moved toward her. If only they could re-experience the kiss from a few minutes ago. Her cuddling with him one minute, then shooting daggers at him was confusing.

"You kiss me like … like that … and bring me flowers. Love notes. You decide when we—"

She didn't finish the statement, but he knew. His face flushed hot.

"I didn't bring you flowers, or give you that note, to try to get you in my bed, if that's what you're implying."

"No?"

"I won't lie and say I never imagine us taking the next step. If we're being honest, I do. But there's more to us having a real relationship than sharing a bedroom. I'm willing to wait for intimacy. However"—he let his voice take on a more serious tone—"I'm no longer willing to do nothing while I wait."

"Meaning?"

"We're married. Sometimes, I want to kiss you like a husband wants to kiss his wife. Like we just kissed." He gave her a slow smooch just to demonstrate.

She didn't push away, but she didn't give herself to the embrace as she did earlier.

He sighed and took a step back. "I stopped by to bring you flowers because you're my sweetheart." He smiled, hoping she saw he meant what he said. "Making out was an added benefit."

"So you expect kisses now, too?"

"Maybe I do." He grinned cheekily. "Two or three a day of what we shared a few minutes ago will be fine."

Her dropped-jaw expression was priceless!

All the way back to the project house, he kept thoughts of kissing his wife close to his heart.

* * * *

Paige smoothed the note Forest had given her over the kitchen counter, reading it three times. He thought she was the best thing that had happened to him? He thought about her at work? Her lips curved upward. Yeah, she'd been thinking about him too. About his kisses. About him sleeping in the room next to hers.

But his expectation of two or three long kisses a day? Huh-uh. Too dangerous. Too soon she'd find herself caving in to everything she was trying to hold back between them.

Although, with the way he held her close to him a little while ago, the intoxicating way his lips brushed pudding soft over hers, she might not want to resist him at all. Wasn't that exactly what she had to watch out for?

Twenty-three

Peter Cedars took long strides down the sidewalk in downtown Ketchikan, Alaska, peering into every shop he passed, searching for Ruby, his wife. Some might call him a burly man—wide shoulders, solid torso, tall, and he'd let his whiskers grow for a week. His jacket smelled slightly of fish scents and diesel, things people in this island town were used to.

At each place where he stepped in to inquire if Ruby had been in recently, or if she possibly worked there, he received a similar answer. No, they didn't know Ruby Cedars, or Ruby Tate, her maiden name. No, she didn't work for them.

Then he hustled into the next shop or business, asking the same question, getting a similar reply. Emotionally dog weary, he returned to his fishing boat, the *Lily Forever*, and crashed on the bed in the lower cabin for a couple of hours.

Lying on the custom-built bed that conformed to the shape of the bow, he stared at the white ceiling above him. He pictured his fiery, vivacious, redheaded wife, the independent woman who'd often manned the helm of his fishing boat, being somewhere in town angry at him, and frustration welled up in his chest cavity.

Before she left, why did he allow his temper to escalate until he was shouting at her? Of course, she shouted right back at him. Called him stubborn and prideful. She was right about that.

Why did he get so steamed when the woman he'd promised to love above all others pushed for answers about his past? She said she wanted to understand his heart, to know him better, yet he took her statement as an invasion of his privacy. Why couldn't she accept him without digging into his past?

Like a fool, he blew a gasket and told her to leave and not come back. He had to find her and apologize. Although, he still didn't want to talk with her about the reasons he fled to Alaska to fish with his uncle when he turned eighteen. Or how he left his family with hardly a word of explanation. Why stir up those old resentments?

He'd left several voicemails on her phone. Texted her a dozen times. Yet no response had come back, other than the brief text stating she was safe. Where was she? Was she trying to drive him crazy with worry?

He shoved off the foam mattress and headed up to the galley. He needed a cup of dark black coffee. His sixth for the day.

Thirty minutes later, he stepped into a souvenir shop across from the docks where passengers disembarked from cruise ships in the summer months. He immediately felt out of place among the aisles filled with sparkling jewelry and Alaskan memorabilia.

"Can I help you?" a thirtyish blond wearing a nametag of "Stacy" asked, her eyes lighting up like he might be interested in buying out the whole store. Must be a slow business day.

He decided to try a different tactic here. Instead of asking about Ruby right off, he'd buy something, get on the clerk's good side, then ask for information. "I want to buy something nice for my ... wife." Why the hesitation? Ruby was still his wife. Just because she left him ten days ago didn't mean she was staying away for good.

Keep telling yourself that, buddy.

Stacy grinned at him, probably imagining a huge commission. "You've come to the right place." She waved him over. "What kind of jewelry are you looking for?"

Hmm. Ruby didn't wear much jewelry. They were minimalists by necessity of living in a small boat cabin, so neither of them kept trinkets. Still, he wanted a nice gift to give her when he found her. For when they made up. And they would make up, he was certain of it. "Something not too fancy. A unique piece, perhaps. My wife doesn't wear much jewelry."

"Oh?" Stacy squinted at him.

"We're fishermen. Live in a small space." Why was he explaining their livelihood and living arrangements to this stranger?

"Would you rather choose something else?" She nodded toward a tall shelf of merchandise. "We have mugs, plaques, T-shirts."

Souvenirs for tourists. No, he preferred something meaningful for Ruby. Not that jewelry would be significant to her when she didn't normally wear it. Although, she put on a tiny cross when they ate at a restaurant once.

"I'd like a necklace."

"Okay. Have a look." She swayed her hands toward the display cases.

He leaned over the lit glass shelves and perused the delicate pieces mostly made of jade. Some of the necklaces and bracelets had gold nuggets or black diamonds. He whistled. How much would a jade necklace set him back?

"Do you see one you like?"

"Not yet." The longer he stared at the shiny gold-lined jewels, the more they looked the same to him. "Is this all you have?"

She raised her eyebrows.

"These are great, but would you have any that aren't so fancy? Something more original, maybe?"

Stacy stared at the massive shelf of golden merchandise. Then pointing her finger in the air like she had an epiphany, she said, "I'll be right back." She dodged into a curtained-off area with an "employees only" sign attached to the fabric door.

Peter leaned over the glass case again, perusing more necklaces. None caught his eye. None were like his Ruby.

A few minutes later, Stacy emerged with something gingerly held in her hand. "I have just the thing. The clasp on this one broke, and our in-house jeweler fixed it." She paused before showing him. "It's expensive, I must warn you, but one of a kind."

"Sounds good." Cost wasn't an issue. Whether Ruby might like it was what mattered.

Stacy slowly opened her palm. A ruby set in a bed of gold latticework gleamed on her hand. "This stone was found at a local quarry."

"It's gorgeous. May I?" He reached out to pick up the necklace.

"Absolutely." She dangled the chain and the ruby caught shards of light.

He fingered the fragile chain and rested the ruby against his palm. The coolness tickled his skin, reminding him of a kiss. Like Ruby's morning kisses against his scruffy cheek. The agony and the beauty of the remembrance hit him so hard he gasped.

"Are you okay?" The clerk's eyes widened.

"Uh, yeah." He gulped. Cleared his throat.

"Good. So, this one is unique," Stacy continued her spiel. "I'm sure your wife would love it since it was designed locally."

"I'm sure she would." He imagined settling this necklace around Ruby's neck and fastening the clasp. Her smiling up at him and kissing his cheek. Her forgiving him would resolve so much between them. If only a piece of jewelry could make that happen, he'd pay an exorbitant price for it. "I'll take it."

"Excellent!" Stacy grinned like she won the jackpot. "Don't you want to hear the price first?"

"Oh, right, sure."

She told him a large sum, and he whistled again.

"Oh, well. It's my peace offering."

"Are you in the dog house?" she asked in a teasing tone.

He tensed. He'd always hated the term "in the doghouse" as if he were a misbehaving animal. But he forced himself to relax. Stacy didn't mean anything by it. "You might say so."

Ruby, where are you? Come home to me.

Would she accept him back, accept that their relationship was as unique as he hoped this slightly irregular ruby might symbolize?

In the busyness of the transaction, he almost forgot about the question he meant to ask Stacy. He handed her the necklace to be wrapped. "Do you have an employee named Ruby?"

"Ruby Tate?"

"Yes!" His heart jumped into his throat. So she was using her maiden name. "You know her?"

"Sure. How do you know her?"

"She's my wife."

"You're Ruby's—?" She almost tripped, then righted herself on her way to the cash register, apparently in a rush to finish the transaction now. "Do you still want to buy the necklace?"

"Yes, of course. Can you tell me where Ruby is?" His gaze darted around the store. If she were here, he would have seen her.

"I can't comment on the whereabouts of employees, or previous employees."

"Previous?"

Stacy placed the necklace in a small white box and wrapped a narrow gold ribbon around it.

Peter pulled his wallet from his back pocket and removed a debit card. "How long has it been since she stopped working here?"

Putting the necklace box in a decorative red store bag, the clerk didn't answer his question. She ran his card through the machine.

"Please, she's my wife. I'm worried sick. I haven't been able to find her. Can you tell me anything?"

She stared at him as if scanning his brainwaves for motives or sincerity. "You seem like a nice enough guy." She handed him the card. "She left three days ago."

Three days. He exhaled sharply. "Where'd she go?"

"She was going south."

He groaned. "South" meant the lower forty-eight. A lot of ground for him to search.

"Thanks for your help. And for telling me she was here." Lifting the bag, he strode to the door.

"Wait." Stacy followed him. "There's one other thing."

"What's that?" He glanced over his shoulder.

"She said she was leaving to get to the source of her husband's pain."

The source of—? Oh, no. That meant only one place.

Basalt Bay.

Twenty-four

After Forest left early for the deputy's office, saying he was expecting news about his case, Paige rolled out her blueprints onto the kitchen table. A small piece of paper unfurled with the prints. Another note from Forest? Groan. But then an unstoppable smile spread across her mouth. How could she be annoyed with a man who hid love notes for her?

Yesterday, he gave her one with the flowers. Then she found one on her pillow last night—*I am so in love with you, Paige Harper!*

Her heart throbbed harder just thinking of Forest sneaking into her room and setting a message from him on her bed. Where might one turn up next? She was half-tempted to turn the house upside down looking for more.

She uncurled this one. Had he put it in her blueprints last night or this morning?

Paige—You are everything I could ever dream of in the woman I want to spend my life with. Have a lovely day! Remember, I'm thinking of you. I love you.

He was so sweet. Was he trying to wear her down? She clutched the paper to her chest. Sighed. She wasn't ready to embrace everything about marriage yet, but reading these endearing notes was a nice beginning.

She tucked the paper into her pants pocket. What if she returned the favor and left him a message somewhere? If she did, what would she say? He was obviously trying to reach her heart by giving her notes and flowers. His kisses were already out of this world.

But then she remembered their past. How she previously gave in to romantic emotions before knowing Forest well enough. Look how that turned out!

Groan.

Why couldn't she just say what she needed to say to him and ask about his feelings for Elinore? Then, maybe, they could get on with their married life. It wasn't like she'd never cared for anyone else. She had boyfriends in high school. Had liked Craig a lot. But she'd never felt for anyone else the way she felt about Forest, three years ago, or now.

However, the way he discarded her in the days following their marriage left her with insecurity issues. She hated that about herself. She wanted to be a strong and independent woman. Self-controlled. Not needing anyone.

Yet here she was wanting Forest's kisses, daydreaming about him, thinking of what she'd pen in a message to him, instead of studying her business plans like she should be doing. Instead of keeping herself at arm's length from him. But did she want to live her whole life with her guarded wall firmly in place?

Maybe she would leave a note for him on his pillow.

My darling husband. Er, no. Too much. *Thank you for the sweet notes you've given me. I thought I'd try writing one too. Seeing you look into my eyes thrills me. When I hear your car pull into the driveway, my heart pounds like crazy. I love being in your arms. Tasting your kisses is—*

Ahem. Scratch that last line.

While it was too soon to tell him flat out that she loved him, there was no hiding the truth. She was getting closer to being in love with her husband.

Twenty-five

By the time Judah sat down to eat breakfast with Paisley, Ruby had already left the cottage. Stuffing a bite of a cream cheese bagel into his mouth, his phone vibrated. He chewed quickly and checked the screen. The DNA company's logo popped up in his email notification. And with it, a heavy sensation settled on his chest. Was Craig his brother?

For a moment, he closed his eyes, picturing his previous supervisor at C-MER, the same one who'd kissed Paisley and caused terrible problems between them, sitting in jail. Perhaps, having wasted his life trying to appease a man who could never be pacified. Was Edward Craig's father too? Were they supposed to be one big happy family now?

He groaned.

"What is it?" Paisley clasped his hand across the counter where they'd set two bar stools to make an indoor dining space. "I can tell something's wrong. Are you worried about your mom being nominated for mayor?"

"I'm not thrilled with her involvement in Basalt Bay politics. But that's not it. The DNA results are back."

"You got an email?"

"Yeah, but I didn't read it yet. I've been so busy I've hardly thought about the results. But this"—he tapped the phone screen—"should answer some of my questions."

"Are you nervous about finding out the truth?"

"I suppose."

He loved this time together with Paisley. Starting each day as a married couple filled him with so much peace and happiness. His life had changed tremendously in the two months since she returned to him. More so in the three weeks since they renewed their vows.

Thank You, Lord, for this miracle of reconciled love. For putting our hearts back together as one. I can't thank You enough.

"It'll be okay, either way. You know that, right?" She ran her palm over his arm.

"I know. But thanks for the reminder."

"I'm here for you." She kissed him lightly on the mouth. "If Craig is your brother, it isn't like it's any surprise to the Lord. Like you've told me, He's looking out for our good all the time. Even when we don't realize it."

"You're right." He finished his bagel and downed his coffee.

"Do you mind if we pray about it? I mean before you read the email?" She tugged on his shirt sleeve. "Us praying about Craig and about the election together seems like a good idea."

He loved how she was initiating prayer between them more often.

"Sounds great. Let's do that right now." He stood and pulled her with him. Wrapping his arms around her shoulders, he whispered, "I love this. Praying with you is such a blessing. I love you."

"Love you too."

He led them in a prayer for God's guidance in their lives, and for Craig and Edward to have a spiritual transformation. And for God's will to be done in their sentencing. Paisley added a prayer of thanksgiving for their marriage, then she prayed for Ruby and Peter's marital healing.

Afterward, she grabbed Judah's cell phone off the counter and pushed it into his hands. "Please, read it. I can't wait another second to hear the results." She grimaced. "If he's your brother, will we have to invite Craig to family dinners? Thanksgiving? After he gets out of jail, that is."

"I don't know." It was still too much to take in.

Her panicked expression and her question reminded him of what was at stake. She and Craig had a past that could get messy if he wound up being Judah's brother. But, as she said, he was in jail. They'd face the rest with God's grace and wisdom the best they could.

Tapping the email icon, he opened the document with one hand and tugged his wife against his side with the other.

Paisley wrapped her arms around his waist and leaned her cheek against his chest. "What does it say?"

"Just a sec." He scrolled through the opening lines, finally reaching pertinent data. He inhaled as he absorbed the words. "The DNA is a 49.5 percent match."

"So he's your—"

"Yep, brothers." He'd sensed this might be the outcome. Hadn't his mother even thought it was true? Although, he hadn't wanted to believe it. Inwardly denied it.

"Craig Masters is a part of our family," Paisley said in a stage whisper.

"You okay?" He smoothed his fingers over her hair.

"I will be."

He hugged her. This news would take time for them to adjust to. "This means I have two family members in jail."

"That's right. Sorry."

"It's okay. We'll both be okay."

A burden to pray more for his family pressed on his heart. What could he do to show God's love and grace to these two men—father and brother—who'd made such bad choices that affected the Grant and Cedars families?

Twenty-six

Forest strode across the floor of the deputy's office for the umpteenth time. At least his foot felt better today. He was impatient to examine the contents of the envelope that should be arriving any minute. Then he'd find out for sure if Evie was Craig's mom. Still running searches for her current address, he'd come up empty. If she were using a fake ID, which he thought she might be doing given the trouble he was having finding her, it would complicate things and cause delays.

His phone vibrated. Judah's name displayed on the screen.

"Hey," he answered. "Sorry I haven't started on the roof."

"No problem. Did you see the results?"

"The DNA results?"

"Uh-huh."

"Not yet." Forest crossed over to the computer and messed with the mouse, trying to quickly bring up his inbox. "What's the verdict?"

"A positive match."

"Wow." Forest read "DNA" in the subject line of an unopened email and tapped it. He skimmed the results. "Yeah, that's what it looks like. You okay with this?"

"Have to be, huh?"

"Do you want to tell Craig? Or should I?"

"Go ahead." Judah mumbled something away from the phone, probably giving James or Ruby instructions. "Sorry. Hey, we're busy here. Even if the ban on visitors to the jail was lifted, I don't think I'd make it over to see him today. If you want to share the results with Craig, since you have access, that's fine. Maybe do it privately so Edward doesn't make a scene, okay?"

"I can do that. No problem."

"It'll make Thanksgiving dinners interesting." Judah chuckled in a humorless tone. "Can you see us sitting side by side—Craig, Paisley, my mom?" He groaned like he had a belly ache. "We'll have to depend on God's grace and mercy more than ever to act loving in that situation."

"That's the thing to focus on. God's grace." This news had to be a shock for Judah. "At least, Edward won't be at any holiday dinners for a long time. I can't say the same about Craig."

Forest couldn't share anything about the case with Judah. But he was hoping Craig would turn on Edward and confess what he knew. If the birth certificate showed Evie was his mom, and the DNA results already proved Edward was his father, Forest would have several facts to discuss with Craig. It was likely he knew more about the kidnapping than he was letting on. But with a nudge in the right direction, perhaps he'd break and confess what he was privy to.

"James needs assistance, so I have to go," Judah said. "Just wanted to let you know in case you hadn't found out about the DNA."

"Thanks, man."

The call ended and Forest pondered the news. So Craig and Judah were half-brothers.

He fixed a cup of Brian's nasty-tasting coffee and tried forcing it down. Over the three weeks since he arrived in Basalt Bay, he'd endured the awful brew enough times he should be used to it by now. Nope. He scowled at the bitter taste.

Hearing a truck pull up outside, he rushed toward the door with only a slight limp and yanked the handle open as the delivery guy arrived.

"Thanks." Forest reached for the manila envelope.

"No problem. Have a good day."

Carrying the mail back to his desk, he tugged out the single sheet of paper. "COPY" had been watermarked across the page. He skim-read the information.

Craig Raymond Masters

Born: July 26, 1985

Mother: Evie Lynn Masters

The father's name was blank.

So Evie was Craig's mom. The DNA test proved Edward was his father. Forest had the information he needed to talk with Craig.

Were all three of them—father, mother, son—in on the attack against Paisley?

Twenty-seven

As Peter drove the rental car down Front Street in Basalt Bay, the flood-damaged buildings and boarded-up shop windows were a somber sight. He'd been worried about his family during the news reports of the double hurricanes, but he hadn't considered how devastated the whole town might look. Some things, like the brightly colored roofing shingles lying next to weathered gray ones, made it obvious things were in a state of repair. New windows and doors shone from some of the paint-chipped storefronts. Others still looked damaged.

Where was Ruby? He wanted to find her right off. Was Bert's diner the same gossip hub he remembered? Someone might know something about her there. He'd hit the food joint and inquire. Maybe grab lunch.

He never meant to cause his wife such angst that she'd leave him. Every marriage had its share of disagreements and disappointments, didn't it? He'd never observed a truly happy marriage. His parents barely tolerated each other. Aunt Callie had been single her whole life. Many of his friends, or his friends' parents, were divorced.

That's not what he wanted for him and Ruby. He loved her. Wanted her with him more than his next breath. Had he ever expressed those feelings to her? Or did he convince her by his actions and words that he'd rather be single than to be with her? What a bullheaded idiot. He was stubborn and thick-skulled, just like she said.

Opening the diner door, the jangle of the bell, the scent of fish and grilled meat, and seeing a few familiar faces sent déjà vu crashing through him. So did hearing his name shouted across the diner.

"Peter? Peter! You're home!"

Paisley charged at him and flung herself into his arms, squeezing her arms and legs around him like an octopus. Chuckling, he hugged her back almost as tightly. Her hair smelled of bacon and french fries.

"I'm so glad to see you," she said, stepping back from their embrace.

"Hey, sis."

She socked his arm.

"What's that for?"

"For not calling. Not texting to tell us you were alive. Or that you were married!"

He shrugged. "Sorry."

Laughing, she linked her arm with his as if all was instantly forgotten and tugged him deeper into the diner, presumably to find a table.

"That you, lad? The prodigal has returned!" Bert bear-hugged him, clapping him on the back. "Where you been all this time?"

"Fishing in Alaska. Buying a boat."

"So, you made something of yourself, did you?" Bert nudged Peter's arm with his elbow.

"Sort of."

It felt weird stepping back into the old town after twelve years and hearing Bert call him "lad" like he was his long-lost son.

"How are things going here?" Fighting back unexpected emotion, Peter nodded toward the room that looked the same as it had a dozen years ago.

The gray-haired man's smile stretched wide. His salt and pepper handlebar mustache twitched like bunny ears. "Trying to keep the place afloat. Mother Nature knocked me down twice. But we know it ain't how many times you get thrown overboard, is it?" Bert pounded his back again.

"I guess not."

Was Bert conveying a message? Did he know about Peter and Ruby splitting up? Did everyone? He glanced around the room, catching a couple of gazes. Returned a few nods.

"No, sir. It's how many times you climb back into the boat." Bert squinted at Paisley. "Find your brother a booth and serve him lunch on the house."

"That's not—"

"I insist." Bert shook Peter's hand, then meandered through the diner, greeting customers in his boisterous way that was almost a legend associated with this eatery.

"Here's a clean booth." Paisley wiped a smudge off a table with a damp cloth.

"Thanks." He dropped into it, feeling the springs in the seat beneath him.

"Why if it isn't Peter Cedars." Maggie Thomas stopped by his table and scowled down at him. "I'm shocked to find you sneaking back into town."

Sneaking? Even as a thirty-year-old and with Peter being a grown man, the woman had the power to make him want to disappear into his seat. "Hello, Mrs. Thomas."

"I suppose you're here to drag your wife back to Alaska like some caveman."

Peter's stomach clenched. Maggie Thomas knew he and Ruby were having difficulties?

"Mrs. Thomas, I hope you enjoyed your salad." Paisley patted the woman's arm, steering her away from Peter's table. "Let's give my brother some time to adjust to being back in town, shall we?"

"He should know what folks are saying."

"We can't help what other people say." Paisley cast him an apologetic grimace and nearly dragged the woman toward the door.

That was awkward. What were people saying about him and Ruby? Where was she staying? At Maggie's inn? Considering the innkeeper's comments, that made sense. He should go and find her. Beg her forgiveness. He stood quickly.

Paisley rushed back with a carafe of coffee and a mug. She dropped the cup on the table and filled it almost to the brim. "Let me get your burger before you take off, okay?"

"I need to see Ruby."

"Sure. But you just got here. Don't let Maggie get under your skin."

Hadn't he always let Maggie get under his skin?

When his sister tugged on his shirt sleeve, he groaned and dropped back onto the booth seat. It had been a long trip, and he was starving. He could use a gallon of coffee too. "Where is she?"

"Why?" Paisley sank onto the opposite bench.

"Tell me where my wife is."

"Don't get all fiery with me, Peter Cedars." She glared at him and crossed her white-sleeved arms. "Why didn't you tell us you got married?"

She was one to talk. Her and her secrets. Paige's too. They were quite the family of secret keepers.

"I meant to." He took a swallow of hot coffee. "Never got around to writing. Or calling."

"I wish you would have. She's quite lovely."

The warm sincerity in her words and expression hit a nerve.

"I know." He sighed.

Paisley seemed less intense or moody than he remembered her as a teenager. All grown up, he hardly recognized her. Although, that sparkling enthusiasm in her gaze let him know she was still game for mischief like she'd always been. If only they were young and carefree, spending whole days playing on the beach, like when they were kids. The world seemed a better place back then.

He brought the mug to his lips again. "Where is she?"

"Can I get your food first?" She reached across the table and clung to his free hand. "Please, Peter, don't leave town until we have a chance to talk. I've missed you."

He hated making promises he might not be able to keep.

"Promise me you won't disappear into the night again, okay? I hope you'll see Dad, too."

"Fine. Now, bring me the burger already!"

She hopped up and buzzed away laughing.

For a few minutes, he watched the rolling waves of Basalt Bay Cove through the window. The churning of the sea made him yearn to be back on his boat. Back to the solitary peace of working and living on the *Lily Forever*. How he'd hated being sandwiched between two strangers on the jet coming south. Hated driving out of the Portland traffic congestion. What a mess the road system was these days. He preferred the open spaces of the ocean.

Paisley dropped a delicious-looking double stack of burgers and veggies atop a bun and a heaping mound of fries in front of him.

"Wow. Smells great." Good thing he stayed.

"Enjoy Bert's finest."

"I will. Thanks, Pais." He dumped ketchup and mustard on the bun, then holding the burger in both hands, chomped into it. Mmm.

She patted his shoulder. "It's good to see you, big brother."

"You, too." Glancing up, he noticed a couple of scars on her face that hadn't been there twelve years ago. "What happened to you?"

Her hand flew to her cheek. "Oh, that." Face reddening, she shook her head as if shaking off a bad memory. "A tale for another time. I'm better now."

"I guess we both have things to explain before I leave town, huh?"

"Right-o." She grinned at him again.

"So, where's Ruby?"

"Working with Judah, my husband, and our new brother-in-law, Forest."

"Working how?"

"Can I have a refill, miss?" a customer at the next table called.

"Be right there." Paisley grimaced in Peter's direction. "Eat up. Then I'll tell you where you can find her."

Groaning at the delay, he stuffed a couple of fries into his mouth and watched her scurry around the diner, filling coffee cups and taking orders. Then, focusing on his burger, Peter chomped down the best food he'd had since Ruby left him.

Twenty-eight

Ruby lay on her left side on the vinyl flooring to get eye level with the baseboard's nail holes. Each tiny gap needed a smidge of putty before she could finish painting the boards.

Over the last couple of days, glass workers had installed new windows throughout the house, including the large one in the dining room. Yesterday, an electrician put in a lovely rustic chandelier with carved wood arms and Mason jar fixtures that shone brightly over the faux wood vinyl floor. The living room was coming together nicely, and she felt pride in her work. Crawling a few feet, she put putty in the next section.

"Ruby?"

She stilled. That husky male voice haunted her dreams. Peter was here?

Pushing up off her knees, she stood. "Peter."

"Hey, Rube."

The sight of him filling the doorway, his scruffy face and wind-tossed hair, his uncertain smile, made her want to run into his strong arms. She didn't. But how she longed to let go of her frustrations with him long enough to dive into his embrace. Kiss his soft mouth surrounded by a beard that looked a couple weeks old. She wiped her hands down her dirty work overalls, needing something to do.

"This is a surprise. What are you doing here?"

"I could ask you the same question." He thrust out his knit hat like a pointer toward the room. "Did you do all this?"

"Most. Not all."

Judah and Forest clomped down the stairs, yakking about upstairs paint colors. They came to a sudden stop, their gazes rocking between Peter and Ruby.

"Hey, guys, this is Peter," she said.

"What? Oh, hello. It's great to meet you." Judah strode forward, hand extended, smiling broadly. "Welcome to our project house. I'm Judah, Paisley's husband."

"Nice to meet you." Peter returned the handclasp.

Forest shook his hand next. "I'm Paige's husband, Forest."

Peter stared at him with a brooding expression that bordered on a glare.

What was that about?

"Have you seen Paisley?" Judah asked.

"Yep. At Bert's." Peter glanced at Ruby. "She told me where to find my wife."

So, he took time for lunch before looking for her, did he?

All three men turned toward her as if expecting her to say something or explain. She had nothing. Peter coming to Basalt Bay today hadn't crossed her mind.

"How long are you staying?" Judah asked.

"Can't say for sure." Peter shrugged and glanced at her again.

Did he come here to coax her back to Ketchikan? Back to his boat? As what? Worker and unappreciated lackey? She clenched her jaw. If that was his reason for seeing her today, she had some choice words to say to him.

"I'd better get back to it." Judah briefly met her gaze and trotted into the kitchen.

"Nice meeting you." Forest nodded at Peter and scurried after Judah.

"I wish you would have returned my calls." Peter stepped toward her. "I've been worried about you."

"Have you?" she spoke aloofly.

"Of course, I have. I've missed you, Rube."

He shouldn't call her that nickname. Shouldn't act as if nothing were wrong between them, when everything was wrong. How did he even know to look for her in Basalt Bay?

Outdoors, raindrops splattered against the window. Judah had said a storm was coming in from the north, so they didn't have to be concerned about it turning into another hurricane. A relief. On top of Peter's arrival, she didn't want to worry about a bad storm.

"You should have called and told me where you were."

Should have? Her shoulder muscles tightened. A rude comeback hovered on her tongue. *I left you. I didn't plan to call you about anything.*

"I texted you that I was safe."

"Right." He snorted. "I hunted everywhere in town for you. I was sick with worry, knowing I caused this problem between us."

At least he accepted that much of the blame.

Crossing her arms over her middle—not because she needed physical protection from him, but because her vulnerable heart needed shielding—she waited for him to finish. Maybe then he'd leave and give her a chance to think over what his arrival might mean.

"Aren't you going to say anything? Why did you come to Basalt Bay without telling me? Without trying to"—he shrugged—"talk or something?"

He had a lot of nerve mentioning talking when he resisted conversing with her most of the time.

"I had my reasons." She lowered her arms.

"To find the source of my pain, right?"

A breath expelled from her lungs. Stacy, her brief, previous coworker, must have told him that.

"What does it mean? What pain?"

"If you didn't know, why come here looking for me?" She locked her gaze on his. "Why look for me at all?"

"I can't believe you'd ask me that."

"No? Then explain." She leaned her weight on one leg, crossing her arms again.

"Ruby—" Groaning, he trounced over to the window.

So, he didn't really want to talk? Didn't want to uncover the problems between them. Why come all this way then clam up?

"I have work to do, anyway. Where are you staying?"

He whirled around fast. "I came all this way and you're going to keep working?"

Before she could get an answer out, Judah leaned around the doorframe from the kitchen. "Everything okay in here?" He lifted an eyebrow and glanced between her and Peter.

"We're okay. Thanks, Judah."

Familiar with Peter's loud, often rowdy voice, she didn't fear him. He'd never touched her angrily. His lack of words, his cold shoulder, were the things destroying her and their marriage.

Judah nodded and disappeared around the wall again.

"How long do you plan to carry on here as if you don't have a life with me?" Peter's strained expression surprised her. Vulnerability was unlike him. "What's your plan? You must have one."

"I've enjoyed helping Judah and your family. My plan is to keep working and finish what I started." She shrugged. "Then I'll figure out what to do next."

"That so?" He gnawed on his lower lip, his bearded chin moving up and down. "Paisley says Aunt Callie's going to live in this house."

"She is." Ruby smiled, her first since her estranged husband entered the room. "She's quite the powerhouse, but I like her a lot."

A less uncomfortable silence settled between them.

Forest walked through the living room. "Peter, if you need a place to crash, you can stay with Paige and me."

"Thanks." Peter stared hard at the other man. "How long have you two been married?"

"Just one week." Forest grinned. "I'm sure Paige would extend the invitation if she were here. She'll want to catch up with you." He nodded once at Peter then jogged up the steps.

"Why did you glare at him?" Ruby asked. "Earlier, too."

"Concern for my little sister." Peter ran his hand over his chin bristles. "Something she said in her letter made me think whatever they have isn't a love match."

"Are you crazy? Forest is head over heels for Paige."

"Maybe. Time will tell." He exhaled. "Need any help here?"

"Seriously?"

She'd rather he left so she could think. But he came all this way. And she wasn't one to turn down assistance.

"Wherever you are, I plan to be there too." He touched her sleeve. "If you're planning to stay until this renovation is finished, I'd better help get it done so you can come home with me."

His words sent a fire coursing through her. If he thought he could follow her here and tell her what to do, decide when it was time for her to go home, he had another thing coming.

He undid the clasps of his coat and tossed it on a chair. "Tell me what you need me to do, and I'll do it."

She almost laughed out loud. If only resolving their problems were as easy as telling him what she needed.

Twenty-nine

"What do you mean, we'll have to sleep in the same room tonight?" Paige dropped her sketching pencil and glared at Forest, who'd come home unexpectedly.

"I wanted to give you a heads-up. I invited Peter to stay with us."

"That's fine, but—"

"Did you say something to him about us? Something that might make him dislike me?" Forest took a glass out of the kitchen cupboard and eyed her over his shoulder.

"No. Why?"

He ran the faucet, leaving his finger in the stream to check the temperature. "When I introduced myself, he acted like he already had a grudge against me. It was weird."

When Paisley called earlier to tell her Peter was in town, Paige was thrilled to hear their brother was back. She hadn't seen him in twelve years. But why would he have a beef against Forest?

"He knows I had a child on my own. Maybe he has concerns about your involvement now."

Forest squinted at her as he filled his glass.

"I wrote to him about our marriage and divorce." She stacked a couple of sketches into a pile. "Maybe he doesn't like your being back in my life. Big brother stuff. Nothing to worry about."

"Okay. His staying here will be good, then. I can show him I'm not the cad he might think I am." Forest guzzled the water. "Where's Piper?"

"At Necia's for a playdate." She strode to the other side of the kitchen table. "Now, tell me, why did you say we have to share a bedroom?" She wasn't letting that comment slide.

"So your brother doesn't suspect our marriage is anything other than normal."

"Are you suggesting we pretend to be happy newlyweds while he's here?" She nearly choked on the question.

"Would that be so difficult?" Forest's gaze held a challenge. "Maybe after our kiss yesterday, after the note I found under my pillow this morning"—his serious look transformed into a grin—"it might not be too hard for you to pretend you like me. Hmm?"

Her face burned. Of course, she enjoyed his kisses. And she did leave him the note. "I don't have to pretend to like you, Forest."

"No?"

"I like kissing you," she said boldly. "I enjoy your notes. Even writing one back was fun. It's the intimacy I'm not ready for. The sharing of a bedroom and what that means." Admitting that much made her heart pound like crazy. "But if we must create an atmosphere of a real marriage for Peter's sake, fine. I'll put him on the futon in the guest room, and you can sleep on my bedroom floor tonight."

Setting down the glass, he leaned both hands against the table's surface. "Who don't you trust, Paige? Me? Or you?"

"That's not fair." He was the one pushing for them to sleep in the same room. Not her.

"Since we're legally married, I say we can share a bed safely. Pile up pillows between us, if it makes you feel better. Then I won't accidentally bump into you while you're sleeping." The merriment in his gaze said he was enjoying this discussion more than she was.

"With the way you snore, I doubt I'll be able to sleep at all."

"Sorry about that. Now, I'm going to grab a sandwich and head to work." He glanced at the clock. "I got called back to the station, but I wanted to stop and talk with you about your brother staying here. About us sleeping together."

"Forest!"

His laugh made her blush even more.

Could she pull off a charade of marital bliss for her brother's sake?

Thirty

After Forest left the house, still feeling a bit of humor over Paige's reaction to his announcement, he headed for the deputy's office. An hour ago, he'd gotten a call from Brian saying Craig wanted to talk with him. Earlier, when Forest told him about the DNA results and showed him the birth certificate proving Evie and Edward were his parents, Craig acted like he didn't care. Smirky and snarky, he was a hard man to read. So this callback was a surprise.

Forest strode into the office and found Brian pacing in front of his desk, his black shiny shoes clacking a rhythm against the floor.

"What's going on?"

"Good. You're here." Brian rocked his thumb toward the closed interrogation room door. "The prisoners were shouting at each other like maniacs. Yelling as if they'd tear one another's throats out, if they were able to reach each other, that is. I removed Craig. He shouted accusations and expletives at Edward all the way across the office."

"What caused the ruckus?"

"You."

"Me?"

"Whatever you spoke to him about earlier. His mom. Edward being his out-of-wedlock father." Brian wrinkled his nose like he'd caught a bad smell. "Granted, he used more colorful words. Plenty of hate and angst boiling between those two."

"Maybe we're getting somewhere." Forest took off his coat and drooped it over the chair at his desk. Then he tried to mentally prepare himself to question Craig again.

"I called Sheriff Morris and explained what's going on." Brian dropped into his chair. "He wants a call from you as soon as you see Craig."

"Will do."

"One other thing." Brian pointed toward the door to the jail cells. "After such a volatile explosion, and considering their father-son connection, one of them will be moved to another facility today."

"It's about time. Edward, I hope."

"That would make my job easier," Brian said.

Inside the interrogation room, Forest crossed to the chair opposite Craig, whose head was lowered, not making eye contact, and sat down. "Hello."

No movement or response.

"What's going on?"

Craig lifted his face slightly, his features dark and foreboding. His hair poked up in tufts.

"Why did you wish to see me?" After a half-minute of silence, Forest asked, "Are you going to explain? Or are we going to sit here and say nothing? I heard you and Edward had a verbal brawl."

Craig swallowed noisily. "It's over. Gone. The control. The secrets. The plan."

"The plan?" Forest sat up straighter.

"When Mia told me she thought Edward was my father, I didn't believe her. Didn't want to believe her." Craig grimaced. "I'm not like him. You can see I'm not, can't you?"

"Okay." Forest waited for the man to reveal his story at his own pace, glad he was opening up, finally. This was Judah's brother, which meant he was Forest's relative by marriage, too.

"His dominance over me all those years makes sense. As mayor he wouldn't want an embarrassing son. Not one who wasn't perfect like Judah."

Forest didn't comment.

"You know what?" Craig's volume escalated. "He's a monster! A raving mad monster! How could I have thought he cared for me as a mentor? He had the gall to act like he cared, but all he wanted to do was control me. Just like everyone else." The man's glare homed in on Forest. "Like he's done with Judah, Bess, Mia, even Paisley." He said her name softly.

Forest gulped. He wasn't recording this conversation when he probably should have been. He just sat and listened, recognizing heartbreak when he heard it in the man's voice, in the way his gaze pinged around the room as if searching for one thing worth looking at and not finding it.

"It's over," Craig mumbled again. "Thinking I need his approval. That he'd bring me up the ranks. He guaranteed me a lead position in C-MER. Promised if I kept my nose clean, did exactly as he told me to do, he'd give me a job at City Hall, too. Lies! Anything I wanted, he said he'd give me if—" His face collapsed into a silent wail. "I'm disgusted with myself. He had me do things—" He leaned over and spit on the floor. "To Paisley. Things I'm ashamed of."

Forest's gut clenched.

"I'm sorry. So sorry. I want to tell her that."

"And Paige?"

"Huh?" Craig jerked. "What about her?"

Forest shouldn't make this personal, but he couldn't seem to stop himself. "Did you do things to Paige that Edward forced you to do?"

"No. I would never do that." Craig glared at him. "No matter what Edward said, I never would have harmed her. I cared for her and Piper like they were my family, my wife and child. I wouldn't let him near them."

Craig's claim to his family struck a nerve in Forest.

"Other than one thing."

"What's that?" His fists clenched.

"I warned her about the gallery. Tried to get her to leave, give up and do what the derelict on the mountain wanted. What he demanded of me, her, and everyone else. If I didn't try to get her to succumb to his taking over the building, he threatened to expose—" Craig's face contorted. "But I never would have allowed him to hurt her or Piper. I promise you that."

Forest's muscles relaxed a little. "But you allowed him to hurt Paisley?"

"No. Yes. I mean—" He groaned. "I didn't know the extent of his barbaric nature. I stopped it as soon as I had an inkling." He let out a low growl that sounded like an injured animal. "I hate that I'm made of the same cloth as him. Forty-nine percent. Isn't that what the DNA proved? He's a rabid dog, and I'm just like him."

"No, you aren't." Forest reminded himself he was still dealing with a criminal. But he felt compassion for the other man too. Anyone caught in Edward's web seemed to have gotten there by being coerced into some scheme or wrongdoing. "You're here. Doing what's right, now." He didn't know where those gentler words came from. But for Paige to have cared for this man, he doubted Craig had ever done anything harmful to her or Piper. He needed redemption and grace. Just like Forest had.

Craig breathed heavily. "I need to see her."

"Who?"

"Paige."

"I don't know about that." Forest remembered what Judah said about Craig possibly coming to Thanksgiving dinner. He'd rather the other man never sat at the same dinner table with Forest's wife and child, especially knowing he thought of them as his family. But where was the grace he pondered before? Where was God's love? He released a slow sigh.

"I need to tell you, tell her, about my mom." Craig cleared his throat. "I want to explain. After all the lies from my parents, there's no reason to hold back or protect either of them ever again."

This was good news. Exactly what Forest hoped for.

"Where is Evie? You know where she is, don't you?"

"If I tell you, if I turn against Edward to the district attorney, I want you to make certain they go easy on her. It isn't her fault. She's sick. Deluded into thinking—" Craig shook his head as if he couldn't even say whatever it was. "He's controlled her for years. She thinks he loves her. But that's a lie too. Please."

"I can't make any promises."

"Edward forced her to do things too. Aggressive things that seemed out of character for her. I thought she tried hard to please him because he kept me from jail when I stole some things in junior high. Got into trouble with drugs in high school, too." Craig's facial features tightened up. "That she had to toe the mark to keep this powerful man from exposing the truth about me. The guilt of that has hung over my head for years."

"So, she's been working for him?"

"That's where the money came from that we lived on when I was a kid. Her doing odd jobs for him. Some questionable." Craig swallowed and frowned. "I never imagined Edward Grant was my father. She told me my father died in a motorcycle accident when I was a toddler. That Edward had been kind to a single mom down on her luck. Makes me sick.

"Even when Edward helped with my college tuition, I thought it was to keep that noose around my neck—*'Get good grades or I'll turn you in to law enforcement. Your mother will suffer.'* If I didn't do everything he wanted, and keep my mouth shut, he'd expose my theft and drug use, or else stop providing for my mom. He even threatened to report her crimes to keep me in line."

"Sounds like it's been rough on you." Forest linked his hands together over his knee. "What are you willing to do to make things right?"

"I, well, I have a plan." Craig took a deep breath. "If I go through with it, I want two things in return."

"Is that right?" Forest wouldn't agree or disagree, but he was interested in keeping the dialogue going. "What do you have in mind?"

"I'll tell you what my mother's been up to—"

"Yes?"

"What Edward has put her up to. In exchange I want my freedom." His voice got quieter. "Community service to the end of time is fine. I can't bear to be in that jail cell for another minute."

Forest had been working on the case for three weeks. Now things were finally splitting open. When this was over, he and Paige would be free of the threats and warnings. Free to live their lives how they wanted ... together as a couple, as a family. That made him want to push for more from Craig.

"Start talking."

Thirty-one

Paige scooted as far as she could get to the edge of the queen-sized mattress in the master bedroom, her back to Forest. Behind her, he was already snoring. How could he fall asleep so quickly under these conditions? Too bad she didn't stuff pillows between them like he suggested since that might have absorbed his noisy breathing. At this rate, she wouldn't get any sleep tonight.

They'd set up Piper's small-sized bed near Paige's closet so Peter could have privacy in the other bedroom. All evening, Paige had enjoyed visiting with her older brother who left when she was only fourteen. Even before then, she hadn't felt a kinship with him like he had with Paisley. Now, she wanted to hear all about his fishing stories and Alaskan adventures. She appreciated every minute she got to spend with him.

But she sensed a reticence in Peter whenever he spoke to Forest, just like Forest had told her. Was he feeling belated protectiveness for her? Angry with Forest for abandoning her before? Surely, he didn't sense their present marriage was fake.

Ever since Peter arrived at their house, Forest had been pouring on the charm and affection toward Paige. When he slid his arm over her shoulder and tugged her against his side in front of her brother, she forced herself not to tense up or act surprised. But when he linked their fingers together, even bringing her hand to his lips and kissing it, she might have jerked back a little. Did Peter notice that?

She was thankful for Forest's thoughtfulness, the way he volunteered to clean up the kitchen after dinner so she and Peter could visit in the living room, the way he read Piper stories so she and Peter could take their coffee outside and chat. Even if she were an outsider looking in, she'd think the man was behaving like a warm and loving husband.

Husband.

She found another note, too. This one was tucked into her book on the nightstand.

I love you, Paige. Your smile, even when it isn't for me, makes me happy. Hearing you laugh is like music to my soul. I'm so glad you chose to marry me.

Oh, Forest.

The mattress jiggled and his warm fingers stroked her shoulder. She froze.

"Paige?" he whispered.

"Hmm?"

"Thank you."

"For what?"

"This. Letting me be here with you."

He stroked her hair, skimming his fingers over her sweatshirt-covered shoulder, the ticklish sensation bringing all her nerve endings to attention. Now she'd never get to sleep.

"I can't sleep." He sighed. "Think I'll go sit on the porch."

"Seriously?" She turned enough to see his eyes glimmering in the darkness. "You were just snoring."

"Sorry about that." Chuckling lightly, he leaned up on his elbow. "I know this is hard for you. Sharing space. Letting me into your life. I'm sorry I hurt you before. That you had Piper by yourself."

"Why are you telling me this now?" In the middle of the night?

He stroked her cheek. "Hearing you laugh with Peter tonight reminded me of all our laughter and fun back in Vegas. How connected we felt. I haven't heard you laugh like that until tonight." A pause. "Then, reading to Piper earlier, I felt like her dad."

"You are her dad. Don't let what Aunt Callie said bother you."

"I know. But for a second, I had this punch-in-the-gut feeling. Like I was a father reading to his kid the way he might have been doing for two years. Only that part of my life has been missing."

"I'm sorry, too."

She reached for his hand. Her fingers grazed the warmth of his T-shirt, the heat emanating from his chest. She pulled back. In the next second, his fingers clasped her retreating ones. He raised her hand to his warm lips and kissed her knuckles one by one.

Oh, Forest. Kiss me. Love me.

She groaned. Why was she thinking such thoughts? She wasn't ready for him to make love to her. This was why she didn't want to share a bed with him. Why she didn't want them kissing. Or touching. Her crazy, wild thoughts zoomed out of control too quickly. No more of that.

What she needed more than Forest's affection was to honestly trust that he would stick by her and Piper, no matter what. That he wouldn't leave during a crisis. The other stuff ... the desire to curl into his side and sleep against his chest, thoughts of kissing his sweet mouth from now until Sunday ... were illusions made from fairytales and daydreams.

The three words that had the power to cool any ardor strummed through her. *Sweet dreams, Elinore.* There would be no kissing tonight.

Forest let out a long sigh. "I have some case stuff on my mind, so I'm heading outside." The bed moved up and down, creaking as he stood. His bare feet made a shuffling sound as he left the room and moved down the hall.

His apology had been kind and humble sounding. The tender way he expressed his feelings about being a dad touched her heart. Yet even though she was attracted to him, and here they were sharing a bedroom, how could she let go of the grievances she held against him? Her abandonment issues? How could she ever forget those three whispered words?

Thirty-two

Peter tossed and turned on the futon in Paige's guest room, replaying, like an awful playlist stuck on repeat, the last arguments he had with Ruby. He was plagued with worries about the *Lily Forever*, too. Thankfully, a fellow fisherman was keeping an eye on her. But he couldn't help wanting to head back and check on his boat, even though he'd been away for only a day and a night. Had he lashed her down well enough? Was she taking in water in the fall rains? If he left, would Ruby return to Alaska with him?

Yesterday he volunteered at the project house to be near her. Unfortunately, they hadn't come any closer to an understanding, other than once again proving they could work side by side and not talk. It seemed they were pros at that.

It was five a.m. Back in Alaska, he'd already be working, fixing some mechanical parts, charting a fishing trip, or buying supplies.

He heard a sound. Probably Paige setting up her easel. She told him she painted in the mornings. Said it was her time to focus on her art before the kiddo woke up.

That's the Paige he remembered. When they were youngsters, she was always doodling or painting on something. She and Mom. A painful sensation burned in his chest. Thoughts of Mom and their disagreements had been pressing in on him ever since he returned to Basalt. He thought he got over the emotional rubbish ages ago. Apparently, not.

Three years ago, when he heard Mom had died, regrets and grief churned in him for weeks. He would have liked to talk things out with her, ask questions that could never be answered now. Death stole his chance to clear the air with one of his parents, although he certainly had plenty of opportunities and didn't take them. Maybe that's what was eating at him now. Here he was in Basalt and hadn't cleared the air with Dad yet, either.

Groaning, he pushed off the uncomfortable futon and trudged into the kitchen. Sure enough, Paige was painting. With her back to him, he peered over her shoulder at the canvas she was working on. "Wow. That's magnificent, Paige."

She whirled around. "Peter. I didn't hear you come in." Pointing the tip of her paintbrush dipped in dark gray paint toward the picture, she smiled. "Recognize this?"

"Sure do. Haven't seen the old lighthouse in twelve years, but I'd know it anywhere."

"I'm touching it up, otherwise it's finished."

"I'm impressed with your work. I'd display it in my house, if I had a house." He gulped, thinking of Ruby's desire to own a home of their own. Something he'd denied her.

"Thanks." Paige continued painting.

The idea of a place to hang pictures and settle down with his wife filled him with such a strange yearning. A home to call their own. Children born of his and Ruby's love. Why had he grumpily told her no about both things?

He crossed the small space to the Keurig. Prepping his coffee, he looked forward to his first gulp of the black brew. He'd down four or five cups before he was satisfied. One of the perks of early morning rising and working in the chilly Alaskan air was lots of hot coffee. Lots of time to ponder things, too. As soon as he took a couple of swallows, he leaned his backside against the sink and watched his sister paint.

"How's the gallery coming along?"

Paige eyed something on the canvas with a frown. "It's okay. If you want some work, I could use the help." She raised an eyebrow. "I don't want to take you away from Ruby, but seriously, I can't find a contractor who's available for a month."

Peter hated that everyone in town seemed to know he and Ruby were having marital problems. But why else would he be here in Basalt alone, staying in his kid sister's house?

"Sure, I could pitch in." Why not be useful while he was here? Although, his priority was working things out with his wife. For now, that meant working alongside her on the project house. But he could squeeze in a few hours to help Paige before heading north.

"Any changes between you two?" Paige pursed her lips and met his gaze in between paintbrush strokes. "If you don't want to talk about personal stuff, that's okay. We all have our problems."

Did she mean Peter and Ruby? Or was she talking about her and Forest? They seemed happy enough, contrary to what Peter first thought. Last night, he caught them leaning toward each other and Forest kissing her cheek. He'd also seen dark shadows beneath his sister's eyes. Maybe things weren't all rosy for the newlyweds. But what did he know? He drank his coffee cup dry and went back to the machine for a second cup.

"No changes," he said stiffly.

He was a man of few words. Being open and communicative had always been difficult for him, but he and Paige were siblings. He felt the urge to talk to someone, and she was here.

"Things have been rough between me and Ruby for a while."

"I hope you can work it out."

"Yeah. Me too." He returned to his perch against the sink, sipping his hot drink and brooding. "We're great coworkers, at least we have that going for us."

"Coworkers?" Paige made tiny brush strokes along the base of the rocks in front of the lighthouse.

"We worked on Uncle Henry's boat. That's where we met. Laughing, talking, sharing in job-related experiences. Then we fell in love." He stared into the dark brew. In his mind's eye, he saw Ruby dancing with him at a club. Her telling him he was someone she'd like to get to know. Someone special. Their first kiss had shot dynamite through his system. All he'd wanted to do was kiss and kiss Ruby Tate. A detail he wouldn't mention to his sister.

"Then?"

"Oh, right. A few years later, we got married. But then I messed up and became me again." He coughed hard, a pain searing up his chest.

Paige dropped her brush into the water. The murky liquid swirled as she turned the paintbrush counter-clockwise. "What do you mean you became you? Like you hid your true self from your wife?"

"Sort of." Peter drank from his cup, appreciating the hot liquid sliding down his throat. "She says I'm emotionally constipated."

"Ouch."

"Exactly. But I get it. I turned into myself. Outside, in. Didn't talk. We didn't laugh or go out. Just worked and worked." He gazed through the window into the early morning darkness. "I don't know why I did that. Self-preservation, I guess."

"We all deal with emotional stuff differently." Pointing to her canvas painting, she said, "I religiously paint every morning from five to seven. Losing myself in art helps me cope. Call it therapeutic. Although, it hasn't mended me completely." Her eyes glistened beneath the kitchen lighting. "I'm still searching for answers too."

"Things not going well between you and Forest?"

He wanted to comfort her, but they weren't close enough to embrace. Not his style anyway. More emotional constipation, Ruby would probably say.

"It's a long story." She nodded toward the canvas. "What do you think of the colors?"

"Great."

She obviously didn't want to talk about her and Forest, so he said, "I plan to go by Dad's later today."

"That's good." She wiped her brush against a clean cloth. "He's been asking about you. Need any moral support?"

Chuckling, he ran his hand over his short beard. "I should face him myself, being the grownup I am."

"If you need a buddy, I'm here for you."

"Thanks. I appreciate your letting me hang out here."

"Any time."

Over the years, he'd faced tough fishermen in brawls, wrestled two-hundred-pound halibut on board fishing vessels, mastered rough seas, and kept his boat afloat in horrific storms. Why was he so nervous about seeing his father?

Thirty-three

Before leaving for work, Forest sat with Piper on the couch and read a couple of books to her, mostly pointing out pictures. He closed the bear book with its ratty edges and sighed. While he liked his job with the task force, and he enjoyed the creative work at the project house, part of him wanted to stay right here with Piper and keep reading to her.

Piper patted his hand. *"Mow* books?"

"Sorry. I have to—" Why not prolong this time with her? "Sure, princess. One more book."

She picked up the horse book they already looked at twice this morning. He fingered through the pages as she made neighing sounds and chattered about "hosies" in the "bawn."

Noticing movement in the room, he glanced up. Paige leaned against the entryway between the kitchen and living room, watching them with a half-teary, half-smiling expression.

His thoughts returned to last night's interaction, his touching her shoulder, his wanting to take her in his arms and kiss her. He'd made light of them sleeping together. Of putting a pile of pillows between them to keep them apart. But it had been harder than he thought to be self-restrained, to not kiss her like he wanted to.

That's why he'd gone outside. To cool off and distract himself with thoughts about the case.

Edward had been taken to the Florence jail yesterday. He balked and shouted at Deputy Brian, accusing him of every false offense under the sun. But the deed was done.

Then there was Craig's idea to get a confession from Evie. His plan had merit. However, his depiction of his mom's unpredictable behavior as she fulfilled Edward's demands in the past troubled Forest. He knew firsthand that things could go wrong in a sting.

Paige sure looked lovely in the morning light. Although, she always looked lovely to him. If only she were willing to accept him into her heart as her husband, as the man who wanted to love her for the rest of her life, it would be a gift he'd treasure forever. Man, he wanted to walk over and kiss her. Tell her how much he wanted— He groaned. Those were thoughts better saved for another time, or he wouldn't want to leave at all today. He had work to do at the deputy's office. Hard labor to be accomplished at the project house. Still, his gaze lingered on his wife for a few extra seconds.

The words from the note he'd found in his toiletries bag this morning rattled through his thoughts, teasing his senses. *Each day we're together, I grow fonder of you. I know we can't go backward to find what we lost, but I wish for that time and what we had. Thank you for being patient with me.*

She was growing fonder of him? That almost sounded as if she loved him. He liked how vulnerable she was being in her notes. She wished for what they had? So did he. But he'd like to stir up that remembrance in her with what they could have right now.

He'd hide another love note when he got back from work later, being careful in its placement so Peter didn't find it. What should he say this time? *My darling Paige—*

"You'd better get going or you're going to be late," she said, sounding cute and wifely.

"Yeah, I know." He cleared his throat and closed the book. "Mommy says I have to go to work, Piper."

"No. *Mow stowies.*"

He extricated himself from the pile of books and removed his arm from around her.

Piper stared up at him with watery eyes. "*Mow* books!"

"Piper." Paige rushed over and picked her up. "Forest, I mean Daddy, has to go to work. You need to get dressed. Mommy has things to do, too."

"Books! *Mow* books." Piper's loud tone turned into ear-piercing shrieks.

Paige bounced her on her hip and went to the mantle, pointing out pictures. Still, the crying and broken-hearted pleas for more books continued.

Forest felt helpless. Not only did he hate seeing women cry, he hated hearing his daughter cry also. Had he caused this reaction by continuing to read to her? He scooped up the books into a pile and set them on the coffee table.

"There's Piper." Paige pointed to a baby picture. "There's Mommy and Papa."

"Papa—" Piper wailed. "I want Papa!"

She could twist Forest's heart in knots with those big tears. Suddenly, she arched backward, reaching both hands out toward him. "*Daee. Daee!*"

"Oh, princess." He crossed the space between them. "I'm right here." He picked her up, hoping Paige didn't mind him interfering. "I'll always be right here." He met Paige's glance. Did she get his message too?

"*Mow* b-books?"

"I can't read more books right now. I have to go to work with your Uncle Judah."

"Unca Dzuda?" Piper sniffed.

"Uh-huh." Forest walked into the kitchen, bouncing her like Paige had been doing. "Later when I come home, we'll read more books, okay?"

She nodded and wiped both fists beneath her eyes.

"You have a nice day with Mommy." He kissed the top of her head and turned to find Paige watching him with that soft look on her face. He handed Piper to her. "I'll see both of you lovely ladies after work, all right?"

"Okay." Paige clasped his hand. "Thank you for spending time with her and for being here with us, even if we have to work through the screaming part. And the other stuff."

"Sure. It's an honor."

She stared at him so intently. What was she thinking? Did he dare close the gap between them? Maybe his stepping up and becoming fatherly was another way of assuring her that he was serious about being here for her too. Time to take a chance. Wasn't their love worth him risking his pride? His own fear of rejection?

Taking Piper from her arms again, he set her on the floor and pointed at a ball under the chair. Then he slid his arms around Paige.

"What are you—"

Her soft lips parted as his landed perfectly on hers. Pulling her to him, he kissed her fully, deeply. He'd warned her there'd be more kissing.

"Forest." She glanced toward Piper who was kicking the red ball.

"It's okay." Gazing into her dark eyes, he swept her hair back with both of his hands. "Kissing and holding each other is a part of our lives now. It's okay for our daughter to see us kiss. For her to see me being in love with her mama. That's a healthy part of our homelife. You sure are cute when you blush." He kissed her hot cheek. "I can't wait to see you after work."

"I'll, um, look forward to it, too."

There were things he and Paige needed to talk about. Mainly Craig's idea that involved her in a way Forest didn't approve of. He'd have to discuss it with her this evening. For now, he just wanted to focus on the two of them. Even as he kissed her goodbye, lingering a little longer, it seemed they were taking steps toward a real marriage. And he thanked God for that.

Thirty-four

Peter pulled his rental car up to his childhood home and peered at the aged, battered house he once thought was huge. Now, it seemed shrunken. Even the yard appeared minuscule. How had they ever played Annie Over on this property?

Wait. Why was Ruby here?

She sat on the porch steps of his father's house, looking lovely in her overalls and a thick golden sweater. But finding her here, waiting for him, shot tremors of annoyance through him.

Surely, she wouldn't gloat over whatever was said inside the house. But hadn't she come to Basalt to discover his "source of pain?" And here she was, ready to watch him suffer? No, he didn't like that one bit.

Ruby stood. "Good morning, Peter."

"Hey." He stuffed his hands into his jacket pocket, his shoulders hunched as he strolled toward her. "Why are you here?" That probably sounded abrupt. He should have asked how she was doing or commented on how pretty she looked with her long red hair flowing over her shoulder.

If he could forget about her leaving him for ten seconds, he might be able to take her in his arms and kiss her like he hadn't in a long time. A ridiculous thought considering they hadn't been affectionate once since he arrived in Basalt.

"A little bird told me you were coming here."

Paige, no doubt. He groaned.

"I'm here for you if you need my support."

She was here for him? Probably more to satisfy her own curiosity. He bit back the urge to say something along those lines.

"Ready?" She knocked on the door.

"I guess." Peter moved up the uneven stairs.

The door opened and Dad's eyes squeezed closed like the sun was too bright.

"Good morning, Paul." Ruby embraced Dad, apparently already on hugging terms with him.

"Nice to see you." Dad winced at Peter.

"Dad." Peter extended his hand. No hugging necessary.

Dad shook his hand, not as firmly as he would have twelve years ago. "Welcome home, Son. Good to see you too." Then his father's arms wrapped around him in a hug that felt both restrained and welcoming. The older man's arms shook around him.

Stunned by the emotion zinging through him, Peter stepped out of Dad's embrace. Glancing at Ruby, he saw a soft smile creep over her lips like she approved of the father and son exchange. Maybe her being here wasn't all bad.

"Come in. Come in, both of you." Dad backed into the house and held the door open. "I still have some of the coffee cake Paige dropped off a couple of days ago. Want any?"

"I'm fine," Peter answered as he entered the old place.

"I'd love some. Thank you," Ruby said.

"Okay, great." Dad shuffled through the living room and disappeared around a partition wall.

His departure gave Peter a few minutes to acclimate himself to being back here. The room smelled about the same. The furnishings were different. The floor looked new and didn't creak as it had when he was a kid.

Mom's garish pictures were still on the living room walls. The frames were battered and oddly swollen as if they had water damage. The faces with their oversized noses and eyeballs appeared even more unusual than Peter remembered.

"Have a seat." Dad shuffled back into the room and handed Ruby a small plate with a piece of brown cake on it.

"Mmm. Looks great. Thank you." She dropped into the eclectic-looking chair across from the couch.

Peter sat in the only other chair in the room. He would rather have remained standing. Easier to dodge out the door. Hopefully, Ruby wouldn't ask any embarrassing questions.

"You want some coffee or tea?" Dad shrugged a couple of times.

"No. I drank a gallon's worth already." Not quite, but close.

Ruby chuckled. "I'm fine too. Thanks, Paul."

Dad settled onto the lumpy-looking couch cushion as if trying to find the comfiest spot. "I was happy to meet your beautiful bride."

Peter glanced at his wife. She was a beauty, and he was still attracted to her, even annoyed as he was with her. Too bad he'd taken their relationship for granted. Acted like she wasn't his wife most of the time. Barked at her like she was a worker who didn't know what she was doing.

He gritted his teeth. Man, he had a lot of angst running through him today. Too many thoughts he could do without.

"How have you been, Dad?" He leaned forward, elbows braced against the overstuffed chair arms.

"Getting older." Dad's chuckle sounded frail. "I heard you were staying with Paige and Forest."

"I am."

"How's the fishing business going?" Dad adjusted his black glasses. A nervous gesture?

"Fine. I own a boat."

Ruby winced, and he felt a jolt charge through him.

"Oh, we, that is, own a boat named the *Lily Forever*." He gave her a tight smile, hoping it sufficed as an apology for omitting her in the boat's ownership.

"Who's Lily?" Dad scratched at his ear.

"That was her christened title before we bought it."

"I see. Henry always went on and on about his boat."

"Yeah, he loved his *Merry J*."

Silence filled the room. Peter glanced at those unusual paintings again, remembering how much he disliked them when he had friends over back in high school.

"The house took a bad hit during the hurricanes, huh?"

"Sure did." Dad pointed toward the stairway. "Judah and Paisley helped me get the old girl back up and running. Otherwise, the place would look much worse."

Interestingly, he referred to the house in a feminine gender much like fishermen did with their boats. Like Peter did with his *Lily Forever*. Ugh. He did it again. Even in his thoughts, he claimed full ownership of his boat.

"I wish you would have called. Gets lonely here by myself." Dad took off his glasses, blew breath over the lenses, then rubbed them with the edge of his green flannel shirt. "Mom and I both missed you."

Peter hated this emotional awkwardness and the tiptoeing around why he left. How did Dad feel after all these years of silence? Betrayed? Peter knew the feeling.

Needing to move and expend some energy, he stood and stalked the perimeter of the room, feigning interest in the dark moods of the paintings. "This one's something, huh?" He jabbed his thumb toward a guy's face that looked like an apple with Pinocchio's nose protruding from the stem.

"Your mom loved her art." Dad shook his head. "That's why I don't have the heart to get rid of them, even damaged as they are."

"Makes sense." Although Peter wouldn't have any trouble tossing them out.

Ruby cleared her throat and nodded toward the chair he'd vacated. What? Was she pushing her agenda? Meddling in the gaping emotional chasm between father and son? Was she hoping to hear some tell-all confession? That wasn't happening today. Never, if he could help it.

"How long are you staying in town?" Dad asked.

"That depends." He glanced at Ruby but remained standing. "What do you think of Aunt Callie moving into the project house?"

"Her and her ideas." Dad rolled his eyes.

"I'm surprised you weren't over there wielding a hammer yourself."

"Why would I? Plenty to keep me busy here."

"Sure, but even James is working out there."

"I don't have the energy I used to." Dad yawned. "Besides, I don't want Callie telling me what to do."

"You two still don't see eye to eye, huh?"

"Nope." Dad stared glumly out the window. "She's bossy and snoopy, same as always."

His dad had lost weight. Paige told him about Dad's diabetic health scare. As far as she knew, he faithfully took his meds and ate healthier. But considering his frailness, was that so?

"Would you be interested in coming out to the project house and having a look around?" Peter stuck his hands in the back pockets of his jeans and rocked on his heels. "I'd give you a grand tour."

Ruby smiled and nodded.

"You can find out for yourself what mischief your sister's been up to."

"Like I care." Dad made a sucking sound as if cleaning out a back tooth. "I heard how she blamed James for a paint color error."

"That was unfortunate," Ruby said, "but it wasn't James's fault."

"Of course not. She's always butting her nose into matters she has no business in." He huffed. "Like this mayor stuff. A whole heap of nonsense if you ask me."

The room grew silent again.

Why was it so difficult to keep a conversation rolling with his father? Even with his aunt's meddlesome peculiarities, at least she'd been a constant in Peter's younger years. The way she sat on their porch, chatting with him and Paisley as they ran to and from the house, made her a fixture in their family. She'd been an unshakeable cornerstone when everything else was crumbling. Too bad she and Dad weren't even talking now.

"Paul, I wondered—"

Something about Ruby's tone set Peter on edge. He shot her a warning look.

"—about Peter's mother. What did she—"

"Oh, look at the time." He strode to the door. "We'd better get to the project house. Nice seeing you, Dad."

"Oh, sure."

"But Peter—" Ruby sent him a disparaging glance.

He wasn't going to stand here while she pried up emotional stuff from the past. It wasn't any of her business!

Dad followed him onto the porch. Peter extended his hand, and they shook. They weren't talk-it-out men. Even so, he felt something pass from his father to him. Perhaps respect, he couldn't be sure.

Maybe he'd come back and visit with Dad another time—by himself.

Thirty-five

A half dozen women traipsed up the stairway and disappeared into the planning room. Judah was tempted to follow them and listen in on their discussion. Instead, he stood at the bottom of the staircase hoping to catch a few words. What was going on up there? What were they planning in that room?

"I say we move forward!" Callie's voice boomed through the closed door. "You have the nomination, Bess. Let's not twiddle our thumbs and do nothing. It's been five days since the community meeting. We must act quickly!"

"I say we do this in the right way." Mom's softer voice was still loud enough for him to hear. "I won't be bullied into anything, or into not doing anything, either."

Clapping followed.

"What's going on?" Ruby jogged down the stairs, peach and ivory paint splatters decorating the flannel shirt she wore over her overalls. "Are you eavesdropping on your mom's meeting?"

"Guilty. I shouldn't be listening, but here I am."

She cocked her head to one side, peering at him. "I can hear them plainly in the room where I was working. You should go up and check on my paint colors for Kathleen." She winked then walked past him. "Wouldn't want any more mistakes like we had with Callie's room."

"Good idea." He jogged up the stairs and trudged past the closed planning-room door.

Inside Kathleen's bedroom, the soft blending of what she referred to as a peaches-and-cream color was coming along nicely. The multi-hued spring-looking walls were taking Ruby longer to complete than regular painting, since she was blending small sections at a time. But with Peter, and even Paisley, pitching in, they were getting a lot accomplished on the second floor.

"Are you planning to sit idly by while Mia Till takes over?" Callie's voice rose to a crescendo.

Judah's stomach lurched. Why was Callie so adamant about Mom running for interim mayor?

"I'm not doing nothing." Mom chuckled lightly. "We've all been busy, Callie, including you."

"While we've been somewhat busy, Mia is gaining ground, especially with the male constituency," Callie said staunchly.

"Take it easy," Mom said. "We have to be careful. That's why we're here, discussing the process, figuring out the next steps."

Judah felt guilty for listening in on the meeting, but he was curious about what his mom planned to do. He strolled around the bedroom, checking out Ruby's work. She'd done a good job on the white floorboards. The dark peach-colored trim around the windows looked great, too!

"Let me see her!" a woman yelled downstairs.

Mia?

Judah ran for the stairs.

"What are you doing here?" Ruby demanded.

"I need to speak with Bess!" Mia shouted.

"Not without an invitation, you don't."

Reaching the first floor, Judah came to a stop. Ruby stood in front of Mia, hands outstretched. Not many would take on Mia Till. But Ruby had a gritty, confident manner that obviously wouldn't take any guff. Even Mia looked wary of her.

"What's going on here?" he asked, crossing the room.

"Oh, Judah, what a relief." Mia reached for him as if he were saving her from Ruby. "This mad woman is keeping me from speaking with your mother."

Ruby rolled her eyes. "Callie asked me to stop anyone who wasn't on their guest list."

"Mia isn't on the approved list?"

"No, she is not. Give me a second, will you?" Ruby jogged up the stairs, leaving him alone with Mia.

He took two steps back.

"What's the big deal?" Mia thrust out her hands. "Does the riverboat captain think she's the CEO of Basalt Bay now?"

"It's a fishing boat. And she's my sister-in-law. I trust her decisions."

"What, you don't trust me?" Mia's voice went soft.

He did not. But he wouldn't be rude and say so out loud.

"Where's Bess? I need to speak with her," Mia said impatiently.

"Upstairs. But as Ruby said, you're not invited to the gathering. You'll have to wait."

"Who's going to stop me from walking right up those stairs?" She stepped in front of him, her flirty gaze sizing him up. "You?"

"If I must." Backing up a little more, he crossed his arms, prepared to block her access to the stairway, if necessary.

"Mia, what brings you here?" Mom spoke from above, descending the stairs.

Ruby followed her, a grimace etched on her face.

"I want to talk with you."

Mom glanced at Judah as if questioning why he was still standing next to Mia. He strode to the entryway but didn't leave the room in case Mom needed his assistance ousting their guest.

"I thought you should know I've filled out the paperwork. I'm accepting the nomination for interim mayor." Mia grinned confidently like she'd already won. "A number of the town's leading citizens are backing me."

Judah bit back a groan.

"Good for you." Mom managed to smile and look in pain at the same time.

"Also, C.L.—have you met him yet?—will be running too. Why, I have no idea, other than to oppose me!" She laughed mirthlessly. "Will you still be running, even though your husband forbids it?"

"Forbids—" Mom marched to the front door and yanked it open. "Thanks for stopping by and letting me know who'll be in the election, Mia. Whatever I decide, Edward has no part in my decision."

"Hmm. I wonder." Mia followed her to the door, then paused. "Ruby, I saw Peter in Bert's this morning. He's quite the hunky guy. Let me know if you two, you know, separate for good."

Ruby didn't say a word, just stared at her.

"Mia?" Mom nodded toward the exit.

"See all of you on voting day!" She scurried out the door. "May the best of Edward's women win."

"Edward's women? Count me out!" Mom slammed the door, her face darkening. "I shouldn't have said that. Oh, she infuriates me."

"With good reason!" Ruby said.

Callie, Kathleen, Miss Patty, and Maggie tromped down the stairway.

"What happened?" Callie demanded.

"What did that conniving wretch want?" Maggie's tone went shrill. "No doubt, she plans to dominate the city like she does men." She glared at Judah as if he might be to blame.

He lifted his hands. Mia did not dominate him. Although, he couldn't deny her efforts to get him to succumb in the past. Thankfully, that never happened.

"Now, now," Kathleen said in a calming voice as the ladies reached the kitchen and circled the center island. "What happened down here?"

"The vixen is giving Bess a run for her money," Ruby said. "Some guy named C.L. is running too."

"Never mind about him." Callie huffed. "He's an out-of-towner. Bess, what are you going to do?"

Mom stepped into the circle the women formed like she was the last puzzle piece. A stubborn look transformed her face. "There are a lot of things I don't know about being a mayor. But we must stop Mia from succeeding. Stop Edward from controlling the town through her."

"Now, you're talking!" Callie cheered.

"About time," Maggie said. "We have our work cut out for us. The canvassing. Telling folks the ugly truth about Miss Till."

"No smear campaigns!" Bess gazed sternly at Maggie. "I mean it. We're going to speak the truth in love like the scripture tells us to do." She gripped Callie and Kathleen's hands. "We'll fortify ourselves with His grace. Then serve our town in a way that pleases Him. Who's with me?"

As quietly as the rustling of leaves, the women shuffled and clutched each other's hands. Kathleen and Ruby reached out and clasped Judah's hands too. He was outnumbered by the females in the room, but he felt honored to be included in this moment of dedication.

"If I run, I will do so only it if we can be kind and honest about the things we hope to achieve for Basalt Bay together." She met Judah's gaze and smiled. "Are you with me?"

He nodded.

"Let's pray and commit this to the Lord." Mom closed her eyes, the group still holding hands. "Heavenly Father, You've heard what we've debated for days. I am stepping out in faith and agreeing to be a leader in Basalt Bay, if I'm voted in. If this is Your will for my life, I accept the challenge. If it's not Your will, I will gracefully bow out."

"In the meantime," Callie added, "we're going to do everything possible to get our town back on its feet, starting with getting Bess voted in as mayor."

"Amen!" the ladies called out.

Judah whispered, "Amen," too.

He still didn't want his mom thrust into town politics. He doubted it would be an easy win, since there were people in Basalt Bay who didn't want another Grant in leadership. But with her heart for service and how she wanted to help others, the future looked brighter with Bess Grant as mayor. Certainly brighter than if Mia were running things.

Thirty-six

Forest leaned against the doorframe to the interrogation room, arms crossed, tapping his foot against the tile flooring. For the last half hour, he'd been debating Craig's entrapment idea with Deputy Brian. Was another sting foolhardy? Maybe they should forget the whole operation.

The lawman sat in his chair behind his desk, one leg crossed over the other knee, rocking back and forth, appearing too relaxed for the topic. Forest felt anything but calm. Tension scrambled through his nerves, tightening his neck muscles. The thought of putting those he loved in jeopardy tore at his peace of mind. Why was he even considering such a scheme?

"I don't see what you're so worked up about." Brian rat-a-tatted a pen against his desk. Annoying sounds. "Craig will be using one of those newfangled recording apps on his phone. Traps Evie saying what she plans to do, or how she was involved in Paisley's kidnapping. Boom! We take her down." He hit the pen against the wooden desk surface.

"What if she realizes it's a setup and turns violent on Paige?" If that happened, Forest would do whatever it took to protect his wife.

"Worried about the little wife, are you?"

"Yes, in fact, I am." Forest uncrossed his arms. The man's cavalier attitude was getting on his nerves. "I don't want Evie, or Craig, causing Paige difficulty. I don't like putting her even slightly in harm's way. My daughter, either."

"You think Craig will try something?" Brian sniffed and wiped his nose.

"I doubt it. They have a past. Still—"

"I see where this is going." Brian sat up straighter, both feet on the floor. "You're worried he'll be her hero. Not you." He guffawed.

"That's not it at all. Paige doesn't want anyone to be her hero."

"Oh?" Brian's eyebrows rose to the midpoint of his forehead.

Forest groaned as Paige's words from when he first arrived in Basalt Bay raced through his thoughts—*"If you think I need a hero, you're wrong."* He didn't have a hero complex, but he didn't want Craig being a champion to his wife, either.

"We don't know what he might do, given Evie is his mom." Forest shrugged. "Craig could be pulling a fast one on us. What if his idea to trap Evie is, in fact, a trap for Paige? A trap against this case? Isn't that what Edward wants? To stop the proceedings from moving forward?"

Brian tossed his pen onto the desk. "After asking Craig all those questions, having him tell us and again and again what his plan involves, you still think he'll trick us?"

"I don't trust him. A lot is riding on this idea of his." Forest paced across the deputy's office.

"Maybe you should remove yourself from this operation." Brian squinted at him. "You're too emotionally involved."

"No way. This is my case. I'm not abandoning it now." Although Forest was too involved to be rational about putting Paige in a possibly dangerous situation.

"One call to Sheriff Morris, and I beg to differ."

Forest blew out a sharp breath. "All I'm saying is what if things go wrong? You know as well as I do that anything can happen on a sting. Anything."

"True." Brian shrugged, slow and leisurely. "All we can do is prepare the best we can. Cover our bases. Work out the angles. This procedure is going down, regardless of your worries about your wife. Sorry. Can't be helped."

Clenching his jaw, Forest thrust his hands through his hair. Surely, they could come up with a better plan. One that didn't involve Paige.

"Have you explained it to her?"

"Not yet."

"Why not?"

"We just got married. The threats subsided. Good grief. Her brother is in town." He paced again. "She hated the other sting. Now you expect me to ask her to do it again?"

"Not ask."

"Yes, ask." Forest glared at Brian. "If she doesn't want to put herself or Piper in the middle of possible danger, then we are not forcing her into that position. Do you hear me?"

"Loud and clear. But, again, I'll call the—"

"No!" Forest shouted. "If my wife says she doesn't want to be involved, I'll call the sheriff myself. Turn in my badge, whatever." He was dead serious about this.

"Tell her tonight, then." Brian wagged his index finger. "Because if you don't, I'll talk to her in the morning."

Forest groaned. Here things were barely stabilizing between him and Paige. Now he had to discuss something with her that might cause even more turmoil?

Thirty-seven

Forest picked up salmon burgers at Bert's for dinner and had the table set by the time Paige came home from the gallery. While he prepped for their meal, he prayed about what he needed to discuss with her.

"Wow. This is a nice surprise. Thanks, Forest." Paige smiled as she put Piper in her booster seat.

"Sure. Any time."

Piper jabbered about Vi and sand and "wocks." At least he was recognizing more of her words now.

They sat down and Forest led them in a prayer for their food, then they ate quietly. He had a lot on his mind. Would Paige go along with Craig's idea? Would she be enraged at Forest for suggesting it? Did she still have feelings for the other man? Of course, he wouldn't discuss any of this during their meal. He'd rather not talk about it at all. But Brian's threat to come here in the morning if he didn't circled through his thoughts.

"Things going okay with you?" she asked.

"Mmhmm. It's all coming to a head."

"That's good, right?"

"Should be." He took a big bite, filling his mouth with the delicious flavor of salmon and avocado, and avoided her gaze. He didn't want her asking him questions about the case. A few more minutes, then he'd have to ruin the peaceful ambiance in the room. But not yet. "I put a sandwich in the fridge for Peter."

"Thank you. He texted me that he'll be late."

Good. That would give Forest and her the time they needed to talk in private.

After they finished eating and threw away their wrappers, he asked, "Any chance we could talk?"

"Sure. Is something wrong?"

"Just something I need to discuss with you."

"No problem. I'll put a video on for Piper."

A few minutes later, with a cartoon playing, Paige returned to the kitchen and sat down. "What is it?" She folded, then unfolded her hands. "I noticed you seemed troubled at dinner."

"You could say that. I don't think you'll like what I have to tell you." He stroked his forehead, wishing for an easier segue.

"Are you leaving?"

"What? No." He clasped her hand. "Not that, baby."

"Okay." She chuckled. "I don't know why my mind leaped straight to that, but it did."

"I'm sorry too."

"It's my fault. I need more self-control in my thought life." She shrugged. "More trust."

And here he was about to discuss something that might ruin the baby steps they were taking toward her trusting him.

"What I'm about to tell you, if you agree to do it, might be dangerous. It's fine with me if you don't want to participate in it. In fact, you can absolutely refuse."

"What are you talking about?" she asked.

He was explaining this badly.

"Okay. It's like this ..." He quickly relayed the data he and Deputy Brian discussed earlier. Craig's idea for entrapping Evie. His lighter sentencing if he turned on Edward and Evie. A slight possibility of danger for Paige and Piper.

Paige's eyes grew wider as he talked. Her jaw fell open a couple of times.

"If you went along with this, you'd have to try to get Evie to open up and admit her involvement in the kidnapping," Forest said. "Craig would take the lead, but you'd have to play along so Evie doesn't suspect anything."

"You're serious?" Paige's voice rose. "You and the deputy want me to participate in another sting? In my own house?"

He tried to mentally skip over her emphasis on the house being hers.

"I don't like the idea either. But Deputy Brian is pushing this. So is the sheriff."

"What if Evie goes ballistic? Does something unexpected?"

"That's a possibility." He wouldn't tell her his doubts about Craig being a potential loose cannon, too. "I wouldn't be far away. Across the street hiding in the bushes. Deputy Brian, too."

"What if she has a weapon?" Paige pressed her free arm against her stomach. "What if she does something bad to me or Piper?"

"It's possible, but not likely." However, these were questions Forest wrestled with, too. "Do you trust Craig?"

"I guess I still do."

"He'll be in the room with you the whole time." This was difficult for him to say. "He's promised to keep you safe, even if that means going against his mom."

"And Piper?"

"We can stage it during her nap time." Forest smoothed his fingers over Paige's. "Again, I'll be just a few yards away."

"If anything happens—"

"It's a risk. But with Craig beside you, and me close, I'm pretty sure it will all be safe."

"Pretty sure?" She huffed out a breath.

"I'm sorry. I didn't even want to tell you about it."

No reason to mention Deputy Brian would be on her doorstep in the morning if Forest didn't follow through and ask her tonight.

"You say Craig thought this up?"

"Yes."

"And he'll get a lesser sentence for his cooperation?"

Nodding, Forest gazed into her eyes, wanting so badly to see into her heart. Did she still have feelings for Craig?

"That's a relief. I've been worried about him." She sighed. "After all he did to help Paisley, and sticking out his neck for Piper's safety, I'll do what I can to help him. I'm sure he'll do everything in his power to keep us protected, too."

Disappointment flipped over in his gut like a fifty-pound pancake. Paige had so much trust in Craig. Yet she couldn't trust him?

"That's great," he said without much cheer in his tone. "Thank you for being willing to do this."

By dragging Paige into this sting, had he widened the gap between him and her, and put her in a situation of being more dependent upon Craig?

Thirty-eight

The next day, Paige laid Piper down for her nap like she usually did at this time of the afternoon and planned to fix herself a cup of tea. She could use something calming. Maybe chamomile.

A knock at the back door halted her footsteps. Craig?

This morning, Forest told her again that she could back out of the sting if she wanted to. She'd felt his gaze on her all through breakfast. Was he as nervous about the upcoming confrontation as she was?

She peeked around the curtain on the back door.

Craig stood outside. Shoulders hunched, a drawstring cinched tightly around his sweatshirt hood, his deep dark eyes gleamed back at her. "I need to talk to you," he mouthed.

Heart hammering, she opened the door two inches, not releasing the safety chain. "When did you get out of jail?"

Forest had told her what to say, just in case Evie was near enough to be listening.

"Today. Open up, please?"

Even though she knew what was about to happen, her fingers trembled around the doorknob. Unlatching the chain, she pulled the door open wider.

Craig entered and pushed the door shut behind him. "Thanks." His gaze darted around the room as if he was looking for someone, setting her nerves more on edge. He strode over to the coffeemaker. "Do you mind if I—"

"Help yourself."

He'd spent enough time in Paige's house to know where coffee supplies were kept.

She stood behind a kitchen chair, her hands gripping the top edge. What would Craig's mom be like?

If anything went south, Forest told her to run for Piper's room, close the door, hook a chair under the handle, scoop up Piper, and wait for him and Deputy Brian to intervene. And they would intervene, he assured her.

Soon, Craig nursed a cup between his hands and dropped into a chair at the table like he belonged there. Like nothing was unusual about his arrival.

Quite the opposite of how she felt. Her stomach was doing backflips. The air seemed explosive with impending danger. Could she still back out of this? What would happen to Craig, then?

If Forest walked in right now, he probably wouldn't like the cozy scene of her old boyfriend sitting at her table. Even last night, with the way Forest stared at her so intensely when he explained all of this, she wondered what he thought about her helping Craig. Any chance he was jealous?

She dropped into the seat across from Craig. If everything went according to plan, he had an app on his phone that would record their voices. Was Forest listening right now?

"How's this going to work?"

Was Evie going to knock on her front door? Burst through the back door?

Craig didn't answer her question. Instead, he asked, "How are things with you and him?" He said, "him," in a snarky tone. Of course, he knew Forest was probably listening, too.

"Fine," she said a bit defensively. What business was Forest's and her relationship to Craig? "You heard we got married again?"

"Heard it through the grapevine." He gulped a long swig of coffee. "Can't say I'm surprised. I saw Piper's and his resemblance. Wish you'd told me yourself."

She didn't owe him an explanation. Then a thought hit her. "You're out legally, right?" This whole setup made her edgy and suspicious. What if Craig wasn't here to protect her? What if he was still loyal to his mom? Perhaps, trying to coerce Forest and Deputy Brian into letting Edward go free? Using her as a hostage?

A chill swept up her spine. She cast a backward glance toward the living room.

"I'm not supposed to talk about my release. National security, or something." Craig glanced furtively around the room. "A lot has gone down since my incarceration. You're married to him, Paisley's back at Bert's, a new manager is at C-MER, and, oh right, you're reopening the gallery with the guy who threw me in the slammer!"

He sure was grumpy. Turning on his mom and dad was probably difficult for him. Craig guzzled his coffee, his hand shaking—a dead giveaway of his nerves.

"I guess we're related, now, too," he said in a quieter tone.

"I heard about that. How does that make you—"

A scratching at the front door made the hair on Paige's arms and neck stand on end. The sound came again. Was someone breaking into her house?

Evie?

Craig gave her a slight nod.

This was it!

Forest told her to respond naturally, but there was nothing natural about this intrusion.

Paige jumped up and lunged into the living room as the previously locked door opened. A short blond, fiftyish woman swaggered inside, dressed in a sleek black jumpsuit, tucking a tool into her pocket.

"Who are you? Get out of my house!" Paige jabbed her index finger toward the door. There wasn't any playacting involved in her reactions as she charged into the hallway, hands spread apart, putting herself between danger and Piper. "What are you doing breaking into my house?"

The woman cackled. "She is cute, just like you said, Craigie."

"Craigie?" Paige eyed the man standing in the entry between the kitchen and living room, leaning against the wall as if he didn't have a care in the world. Why was he so relaxed now? Had he flipped to Evie's side already?

Paige's stomach muscles tightened. Her fists clenched. If anything went cockeyed here, she was going to sock this woman in the face, then run for Piper's room.

If she screamed Forest's name, would he hear it on Craig's recording app? But, no, that would give everything away. Craig risked a lot to do this. She agreed to participate so he'd get a lighter sentence. So he wouldn't have to spend the next decade in prison. She owed him that much, didn't she?

"Paige"—Craig swayed his hand toward the invader— "meet Evie Masters, my mother."

"Your mother broke into my house! I'm calling the police!" Paige yanked her cell phone out of her back pocket, just like Forest told her to do.

"Wait." Craig grabbed her forearm.

"Let go of me." Even though she'd been told he might grab her arm, when he did so, everything within her wanted to fight against him.

"Listen to my mom, then we'll leave you alone." He stared at her intensely as if communicating something. "I'm sorry." Prying the cell phone out of her fingers, he tossed it on the kitchen table.

She cast a desperate glare between the two. "What's going on here?"

This was staged for her and Craig, but this event was the real deal for Evie. She was the firecracker in the room that could explode at any second.

"You're going to cooperate, that's what's going on." Evie strode to the mantle, peering at the pictures. "Nice family you've got. Cute kid."

"Cute kid" sounded familiar. Ohhh. The note attached to the rock had those words written on it. Was Craig's mom the one who sent the warnings? The one who broke her window?

"What do you want with me?"

"We need to talk with you, that's all." Craig put one hand at her back, his other hand still holding her arm, and nudged her toward the couch.

"Let go of me." Paige tugged against his grip. She wanted to run to Piper's room. This break-in felt unsafe. More so than what Forest warned her about last night. "Why would you allow her to invade my home?"

"I can't explain. I would if—"

"Be quiet, both of you!" Evie yelled. "You listen to me, Paige. You rejected my son, but I'm the one who's doing the talking now. Sit down, or Craigie will make you sit down."

"I won't. You can't make—"

"Sit." Craig pressed his weight against her, forcing her down onto the couch.

She jerked against his hold. Why was he clasping her wrist so tightly? Even playacting, he didn't have to grab her like that. Maybe he was trying to make it seem realistic for Evie's sake, but Paige didn't like it. She gave him her deepest scowl.

"This will go easier if you cooperate," he said.

"So help me, if you don't let me go—"

"Sit still and listen," he said gruffly.

"Thata boy, Craigie!" Evie hooted.

"Why are you doing this?" Paige asked. "I thought we were friends."

"So did I before you set me up for your ex to capture me." Craig's eyes gleamed at her. "Here I thought you cared about me."

"Enough of the mushy stuff! You can do better than her, Craigie." Evie sneered at Paige. "Too bad you didn't like my son better."

"Mom—"

Paige groaned. Edward should be proud of these two. They made quite the trio of family thugs.

Evie squinted at Paige. "You're shocked by this surprise visit, huh? Good." She tugged on her skin-tight gloves. "If you don't do exactly as I tell you, things are going to get a lot worse for you and that little girl."

"Leave my daughter alone!"

Beside her, Craig tensed.

"Quiet!" Evie jabbed her finger at Paige. "From this moment forward, you're going to have a bad case of amnesia."

"What?"

"You're not going to remember anything about your sister's so-called kidnapping." Evie snorted. "When they ask you about the evidence you found in that smutty gallery of yours, say you don't recall. Never saw any evidence. Got it?"

"This is why you're here? To coerce me into silence? I think that's against the law."

"Edward's got me covered, cutie." Evie snickered. "That detective husband of yours sent my man away, but he'll be back. He has a town to run with me by his side." She did a mini-runway stroll across the living room. "Me and him are getting hitched! Congratulations are in order."

"Congratulations," Paige said dully. Who in their right mind would marry Edward Grant?

Evie pointed at Paige. "If you want your little girl to be safe—"

"Mom! No threats."

"You'll do as I say, or else—" She drew her index finger across her throat.

Paige glared at Craig. How dare he allow his mother to threaten Piper! How dare he hold her arm like she was his prisoner! When she got free, she'd kick him so hard his eyeballs would turn inside out. Then she'd take down his mother.

"You have two choices." Evie yanked a narrow foot-long black baton out of a loop on her pants. "The hard way or the easy way. Which will it be?"

"Where'd you get that?" Craig's grip on Paige's arm eased.

Evie clapped the policeman's day-stick against her palm. "Fake amnesia or Craigie's going to hit you so hard you might never recover."

"No, I won't! You said you had to talk to her, so talk. No violence!"

"How could you let this happen?" Paige let the terror she felt implode in her words as she faced him. "Piper loves you. I trusted you."

"I'm so—"

"Shut it, Craigie." Evie jabbed the end of the baton against his chest. "You heard what Edward said. What this will mean for us when he's released thanks to no evidence from this twit. We'll be the family we should have been with his ex and her brat out of the picture. The three of us living in the swanky house on the cliff." A dreamy look crossed her face.

Was she delusional? On drugs?

Craig met Paige's gaze briefly as if conveying his apologies. "No more threats," he ordered.

"Don't tell me what to do." Evie shoved the weapon against his chest.

Craig inhaled sharply.

"Why are you doing this?" Paige tugged against his hold.

"I couldn't stay in that cell another day. I had to get out."

"Silence!" Evie shouted like a drill sergeant. "Don't talk to him! Didn't I say I'm in charge? I'll do anything to get my man out of the slammer. So listen up."

Anything, huh? Maybe if Paige got some answers from Evie, then Forest and Deputy Brian would barge in here and arrest her. Craig too, for all she cared right now. "Did you spray paint a threat on Forest's car?"

"Liked that, did you?" Chuckling, Evie ran her glove-covered fingers over the baton. "I thought it was a nice touch."

"Did you write me those awful notes? Break my window with a rock?"

"Well, honey, it sure wasn't Craigie sending love notes from jail, was it?" She chortled.

Paige had assumed Mia did those things. Wait until she told Paisley they were wrong about her. Evie had warned Paige to remain silent about all that, but she wouldn't.

"What's it going to be?" Evie pointed the weapon at her. "Is Craigie going to have to snatch up your kid until you agree to do as I say, or will you do as you're told?"

"Hey—" Craig barked.

Evie had admitted to the crimes. Why wasn't Forest jumping in and arresting her?

"What would I have to do?" Paige asked, playing along.

"That's more like it." Evie gleamed as if pleased with herself. "When anyone asks about the evidence, tell them you had an accident and have amnesia. Swelling in the brain. Invent new facts. Tell them you're confused." She smacked the day-stick against her hand like she'd cause an accident to make Paige become confused, if necessary.

The woman's scheme was absurd. Wouldn't people know Paige hadn't been in an accident? Would she have to fake that too?

"Pull any funny stuff, and you'll be sorry. Got it?"

"I've got it. Now, leave my house!"

"One more thing. Edward doesn't like you doing business with his ex. That art-gala thingy?" Evie thrust her stick across the coffee table, knocking off magazines and a cup left there from this morning. "Accidents can happen so quickly."

"Mom!" Craig croaked.

Evie slapped the stick hard against the couch cushion. "When anyone asks what Craig told you the night he interfered with Edward's plans, say you don't remember, or something bad is going to happen to your little girl."

"Don't threaten her daughter!" Craig said.

Ready to scream if Forest didn't get in here, Paige decided to ask one more question. "Were you the one who helped Edward get Paisley out of the hospital?"

"Of course." Evie smirked like she was proud of it. "That man couldn't do anything on his own."

A sickening feeling surged through Paige. This woman, Craig's mom, had participated in Edward's wrongdoing toward Paisley. She'd threatened Paige, too.

Suddenly, Piper wailed.

Motherly feelings of protection rose in Paige. She reared up, tugging against Craig's hold on her wrist. "Let me go to her." She met his gaze, inwardly pleading with him, trying to appeal to his nicer side. "Please."

Piper's sobs grew louder.

Craig clenched his lips then released Paige.

"Get out of my house, both of you!" She scrambled down the hall to Piper's room and slammed the door behind her. "There, there, sweetie." Scooping up her daughter, she swayed with her, but Paige's whole body trembled. "Mama's here. Everything's going to be okay."

Forest, I did my part, now you'd better do yours.

Thirty-nine

Forest had been crouching in the bushes across the road from Paige's house, peering through his binoculars, trying to see into the living room. He'd observed Evie's break-in, barely restraining himself from sprinting across the street and cuffing her. But he wanted her charged with more than an illegal entry. Once she went inside the house, the wait became almost unbearable.

Fortunately, he heard everything that was said inside the house. So did Deputy Brian, hiding in the bushes about fifty feet away. Two officers from Florence were camouflaged in the bushes, listening, too.

Brian kept sending Forest hand signals like a baseball coach. Jabbing his finger toward the ground seemed to mean "don't move." His most repeated signal was an intense glare aimed at Forest, as if that would stop him from running across the road and saving his family.

Hearing Evie threaten Paige and Piper sent cold adrenaline spasming through his system. A couple of times he almost jumped up and sprinted to the house, despite Brian's signals.

This was Craig's plan to get Evie to incriminate herself, but what if she didn't? What if something went wrong? If anything violent happened inside, Forest was prepared to charge in there and arrest Evie, even if it ruined the sting.

When Evie gave an ultimatum against Piper, Forest's muscles tightened up and a riotous flood of emotions hit him. Craig had better not allow his mother to come one inch closer to Paige or Piper!

God, keep my family safe.

Every muscle on alert, when Evie confessed to helping Edward, Forest leaped to his feet.

Piper's wail set his heart on fire.

So did the shout from Brian, "Let's go, men!"

Bounding out of the brush, Forest, Brian, and the other two officers charged for the house. Forest and Brian ran for the front door. The other two circled around back.

Before Forest got across the street, Evie screeched, "Craigie, the cops are coming!" She raced out of the house, scrambling across the lawn as if she believed herself capable of outrunning them. Deputy Brian chased her down the sidewalk, and Forest had no doubt the lawman would catch her.

Forest had one goal in mind—reaching his wife and daughter. He met Craig exiting the house. "Where's Paige?"

"In Piper's room."

"Stay right there!" he yelled and charged through the living room. Flinging open Piper's door, he found Paige holding their daughter, rocking her.

"Forest!" Her face crumpled.

"I'm here, baby." In three strides, he had his arms around his wife and daughter. "You were amazing." He kissed the side of Paige's head. "You did great! Got answers. Stayed calm."

"I didn't. I was so scared. My heart pounded like a locomotive."

"Mine too. It's over now. You're both okay."

"When she threatened Piper, I could have punched her eyes out. I wasn't pretending then." Paige met his gaze with a frantic look. "I'm serious. It felt so real. I wanted to kick Craig!"

Forest chuckled, relieved the sting had ended successfully. And safely. "Thank you for being brave enough to see this through. I'm sorry I had to involve you. Never again."

"I agreed to it, but it was bizarre. What Evie expected me to do? I still can't believe it." Paige carved her free hand through her hair. "I feel a mess. All shaky."

He hugged her again. "I'm sorry."

Craig clearing his throat at the door drew them apart.

"The deputy has Evie in custody." His shoulders slumped as he leaned against the doorframe. "Setting my mom up to take the fall was the worst kind of disloyalty imaginable."

"Sorry about that." Forest strode across the room toward him. "You did the right thing."

"Right for me."

"Not just for you. For my family. For Paisley, too. And for justice."

Craig stared at Paige. "Just so you know, I wouldn't have let her hurt you, or Piper."

"I know." Paige swayed with Piper in her arms. "What she said drove me crazy."

"No kidding." Craig gnawed his lower lip between his upper and bottom teeth. "Guess I'm free to go, huh?"

"Not quite. You still have the device." Forest pointed toward Craig's jacket pocket where the phone app was still recording. "Also, we'll head over to the station for a debrief. Set up all your requirements for early release."

"Right." Craig sighed. "Even though my mom helped Edward take Paisley out of the hospital, is there any chance I could talk with her? Try to explain why I did this."

"I'm sure that can be arranged." Forest shook his hand. "Thank you."

Craig nodded, casting a long look at Paige, then strode down the hall.

If it wasn't for Craig, Forest wouldn't have proof of Evie's involvement in Edward's criminal activities. Craig had revealed the fake name his mom was using—Jenn Blanchard—so they could track Evie to the Beachside Inn. Even now, two officers had a search warrant and were combing through her belongings, searching for evidence.

Paige set Piper down and walked over to Forest. "Now that Evie's in custody, what now?"

"What do you mean?" He swept some of her long hair over her shoulder, smoothing his hand over the back of her light blue sweatshirt.

"We married partly due to the threats. If that's all over now, I wondered—"

"How I'd feel about you without trouble hounding us? If I'll stay?" He sighed, weary of her doubts. "How can I convince you that I'm not going anywhere? I love you, baby." He pulled her into his arms, and she came willingly, sighing against him.

"I thought that maybe, you'll ... go."

"Not happening." He held her while Piper frolicked around them. "When I heard Evie threatening you, I wanted to run in here and stop her in her tracks."

"But you didn't."

"We waited for a confession. But if I'd heard any real danger, I would have ruined the trap to save you."

"My hero, after all, huh?" She gave him a cute smile.

"That's right." He grinned.

He had official responsibilities concerning Craig and reports to fill out about the sting, but if he had a choice, he'd stay right here holding his wife.

Forty

The next day, despite Paige's emotional fatigue, Aunt Callie roped her and Paisley into volunteering to do a final cleaning of her house. She said she and Maggie were spending the day canvassing the neighborhood for Bess, which she assured Paige was more important than any housecleaning.

The sisters agreed to their aunt's wishes, since both were cheering for Bess's success, too. Although Paige found Aunt Callie's enthusiasm for local politics a bit humorous. Maybe she should have run for mayor herself! When it came to bossing people around, Aunt Callie was a natural.

For Paige, doing the last-minute clean-up of her aunt's house, focusing on something other than the sting and her marriage with Forest, was a relief. There was no longer any reason for her to stay locked up in her house. No reason to keep watching over her shoulder or worrying about Piper's safety. The gallery should be a safe place for her, too.

So if that was all over, why did she still feel a weight on her shoulders? Still troubled?

Mia hadn't been the one doing the vandalism or sending those aggressive threats, although she had carried some suspicious messages from Edward. Evie was locked up in the Basalt Bay jail all by herself. According to Forest, the trial was going to move forward as planned after Christmas.

Poor Craig. Paige felt sorry for him with his family ties with Edward and Evie. But she was thankful he'd brought an end to the fears that something else bad might happen to her, Paisley, or Piper. Although, what did Evie mean about the art gala and accidents happening?

Groan. No more worrying. The woman couldn't cause any harm now, right? Hopefully, it truly was over.

Wiping the paper towel over a stubborn smudge on the glass, Paige gave the window another spray of cleaner and thought of the note she found taped to her easel this morning. *Hey, baby. You are one of a kind, you know that? I'm so proud of how you helped us set that trap for Evie yesterday. You were amazing! I love you. I'm so happy you're my girl.*

His girl. Was she his? Would he say that if he knew of the grudges she held against him? Of the way she clung to his words, "Sweet dreams, Elinore?" Guilty feelings about that bothered her.

Paisley ran a dust mop across the hardwood floors, humming a church chorus. Then she chuckled about something.

"You're cheery today," Paige said. "Things must be going well between you and Judah."

"Couldn't be better." Paisley stopped and clasped the top of the mop handle with both hands. "I'm blessed to have him back in my life as my husband. I mean, we finally started our honeymoon." She laughed, her cheeks turning rosy. "Sorry. TMI. Everything's good, let's leave it at that."

Paige smiled but felt tears forming in her eyes. Her teary emotions must be due to the release of tension after all that went down yesterday. Or because of Forest's note. Not because of Paisley and Judah's successful relationship. "You're lucky to have each other." She thought of her and Forest sharing the same bed, but not sharing their hearts. Of how unsettled she felt around him sometimes. "Judah's such a … great guy."

So was Forest. But she kept pushing him away, keeping him at arm's length. Holding him, and love, back. Hurting inside. More tears. She swiped them quickly.

"I know." Paisley sighed in that dreamy tone. "Driving back to Basalt two months ago, I thought Judah and I were finished. But God gave it all back to me—him, our love, the beach cabin. My hope. I'd lost that after Misty Gale. Now, I want to have more kids!"

"That's great. I'll get to be an auntie!" Paige gulped, tears flooding her eyes, making it difficult to see. She wanted to have more babies too. Wanted a real marriage and family. Why was this hitting her so hard now? She wouldn't break down. Couldn't reveal her emotional mess. But something within her was cracking. She longed to have what Paisley found. The peace on her face was like a radiant light.

Suddenly, she was sobbing. So unlike her. Crying was weak, and she wasn't weak. She was strong and independent and … she covered her face with her hands and wept.

"Oh, honey, what's wrong?" Paisley wrapped her in a hug. "What did I say? I'm so sorry."

Paige dropped the glass cleaner on the window ledge. She sank to the floor in the empty room and cried. For herself. For Forest. What they lost. What they were trying to get back. What they could have been if they'd never split up. All the things she held against him.

But she didn't want to hold anything against him anymore. Yet, how could she let it go? How could she finally be free of the resentment that sat beneath her ribs like a giant rock?

Paisley sank to the floor beside her and wrapped her arms around her again. "There, there. It's going to be okay."

Paige cried against her big sister's shoulder. It reminded her of other times when Paisley had comforted her when they were little.

"How c-can it b-be o-okay?" She sniffled, rubbing her sleeve over her wet, no doubt mascara-smeared face. "I've ruined everything. Part of me is shoving him away. While the other part wants him to hold me and love me." She sobbed again. "I don't know why I'm doing that. Why I'm so messed up."

"Oh, honey." Paisley set Paige back, her hands on her shoulders, peering at her like a wise old owl in Piper's picture books. "What's happened to make you so sad? Did you and Forest have a fight? I've messed up more times than anyone in this family, yet God's grace and love, sometimes Judah's grace and love, reached my heart. It's still changing me and healing me."

An emotional torrent stormed through Paige like a hurricane tearing apart every shred of self-preservation. The anguish beneath her ribs erupted into a wail. She'd never heard such a mournful cry come from anyone before, let alone herself. How could she make it stop?

"I'm so sorry you're hurting like this." Paisley held her, rocking her, whispering comforting assurances. Praying, too. She sang a song about God's grace being enough for any situation, for any weary soul.

Paige felt like a weary soul. A tired human who'd lost her way. Shuffling against the wall, she let out a long shuttered breath. Paisley leaned back too, clasping her hand like a lifeline. They sat still, neither speaking.

Then, "I can't believe I cried on your shoulder like that. I'm such a baby."

"No, you're not."

"I want what you and Judah have found. I want love and peace and happiness."

"Of course, you do." Paisley's shoulders lifted then sagged. "But, goodness, Judah and I have had our times of pain, too."

"I know. I'm not jealous of you guys." She barked out a sharp syllable that didn't even sound like her voice. "That's a lie. I've been immensely jealous of you and what you have with a man like him. Ever since you came back, I've been jealous of you two."

"Oh, Paige, is that what's bothering you?" Paisley wiped her cheeks. "Now, you have Forest, right?"

"Yes, but he and I—"

"Since you got married, haven't you been happy?"

"It's a farce. The whole ... stinking ... thing."

"I thought you loved him."

"I did. Do. So much I can hardly stand it." Finally admitting it felt good.

"Okay. That sounds better, but I'm confused. Why don't you explain from the beginning?" Paisley let go of Paige's hand but stayed close, their shoulders leaning against each other's. "Pastor Sagle says talking about what hurts us is a part of our healing. Don't worry, I didn't believe him, either." She chuckled.

Paige's secrets had been locked away for so long, how could she expose them? She took a deep breath. Then, as if she were telling a fairytale, she told Paisley the story of Forest's and her brief but dreamy courtship, their spontaneous decision to marry, the darling wedding chapel where they exchanged vows. She skipped over details of their equally dreamy and passionate honeymoon.

"It sounds delightful." Paisley smoothed her palm over Paige's arm. "What happened to cause your breakup so soon after the wedding? Did it happen too quickly? It's easy to get caught up in the romantic side of a relationship, in the physical intimacy."

Paige nodded. "Our coming together was beautiful, like a perfect dance. I thought I'd be with him for the rest of my life. I was in love. So sure of it. Until he ..." Gulp.

"Did he hurt you?" Paisley's arm against Paige's tensed.

"Nothing like that. His offense was whispered words in the night. Then leaving me suddenly." Needing to get this off her chest, she said the next sentence quickly. "One night when he told me goodnight, he called me by his ex-fiancé's name."

"Eeuw. That would be troubling."

"I still hear him saying it in my mind."

"Could there have been a reason?" Paisley shrugged. "I'm not sticking up for him. But some people talk in their sleep."

"At the time, I thought it meant he cared for her more than me." She explained about Elinore's car wreck and Forest leaving her to be with his ex. "And you're right, we married quickly. I didn't know him. I wanted proof he loved me above her."

"Sure you did," Paisley whispered. "It's okay. You can talk things out with him."

"I made another mistake. Married him quickly again. Fell for his kisses."

"How could marrying a lovely man like Forest, a man who obviously has eyes only for you—no matter what he whispered or did in the past—be a mistake?" Paisley put her arm over Paige's shoulder. "I needed a second chance. You don't know how horrible I felt coming back to Basalt, to Judah, to our family. But God ... and Him working through Judah ... helped me see things in a new way. A life filled with grace and hope."

"Hope sounds amazing." Paige pressed her fists against her chest. "I don't know what to do. I'm afraid Forest will leave me again, especially now that the tension of the case has eased."

"Sweetie, I think he loves you too much to do that." Paisley smiled softly. "However, I know what you should do. How about talking to Jesus? All the peace and grace He gave me is available for you, too. He knows your heart, your regrets, everything. He loves you so much. And so do I."

What Paisley said sounded like the things Judah had told Paige over the years. Was she ready to accept God's love? Was it as simple as accepting? Something else still ate at her.

"Our marriage is ..." Embarrassment flooded her. "Even though we have feelings for each other, it's not a real marriage."

"How can it not be real? Oh, you mean you haven't slept together?"

Paige shook her head.

"Even Judah and I waited for a week."

"This is different. Our marriage has been a way for him to stay in my house, protecting me and Piper, and getting to know his daughter." Paige wiped her hand over her forehead. "And it's giving me time to learn to trust him again."

"See there. That's not a fake marriage. Not when you're both working on it." After a pause, Paisley said, "When I was tied up in Edward's closet, fearing for my life and wishing for the chance for a real marriage with Judah, I took a leap of faith and trusted in Jesus. Ever since, God's love has been making a difference in my life."

"I can see that." Could Paige take her own leap of faith? Would that make a difference for her, too?

She closed her eyes. *I want to trust You. I accept You into my life. Help me to forgive and to live for You from this day forward.* A warmth filled her. Peace, maybe. She opened her eyes and met her sister's teary gaze. "I accept God's grace, His love, and what He did for me. I want a new beginning, too."

"Oh, Paige." Paisley hugged her. "I love you, little sister. I'm proud of the amazing woman and mom you've become."

"Thank you. Love you too."

They both sniffed and Paisley chuckled.

"Look at us laughing and crying and hugging."

"It's a beautiful kind of wonderful." Paige grinned, feeling lighter, almost as if the air in the room was easier to breathe. "I guess we'd better finish Aunt Callie's house, or we'll never hear the end of it."

"You're right about that."

As Paige worked, only one thing diminished her new sense of hope. Was she brave enough to tell Forest what had been troubling her for three years?

Forty-one

For the last two days, Ruby had been working beside Peter in the project house, painting walls and installing flooring in the upstairs bedrooms and hallway. Sweaty, thirsty, and in need of a break, she was aware of him casting glances at her like he wanted to say something. Why didn't he spit out whatever he needed to say, had probably needed to say since he got here three days ago, and be done with it? His silence unnerved her. Usually, they were better at ignoring their relationship while they worked. Isn't that what they did on the *Merry J* and the *Lily Forever*?

Cutting the vinyl planks, installing them, then smoothing out the seams, occasionally Peter's arm or leg bumped against hers. She was used to his body being next to hers as they worked. But now, the scent of his musky deodorant mingling with his masculine odor tickled her senses. She leaned closer to inhale the intoxicating scent before she remembered they weren't a couple. She'd left him. Yet, here he was, beside her … smelling so good.

She met his dark, brooding gaze. His pain-filled glint. She didn't break the intensity of their gazes. Didn't shuffle away.

He reached out and smoothed the rough pads of his fingers down her cheek. His throaty sigh sounded like a rumble. He blinked slowly, his gaze traveling toward her lips. One of his eyebrows pulsed upward as if he were asking her if he could kiss her. Why was he suddenly acting caring and husbandly?

"I'm sorry," he whispered hoarsely. He dropped the mallet from his other hand.

"Sorry for—?"

On their knees, he clasped her shoulders and turned her toward him, their noses nearly touching. "I've been a fool. A stubborn idiotic fool."

Did he expect her to agree with him?

"What are you saying?"

Explaining things seemed so hard for him. But having seen him and his father together, neither of them able to express themselves, it made sense.

"Ruby, please come home. I want you back on the boat with me."

Every muscle within her tensed. This was what he wanted to say to her during their first tender moment in weeks? Months? To tell her he expected her to return to his boat?

Groaning, she pushed away from him. "We'd better get this work done." She crawled to the next section between the last vinyl plank they installed and the wall in Bess's future bedroom.

"Then you'll come back with me?"

She lifted her chin. "I'm staying here."

"Our home is in Alaska."

He obviously didn't get why she left him. He said he was a fool, yet he didn't fathom the gulf between them. Until he acknowledged that, and had some true remorse for his emotional distance, there wasn't any hope for reconciliation.

"I left you, Peter."

"Don't you think I'm aware of that every single day?"

His gruff tone sent irritable emotions slamming into her ribs. She didn't want to argue with him during work hours. Didn't want the guys working in the adjoining rooms to hear them.

"Let's keep at this, huh?" She nodded toward the door, hoping he got her message.

"I have to get back to the *Lily Forever*. I can't abandon everything as you did."

His words hit their mark. She stood quickly, nearly staggering. "You want to have this out now? Fine! Let's talk about the way you abandoned our marriage. The way you blocked me out—your wife."

Too bad Forest and Judah would have to hear their argument. Peter wanted a fight, he was getting one.

He stood stiffly, raking his fingers over his bearded chin. "I had to eke out a living and keep the boat in the black. Making sure all the parts of a fishing business run smoothly takes time and manpower."

Excuses she'd heard before.

"You're more married to the *Lily Forever* than you ever were to me."

He flinched. "Not true."

"Yes, it is."

"Can't we make this work, Rube? I still want you with me."

"As what? A deckhand? Someone who's always second-guessing your moods? Someone who jumps at your beck and call? No thanks." He had to have things his own way. Master and worker. Not wife and husband, lovers, as they should have been.

Her only regret was not leaving sooner. But she'd kept hoping, wishing for things to improve, dreaming of a change in their relationship that might bring children into their hearts and home.

Peter stood beside her but didn't touch her. Even so, his closeness made her uncomfortable.

"I don't just want you as a deckhand," he said in a softer tone. "You're not a laborer I'm trying to bleed dry. You're wrong about that. But the boat, our livelihood, depends on me being there. Not putting this project house together like some puzzle." He groaned. "What are we doing here, Rube? What are you doing here?"

Her heart pounded explosively. This was her opportunity to explain, but expressing herself might be the death of them. "I'm trying to do the impossible, Peter. Figure out what went wrong between us so we might have a slim chance of sticking together. So I could try to understand you, understand your past, better."

"Has it helped?"

"Not so far." She crossed her arms, glaring at him. "At least I was willing to try."

"So was I!" he thundered. "I followed you here, didn't I?" He said it like it had been such an imposition.

"You're here following your own plans. Not trying to listen to me or make things right."

"Good grief, woman!" Peter bellowed. "That's exactly what I'm doing! I'm helping you with this project, aren't I? So we can try to work things out. Maybe talk."

His passionate response took her by surprise.

"You don't plan to come home with me, do you?"

"No." She hated hurting him, but it couldn't be helped. "Not before we've worked things out and mended the scars between us." She nodded at him. "Because that bear of a man who acts like work is his food and drink, his breath, isn't the man I fell in love with."

"I said I was sorry about that!" he said in his familiar roar.

"Yet, you still don't get it." She wanted to walk away. Their relationship might already be beyond repair. Yet, a faint nudge to hold on tugged on her like a leash. She'd made vows to this burly man. "Why are you so angry with your father?"

His eyes squinted to tiny slits. "Stay out of it."

"Because a wife can't know her husband's past?" She put her hand on his arm and felt his taut muscles. "You're burning up inside over more than us not getting along. It's obvious in your brooding gaze. In the way you act around your dad. Under all your bluster and hotheadedness, under that drive to make fishing your whole life, you're in pain."

He jerked away from her.

Someone behind them cleared his throat. Ruby turned. Heat flooded her face to find Brad Kiefer, a fisherman friend of Peter's, standing in the doorway, probably having heard those last things she and Peter said.

"Sorry. Didn't mean to intrude." Brad wore green raingear and shuffled his hat in circles between his hands.

"Brad!" Peter clomped across the empty space, his heavy shoes echoing in the stillness, and shook the other man's hand.

"Peter." Brad nodded in her direction. "Ruby."

"Hello, Brad." She wrapped her arms around her ribs, annoyed over Peter's suddenly jovial tones.

"What brings you here?" Peter clapped Brad on the back.

"Judah said I could come up." Brad ran a hand over his full red beard. "High winds are kicking up in Ketchikan. A real humdinger should hit by tomorrow."

"I hadn't heard. Thanks for stopping by and telling me." Peter's whole demeanor changed. He stood taller, shoulders back, spine tight as if he were already prepping for the storm. "How bad will it be?"

"Possible gusts of a hundred miles an hour."

Peter whistled. "Sounds like a bad one."

"Folks say it could be like the Thanksgiving Storm of '68. Not that we were around for that." Brad twirled his hat again. "Thought I'd warn you."

"Thanks. I probably wouldn't have heard until it's too late."

Peter met Ruby's gaze and gave her a long look. He was leaving. He wouldn't stay here and do nothing while his boat suffered peril. Unlike the way he let their marriage fall into disrepair and did nothing to rescue it. But that was unfair. He had followed her to Basalt Bay. But three days was hardly time for them to fix anything between them.

Now, he was going back to the *Lily Forever*, his one true love. Where did that leave them?

Forty-two

Despite the rain that was already coming down in torrents, Peter made one last check of the exterior of his power troller, making sure it was shipshape for the lashing to come. The forecast of heavy rains, while foreboding, wasn't unusual considering Ketchikan was situated in a middle-latitude rainforest. But the strong winds blowing fiercely across Southeast Alaska tonight might mean a catastrophe to the vessels in port.

He'd weathered plenty of storms at sea. In fact, riding out a squall, hunkered down in his boat, was a high like no other. Hopefully, the *Lily Forever* proved up to its name—that it would endure forever.

If only he and Ruby had weathered their marital storms as well. He groaned. Why did he have to come up with a marital analogy at a time like this?

Rainwater splattered his face and the wind plowed hard against him. He'd better hurry with his chores so he could get inside the galley and find warmth. Maybe open a can of chili. That would hit the spot.

He tugged firmly on two safety rings attached to clasps on the outside wall of the cabin. Both held securely. Striding around the back deck, he made sure nothing was loose. He double-checked the fishing gear and the hatch to the hold where ice was stored when he was out trolling. Then he carried stowable parts below deck. He didn't want to lose anything in the storm.

As he worked, thoughts of Ruby coursed through him. She stared into his eyes so solemnly before he left. Did she secretly hope he'd stay in Basalt? Did she figure since he was flying home to check on his boat that he was too engaged in his business to care about her?

Yes, he was single-minded about the *Lily Forever*. That made him a conscientious boat owner. Not a neglectful husband. He'd nearly paid off the troller. Hadn't had an accident aboard ship in the twelve years he worked as a full-time mariner. That had to say something about his honor and diligence when it came to his livelihood.

She'd probably say he should have been as faithful about her, his wife, too. More thoughts he didn't want to think about.

He strode to the port side. Reefed on tie-downs, making sure each rope could take the brunt of excessive force and not break. Splatters of rain tap-danced on the deck. Time for him to get out of this weather and hunker down for the night.

Inside the galley, he removed his coat and hat. Leftover diesel fumes mixed with the musty, salty aromas of the sea met his olfactory senses—the scents of home—and he sighed. Was there anything like living on a boat like this? Sure, the accommodations were tight. That didn't bother him. Why did Ruby think they needed a house on land?

What if she wanted all this, their lives on the sea, to end? She hadn't intimated he had to choose between her and the fishing business. But during one argument, she accused him of the *Lily Forever* being his mistress. As if his being a boat owner was a slap in her face. He'd disagreed then. Still did.

Ducking his head so he didn't hit the low overhang, he shuffled down the couple of steps to the sleeping area. He pulled off his damp shirt and grabbed a dry T-shirt.

Momentarily distracted, he ran his hand over the thick quilt on the bed, letting his thoughts replay times they laid here as a married couple. Nights at sea with the aurora borealis casting a glow through the portals and over the bed, over their skin. Times when they went to sleep in each other's arms to the sounds of orcas and seals frolicking outside.

Ruby. Man, he missed what they had when things were good between them.

A few minutes later, back in the galley, he opened the can of chili and heated it up. He'd wolf it down, then turn in. No doubt he'd be awakened by the storm sometime after dark.

Later, Peter awoke to the swaying of the boat getting a strong pounding of wind and rain. The creaking of the rigging being buffeted above him shot tension and worry through him. Would everything hold? Would he have to go outside and check in the dark? Maybe later. He'd try to keep sleeping until dawn.

But with each slosh of water hitting the boat, his thoughts churned. What if Ruby left him for good? He wasn't going to live in Basalt Bay. This is where he planned to live, here on his boat in Southeast Alaska, for the rest of his life. If she insisted that they own a house on land—if that's what she was so upset about—he'd compromise if it was somewhere along the Inside Passage—Ketchikan, Wrangell, or Petersburg.

Pulling the quilt over his chest, he shuffled deeper into the covers. The wind howled and whined, jerked the troller against its mooring. Rain pelted the portals. Something up top clattered to the deck like a piece of metal might have broken.

He groaned.

Shoving off the bed, a strong gale hit the side of the boat, and he nearly fell over. He gripped a metal clasp attached to the wall to stabilize himself, waiting out the heaving of the sea. The craft pulled against the ropes binding it to the docks so strongly it groaned out an eerie sound.

After a few minutes, the motion eased up, as did the whining sounds. Up in the galley, he tugged on his float jacket and boots. Then grabbing a flashlight, Peter prepared to face the elements in the dark.

He pressed his shoulder against the narrow door, but the suction of the wind prevented him from easily opening it. Shoving harder, it finally gave. He held onto the handle tightly so the wind wouldn't jerk the door off its hinges. After securing the latch behind him, he braced into the gusty conditions and shone his flashlight across the back deck. Then up at the rigging. Nothing looked out of place. What had he heard breaking or falling earlier?

A mighty gust pummeled him, bobbing the boat even though it was lashed down. Heavy rain hit him so hard, his feet slid across the wet deck as if he were on skates. He thrust out his hands, grabbing for the stern railing. The flashlight slipped out of his wet grasp, crashed to the deck, and disappeared overboard.

He groaned and peered into the darkness. Not far from his craft, a smaller boat lay on its side in the sea, a lone tether adhered it to the berth. His instinct was to try to rescue it. To save what could be saved. But it was foolhardy to even be standing outdoors in powerful winds like this let alone wandering out onto the dock. He'd better get back inside. Apparently, the worst of the storm wasn't over yet.

* * * *

Throughout the night, Ruby checked the weather reports for Ketchikan on her phone app. Every few minutes she tapped the screen for updates. Close to a hundred mile per hour winds were hitting the island. Flood-like rain, too. She and Peter had weathered lots of storms. However, that didn't stop her from worrying about him. And the *Lily Forever,* their home.

She sent Peter a couple of texts—*How are you doing? Is everything okay? How's the boat?* He didn't respond. The storm had probably messed up the satellite system. She might not get a response until tomorrow.

What if something awful happened to him? She had no way of knowing if he was okay. Shivers raced over her arms and up her neck. She tugged a throw blanket over the sweatshirt she'd worn to bed. What if Peter was on deck and a large, unsuspecting wave crashed over him, knocking him into the sea? What if the boat capsized and he drowned? Not likely, since it was docked. But still.

She should have gone with him. Then she wouldn't be pacing across the guest room floor in Paisley and Judah's house like this. Then she'd know for herself how her husband was doing.

There was no way she could go back to bed until she knew Peter was okay, especially after picturing him falling overboard and drowning.

She could pray. When she was a kid, her dad made her go to church and Sunday School. But in her adulthood, while she believed in God, she hadn't been faithful to pray that much. Other than desperate times at sea when she called out to Him to rescue them, or to get them through some crisis. Maybe to help them catch enough fish to pay the bills.

This was different.

Lord, it's been a while since we last talked. I'm sorry about that. Please be with Peter. Keep him safe. I'm worried about him being alone tonight. Would You watch over him, and the other fishermen too, during this storm?

Would God listen to her if she prayed only when things were going terrible? She thought of something else.

The people here have been so kind to me. They talk about Your grace and love as if they've truly experienced it. I want that in my life too.

Sighing, she whispered another plea for God's protection over Peter.

* * * *

Still troubled by the scraping sounds above him, Peter decided to head outside to check the rigging one more time. He donned his float jacket and boots again. Grabbed another flashlight. Then fought to open the door as before and trudged onto the deck. At the stern, he shined the light out over a plethora of whitecaps. Had whatever he heard earlier toppled overboard?

Gripping the railing with one hand, he stared through the torrential rain at something bobbing in the dark waves. A piece of his fishing gear? Could be anything from any of the boats in the harbor, except he thought he'd heard something break.

Just then, another screeching sound shot adrenaline through him. He jerked sideways.

Whoosh! Slam!

A metal projectile crashed to the deck near his feet, parts exploding. Something scraped his ankle. Fire burned through his lower leg. His heart pounded like a runaway freight train.

That was close. Another inch and whatever fell could have rammed into his skull. He bent over to discover what might have nearly cost him his life. Unfortunately, he'd dropped his flashlight again. A brief light from somewhere in the harbor revealed the metal outrigger pole that normally pointed toward the sky was lying at an odd angle across his back deck.

Not good. This would take time and effort to repair. But there was nothing he could do about it tonight.

More blasting wind and pelting rain bombarded him. Concerned for his safety, he hobbled back toward the door, one hand holding onto his rainhat. At the cabin door, he yanked on the handle several times before it opened enough for him to slip inside. A dry galley had never felt so inviting. So safe. He stripped off his outer gear and draped each piece on a hook so they could dry off.

Over his years of fishing, he'd had close calls. Tonight was a reminder of life being short. This time, only his ankle had suffered an injury. It could have been far worse. *Someone* must have been looking out for him from above.

Forty-three

"Good morning, Judah." Mom breezed into the kitchen at the project house, smiling, dressed in a navy jacket and slacks. Her shorter haircut was tipped with a frosty color and bounced as she crossed the room to the coffee machine.

Callie followed, moving much slower. "Judah."

"Morning, ladies." Squatting next to the front door, he mended the trim work that had gotten damaged when they were hauling in materials or the new appliances. "Are you ready for this big day?"

"Ready as I'll ever be." Mom finished fixing her hot drink. "Today our citizens will make up their own minds about who should guide the town until the next election."

"If they're smart, they'll recognize it's high time for new leadership." Callie set a teakettle on the stove. "How about you?" She eyed Judah from behind the butcher-block island. "Will you be voting for your mother?"

Nothing like being put on the spot.

"However he votes is a private matter." Mom gave him a smile. "My son supports my decision to do what's on my heart, right?"

"That's right."

Callie harrumphed. "A son ought to do more than say he supports his mother."

Judah clamped his jaw to keep his mouth shut and not respond negatively to Paisley's aunt.

Mom strolled toward the large window where the dining area would be. She stood holding her cup with the morning sunshine pouring over her, and she looked younger, more vibrant than he'd seen her look in a long time.

This being a monumental day for her, win or lose, he should say something encouraging. He shuffled over to her, gazing through the trees, wishing for a better view of the sea.

"Are you worried?" Mom asked before he said anything.

"About?"

"I don't know. Maybe if I win things will be different? More changes in our family?"

He sighed. "I don't want you in the hot seat, deflecting criticisms and sorting out Edward's messes."

"I won't like that, either. But it'll be part of the job." She pointed at the roots of a downed tree. "See those roots still attached to the ground? Every time I look at them, I picture our family. The storms of life rammed into us. But you and I dug our roots deep and held onto each other, our faith, and our friends, too." She ran her hand over his shoulder. "Look at you and Paisley. So in love, married again, full of hope. It's written all over your face. You're truly happy again, aren't you?"

"I am. I want that for you too."

She chuckled. "I'm fine without the being in love part. But peace and happiness, finding a purpose for living again? I'll grab those with both hands and hold on tight."

"That sounds good." He met her gaze. "Just so you know, I will be voting for you. If you win, you'll lead Basalt Bay with wisdom and kindness. I couldn't wish for more for our hometown."

"Thank you, Son. I'll try to live up to those words." She turned the cup in her hand. "We'll leave the rest up to the residents and accept God's plan. Oh, one other thing."

"What's that?"

Did she want to discuss the news he heard about Craig being Edward's son? He'd called her and told her about the DNA results a couple of days ago. She hadn't acted surprised.

"Everything's finalized for the divorce. My lawyer went to Florence and got Edward to sign." She spoke softly like she didn't want Callie, who still stood by the island stirring a spoon in her teacup, to hear. "It's possible I'll be a free woman on the same day I'm voted in as mayor."

"That's good news. It's what you want, right?"

"It's not the happily ever after I once hoped for." She drew in a long breath. "But I'm glad to be moving forward with my life after a troubled marriage. Let's hope for a happier future for both of us."

"Amen." Judah gave her a sidearm hug. Then he resumed his inspection of the trim by the door.

"You know what I'll miss if I get elected?" Mom strode back into the kitchen, chuckling.

"What's that?" Callie asked.

"Working at Lewis's Super. I love my job!"

"Your talents are wasted there," Callie said in a stern tone.

"I disagree." Mom set her cup in the sink. "If anything, any dormant talents I had were awakened when I started working there. I'm thankful Lewis took a chance on me. It was a stepping stone into my new life."

A stepping stone. Judah thought back to the advice Pastor Sagle had given him and Paisley about taking the hurts and the experiences of the past and building a bridge.

Lord, please make something beautiful of the stones of our lives. Bless Mom. Guide her, however the town votes today. Have Your way about Craig being a part of our family, too.

Another stepping stone.

Forty-four

Can you break away and meet me at Baker's Point?

The unexpected text from Paige sent adrenaline spiking through Forest's core. Baker's Point? Why did she want to meet at the same place where he arrested Craig? Was she doing okay in the aftermath of the sting? It had been three days.

Is everything all right? He typed quickly.

Yes. Can you meet me?

Last night, their gazes met across the living room several times. He'd been reading to Piper while Paige was going over the gallery sketches. Each time when he caught her staring at him, she glanced away as if embarrassed by him finding her watching him. But he liked her being attracted to him, if that was the case. He liked the softer look in her gaze too.

Thirty minutes? He tapped across the phone screen.

Perfect. Thanks.

Since Peter had left to return to his boat in Alaska, Paige put Piper's bed back in her room, and she slept on the futon.

Last night, she barely spoke to Forest all evening, just sent him those confusing cursory glances.

What was going on with her?

He was thankful Edward and Evie were in jail, so he didn't have to be concerned about any more threats or violence toward his family. Although, one thing still troubled him. He hadn't resolved Mia's message passing with Edward. What would stop her from continuing to get messages from him in Florence?

What if Forest had missed something?

Just like he'd almost overlooked the note in the bathroom drawer this morning. Paige's words hummed in his brain. *I've been thinking a lot about us lately.* That sent heat waves through his system. *I'm proud of how you've jumped in to being a dad for Piper. How loving you are with her makes me so happy.* He loved being Piper's dad. *I'm hopeful for our future.* Those words took his breath away. If she was hopeful about their future, something must be changing in her heart.

Forest jogged down the stairs of the project house in search of Judah. He found him in the kitchen where he was bent over blueprints at the island. "Would you mind if I took an hour off? Paige asked me to meet her."

"Sure. No problem. Are you going to the community meeting this afternoon?"

"The vote's today, isn't it?" Forest shrugged. "I wasn't planning on it since I haven't lived here that long."

"Participating in an event like this might demonstrate to Paige, and her family, that you plan to stick around. You know, get involved in the town, caring about what she cares about." Judah shrugged. "Just a thought."

Forest hadn't considered that. What did Judah know about him and Paige? Did she reveal something to her sister about their platonic arrangement? He'd be glad when this charade of them having a normal marriage while he proved himself trustworthy to Paige passed. Although, as soon as the thought crossed his mind, he regretted it.

He was immensely grateful for this time to be near Paige and Piper. Even if they weren't living his ideal of what marriage should be, he loved being around his wife and daughter, the three of them finally getting to be a family. He went into this marriage with open eyes, willing to take a chance on a fake marriage transforming into a real one. In time it would— he believed that with all his heart. If only he weren't so impatient!

"No pressure, man. You and Paige must work out your own stuff. Paisley and I are here for you if there's anything we can do." Judah patted him on the shoulder then returned his gaze to the blueprints and frowned.

"Something wrong?"

"I did a walk-through in the attic." He tapped a pencil over the paper. "The roof needs our immediate attention. We've been focused on preparing the rooms the ladies wanted done first, but this roofing business concerns me. Bad leak stains. A couple of holes. Potential for winter problems if we don't get a handle on it."

"Sounds like a whale of a task."

Judah snorted. "Can't be helped, I'm afraid."

"You want me to pick up patching supplies while I'm in town?"

"I'll mull this over. Work out a plan." Judah nodded toward the door. "Go. Meet Paige. Take your time. Don't concern yourself with this today."

"Okay. Thanks, boss."

At the Baker's Point parking lot, Forest turned off the engine and jumped out of his rental. He'd have to return this car and get back to Portland to retrieve his own vehicle soon. Maybe he and Paige could make a day of it. He'd like to introduce her and Piper to his folks and Teal. He had to shut down his apartment too.

He sighed, contemplating what Judah said about going to the town meeting. Would getting involved in the local event send a message to his wife that he intended to stay here with her?

Paige's car wasn't in the lot yet, so he strode down the grassy cliff to the beach. Crossing the sand, he walked until he reached the tideline. The waves rolled in slower here, calmer than at the city beach. Inhaling, he took in the salty aroma of the sea, then exhaled. Something about living by the ocean pleased his senses, relaxed him. He'd like to get a beach cottage like Judah and Paisley's and take walks with Paige and Piper every day. What would Paige think of that?

A car engine turned off. Paige appeared at the top of the cliff and waved. Lifting his hand, he gulped. He loved her so much. Based on the times he'd kissed her since they got back together, he knew she enjoyed them. But had she fallen for him yet? What would he have to do to convince her that he was worth whatever she had to do to commit to their marriage?

Paige smiled timidly as she trudged through the sand toward him.

"You okay, baby?"

"I'm okay." She stopped a few feet away from him, her hands tucked in the pockets of her navy-blue jacket. "Thanks for meeting with me like this."

"Sure. What's going on?"

"I need to talk with you about something."

"Okay."

She nodded toward a flat spot on the beach. "Did you know there used to be a gazebo here where guys used to propose to their girlfriends?"

"Oh yeah?" Propose, huh? She had his attention.

"Sometimes people made baby announcements here, too, or celebrated family achievements. Or said farewells."

Paige couldn't be announcing a baby. He prayed she wasn't here to tell him farewell.

"Too bad it got destroyed during Hurricane Addy." She gazed wistfully at the vacant spot. "Even Judah proposed to Paisley here the first time."

She met his gaze and smiled. At her warm expression, the tight band across his chest dissipated. Maybe she wasn't here to tell him anything negative.

"I'm sorry for not being completely honest with you, Forest."

"What do you mean?" Apprehension tightened his vocal cords.

"There are things I've held onto." She expelled a breath. "Hurtful feelings toward you that I've kept close to my heart like a shield, even when you've tried to make things right. I'm sorry for doing that. For not letting it go so we could heal and try to work things out together."

"I'm sorry for hurting you by leaving before." He wanted to take her in his arms and hold her, but a wariness in her gaze stopped him from acting on the impulse. "I'd do anything for a do-over of that time in our lives."

"Me too." She sighed. "You've done a great job watching over Piper and me, even sleeping in my room while my brother was here to make things easier in the house. Thank you for that." She fingered a few strands of hair behind her ears, and his fingers itched to do the same thing.

"No problem. I wanted to be with you." Still wanted to be with her.

"There are reasons I needed to test this marriage before fully giving my heart to it, beyond the need for protection for Piper, or me." She swallowed hard.

"You mean about me needing to prove myself?" The notion still irked him.

"Partially." She shuffled her dark shoe in the sand.

"You can tell me whatever it is. You're distrustful of me possibly leaving. I get it." He crossed the distance between them and set his palms lightly on her shoulders. "Paige, I promise I won't leave you again. I'm in this marriage for real. You can count on me. It's not a fake marriage to me. Never has been."

"I know you say that, but you called her name!"

"Whose name?" He stepped back, breaking the connection of his fingers on her shoulders.

"Elinore's."

"I don't understand."

"When we were together as newlyweds ... the night before you left ... you called her name, not mine, when you said goodnight." Paige blinked slowly at him, moisture making her eyes shine.

Understanding, then horror, dawned on him. "I called you … Elinore?"

"Yes."

"Is that why you filed for divorce so quickly?" She'd told him she thought he ran off and married Elinore.

"Yes. I thought you went back to be with her." She gazed out toward the sea, the wind fluttering her hair. "It's been eating me up. The doubts. The remembrance of you saying her name like you cherished her. That's what I needed to tell you and get it off my chest. Why I texted you to meet me here."

"Paige—"

"I'm trying to let it go. Honestly, I am. But it's been difficult for me."

"I'm sorry. I can't even imagine saying that."

She nodded, her chin quivering. "Also, I wanted you to know that I talked with Paisley about us. I told her everything. And I … prayed. I'm trusting Jesus to help me forgive you, myself, and all that happened between us. I want to live for Him now, too."

"Oh, Paige, that's amazing." An answer to his prayers. "We can pray together more too."

She nodded. "I'd like us to start over. I mean, if you're still interested."

"If I'm interested?" Relief, then joy, swept through him. "You bet I'm interested." Taking her hand in his, he gazed into her eyes. "I don't know why I would have said Elinore's name when you were the only woman I wanted. I'm sorry I did that. For how it hurt you. She was a friend who I cared about. I've never loved anyone as I love you. I'm crazy about you."

"Thank you. Like I said, I'm letting it go." Her voice shook like she was restraining her emotions. "I've held the hurt and anger in my heart for so long it had a stranglehold on me. I vowed never to be vulnerable to you or anyone else ever again. I was proud of the brick wall I built around my heart." She groaned. "I've tried so hard to be tough."

"Oh, baby." He drew her against his chest, and she wrapped her arms around him. He ran his hands over her back, catching the aroma of her herbal-scented hair brushing his face. He leaned back a little, not kissing her yet, not assuming anything. "Are you saying you want more to happen between us now? I mean husband and wife stuff? You said you want to start over. Your note said you were hopeful about our future. Does this mean you want a true marriage with me?"

"I do," she said softly. "I don't want a fake marriage anymore."

Thank You, Lord!

"That's the best news I've ever heard." With his fingers tangling her hair, he leaned in, their lips almost meeting. Pausing an inch from her mouth, he glanced at the sandy place where Paige said people used to make announcements, the place where Judah proposed to Paisley. An idea hit him. Clasping her hand, he grinned and tugged her over to the spot.

"Forest, what are you doing?"

"Just this." He knelt in front of her and, clutching her hand to his mouth, kissed the ring on her finger. "Paige, will you be my wife for real? To have and to hold all the days of our lives?"

Her lips spread in a wide grin. "Yes, I will marry you and stay married to you for all our days."

"I love you, baby."

"I love you too."

Her soft admission thrilled him. He jumped up and kissed her with all the depth of feeling he had in his whole being, loving the way she melted into his arms and kissed him back. They lingered in each other's arms, kissing over and over, touching each other's hair and cheeks, laughing and grinning.

"What now?" He stared into her sparkling gaze.

She brushed her lips against his cheek. "I want you. Us. A beautiful life together. Forest and Paige Harper."

"Me too." He kissed her again.

A few minutes later, as they walked up the cliff toward the parking lot, holding hands, he asked, "Do you have plans for the afternoon?"

"Piper's playing at Necia's house. There's the town meeting this afternoon. I want to vote for Bess."

"Oh, right. I thought I'd attend also."

"Really? We could go together."

"I'd like that." He'd go to the ends of the earth and back to be with her.

Beside her car, Forest took her in his arms again. "Do you mind if I follow you back to the house? Even if we just talk—"

She met his lips, kissing him, stopping his words, seemingly giving him his answer.

Heart hammering, he let her go and lightly squeezed her hands. "I'll follow you home, then."

This time when he said "home," he meant it.

Forty-five

Holding Paisley's hand, Judah followed the crowd of Basalt Bay residents into the community hall. He tried ignoring the pessimistic feelings that usually hit him whenever he entered this building. He was here to support Mom. Not to dwell on Dad's longtime position as mayor, his rude behavior, or any of the trouble he caused. Hopefully, there wouldn't be any negative uprising about today's speeches and voting.

Mom, Mia, and C.L. would each have ten minutes to try to persuade citizens to vote for them as the temporary mayor. Then the voting booths would be opened.

Judah tried imagining what his father might think of this gathering. Things hadn't gone his way lately. He didn't win his day off. Visitation was still suspended. His place of residence changed to the Florence jail. His old girlfriend, Evie, had been apprehended—Forest told Judah that much. Now, Edward's ex-wife was competing against two candidates for his mayoral seat. He was probably sitting in his jail cell chewing on proverbial nails. Maybe kicking the wall. Was he enraged that the town would dare to replace him and move forward?

Judah and Paisley migrated to their usual places about three-fourths back in the room lined with folding chairs. Easy enough to get out quickly if things went south.

Paisley waved to someone across the aisle. Callie and Kathleen, grinning broadly, waved back at them like Granny did at the end of the old TV show *The Beverly Hillbillies*. These two gals and Maggie were Mom's leading supporters in the door-to-door campaigning and standing on street corners passing out fliers. Mom was fortunate to have such great friends and roommates.

Shaking hands with attendees and grinning like she'd already won, Mia sashayed up the aisle.

Judah wished she weren't involved in this election. How she passed warnings from Edward to him, Paisley, and even Paige, still annoyed him. At least, thanks to Forest and Deputy Brian, she was being kept away from Edward. Judah still had misgivings about her possible involvement in the drawing alterations at C-MER, too. But as far as he knew, nothing had been proven or resolved about the matter.

And it was Evie Masters, not Mia, who was involved in Paisley's kidnapping from the hospital. That made Judah not quite so angsty about his previous coworker being in today's electoral race.

Still, Mia running for interim mayor? He prayed Mom or C.L. would win. C.L. was a newcomer who didn't know much about Basalt Bay, but he seemed honestly concerned about the coastline. Didn't his stopping the work on the dike prove that?

Mia rushed over to Judah and shook his hand, grinning back and forth between him and Paisley. "I'm counting on your vote, you two."

He coughed.

She leaned across him to get closer to Paisley. "However this turns out, no hard feelings, right?"

"Of course not. Why should there be?" Paisley gave her a closed-mouth smile.

"May the best woman win." Patting Judah's shoulder, Mia winked at him and laughingly moved on to the next person.

Paisley's groan coincided with his.

"Aren't you glad you don't work with her anymore?"

"Never so much as right now." He sighed and linked his fingers with Paisley's.

By the draw, Mom would be the first speaker. At exactly three p.m., she stepped behind the podium. The room broke out in cheering and hand clapping. With her dark blue dressy suit and freshly-styled hair, she appeared a mix of confidence and awe. Judah was so proud of her.

"Thank you for coming to this meeting and for your kind support during our brief campaign." Mom gazed out at the audience. "All of you being here, taking part in the interim-mayoral process, and showing such encouragement to me and my team, means the world to me."

Judah glanced around the room, assessing people's reactions. Callie and Kathleen stared forward, their faces almost glowing, their heads bobbing in unison with each of Mom's points. Others leaned toward each other, murmuring and shaking their heads negatively. They were probably some of the ones who wanted the Grants out of local politics.

"If I'm voted in as mayor of Basalt Bay, one of the things I hope to accomplish is to build our community's sense of goodwill." Mom smiled warmly. "We experienced many kindnesses following Hurricane Blaine with the neighborhood brigades—a fabulous idea, by the way. But all too soon we got caught up in our own problems and lives. We forgot to look out for each other. Life is so much more fulfilling when we're thinking of our neighbors, reaching out to make sure our friends are cared for and safe, don't you agree?"

"Hear, hear!" Callie bellowed.

Shouts of agreement crossed the room.

"She's doing great." Paisley leaned into Judah and smiled. "She is."

On the front seat, Mia whispered something to C.L., snickering as if dismissing what the speaker had said. That kind of unsportsmanlike behavior annoyed Judah, even in a political arena.

Mom ended her speech and stepped down from the low platform to a loud rumbling of foot-stomping, clapping, and whistles. She waved to the crowd and smiled in her easy manner.

In a completely opposite display, Mia nearly danced to the podium, several necklaces jangling with her movement. "Isn't she just the sweetest lady?" Her voice came out sounding syrupy and insincere. "Here's what I bring to the table, gents and ladies"—Mia cast a few winks and grins toward attendees— "youth and vitality, clarity of thought, and a new vision for this town. While we all love and respect Mayor Grant—"

Judah clenched his teeth.

"It's time for us to step up and transform Basalt Bay into a modern town. We have to stop living in the past." Her laugh turned brassy. "Like this business of red tape and all the problems with getting our dike fixed. Someone needs to take C-MER by the throat and give it a squeeze." She acted out shaking something with her hands, then laughed boisterously.

Some in the group joined in her laughter.

C.L. glared at her.

"Seriously, people, I've been with the company for years. They do good work. Great work. But I have the inside track on getting things accomplished efficiently. You can count on me." She raised her hands like a cheerleader. "Vote Mia Till for mayor! I'm your girl!"

About ten seconds of silence ensued without any hand clapping or cheers. Had she gone too far this time? Too flamboyant?

But then, some clapping and whistles followed her semi-dance back to her seat.

Judah released a long sigh, glad for that part of the program to be done.

The third candidate strode to the front of the aisle, not bothering to step behind the podium. C.L. faced the group with the same intensity of expression and voice Judah noticed during his visit to C-MER. "You want your town put together post-hurricanes, the business section, including the dike, rebuilt to modern standards, and tourists brought back to town? If you're serious about getting Basalt Bay on its feet, vote for me. Yes, I'm new to town. Some may question why I'm even running for mayor."

That was the truth.

"Let me tell you one thing about me, I will fight for the good of the communities along the western seaboard and protect our coastline, no matter the cost."

Brad Kiefer whistled loudly.

C.L. eyed the group. "The time for small-minded leadership is over."

Did he mean Edward's governing technique had been small-minded? Judah leaned forward, elbows on his knees, listening more intently.

"I may be unknowledgeable about your town's customs, but I promise you this—vote me into the mayoral seat, and I will get the job of restoring this town done." He returned to his front row seat and sat down.

Someone near the front clapped a strong steady beat and most of the group joined in.

C.L. had said some good things. The speeches were over. What would the citizens decide?

Forty-six

Forest stood with Paige beside him in the community hall, their fingers linked. He liked how close she sat next to him during the speeches, even leaning her head against his shoulder. They'd exchanged a few smiles. Every touch of her hand against his arm or his chest buzzed remembrances of this afternoon through his mind.

This was their first time in public as an honest-to-goodness married couple, and he wanted to shout out to the world that he and Paige loved each other to the ends of the universe and back. His joy over their coming together in heart and in intimacy filled him with such hope and happiness, he couldn't stop grinning.

"Hey, you guys." Paisley glanced back and forth between them. "You two look happy. What's going on?"

Forest coughed.

Paige chuckled and nudged him in the side with her elbow. "We are very happy." She hugged her sister. "Everything's good. Thank you for talking with me and explaining about the Lord the other day."

"Of course. I'm happy for you." Paisley kissed Paige's cheek. "I told you it would all work out."

"You were right." Paige laughed.

Judah, who must have observed Paige and Paisley's exchange, shook Forest's hand. "God is good, huh?"

"Absolutely." These people were Forest's family now, too, and he appreciated their kind concern for him and Paige. "What did you think of the speeches? I thought Bess did fantastic."

"All three articulated their goals." Judah shrugged. "I'm biased. Still rooting for my mom."

"Same here," Forest agreed.

"Hi, everyone." Ruby joined their group. Paige and Paisley hugged her.

"Any news from Peter?" Forest asked.

"Nothing yet." Ruby grimaced. "He'll make sure the boat's safe before he texts me."

Forest related to that kind of single-mindedness on the job. But in the future, as a married man, he'd be more diligent to keep his wife informed of his actions. He'd made a gigantic blunder about that once before. Never again.

"Bess sounded amazing." Ruby glanced at Judah. "More human and compassionate than the other two. You should be proud of her."

"I am. Win or lose, she has my vote."

"As well she should." Ruby patted his shoulder. "Something about the guy bugged me. He was a little—"

"Robotic?" Paige asked. "I hope he doesn't win."

"He was right about folks considering him an outsider."
Paisley linked her arm with Judah's. "Why is he even running?
He should have to live here for longer than two weeks to be
considered in an election."

"If it wasn't for the emergency vote, he wouldn't have had
the chance," Judah said.

"Hey, Ruby." Paisley squinted toward her. "Tell my brother
I have a bone to pick with him."

"Oh? Why's that?"

"He promised not to leave town without talking to me."

Ruby sighed. "You know Peter."

A slight awkwardness passed through their group.

Forest wished Paige would return to his side so he could
hold her hand or put his arm over her shoulder. He missed her
closeness already. Winking at her on the sly, he saw a small
smile cross her mouth … her luscious lips he couldn't wait to
taste again.

But they were at a public event. He should be preparing to
vote, and interacting with family and friends, not thinking of
how in love he was with his wife. Not imagining how much he
wanted to take her home and kiss her again in private.

Eventually, they took turns entering the half-dozen
makeshift voting booths. With small-town pizzaz, as each
person dropped their ballot into the box, Callie rang a cowbell
and announced the voter's name. "Forest Harper has voted!"

Chuckling, he and Paige left the community hall with their
own plans for the rest of the afternoon.

* * * *

Paige spread out a picnic blanket on the sand not far from the trail leading from the subdivision to the beach. No doubt Piper would have preferred playing in the sand right by the water's edge, but Paige didn't want her daughter charging into the surf and getting soaking wet. She wanted this outing together as a family to be perfectly calm and peaceful.

She glanced at Forest, the man who loved her and whom she loved, and his warm gaze thrilled her. For so long she'd ached for what she didn't have. For what she lost. Now, Forest was hers, and she was his ... without regrets or doubts.

Piper had a great dad too. Maybe there would be siblings for her. Paige and Forest hadn't discussed it yet, but she imagined he'd want to observe the process of her pregnancy and delivery of his child, someday. Thoughts of holding another baby in her arms sent goosebumps skidding over her skin. A boy with gray-green eyes? Another girl who looked like Piper?

No use getting ahead of herself. But after the way they kissed and held each other back at the house, the way Forest made love to her, she couldn't help but leap ahead to what an intimate marriage with him might mean for years to come.

After setting the lunch basket they'd prepared together on one corner of the blanket, Forest placed three rocks as weights on each of the other three corners. The stones would help stabilize the blanket from getting caught up in a gust of wind.

Since the weather was cool, they were all wearing sweatshirts or sweaters. But it wasn't too cold to enjoy a picnic at the beach. And Piper loved the sand! Paige smiled at their daughter scuffing her shoes into a mound of grit and pebbles and babbling about rocks and crabs.

"Let's eat lunch, Pipe." Paige set out the chicken and fruit, easy picnic food for a toddler.

"Come on." Forest held out his hand toward Piper.

"No. Sand." She kicked at the dirt, sending a puff of dust into the air.

"Come on. It's food you'll like." Paige held up her plate, hoping to entice her and distract her from a tantrum.

"No, *pway.*" She grimaced, showing her teeth and stomping her foot.

Before Paige could respond, Forest scooped up Piper. Like she imagined, their daughter let out an ear-piercing howl. Forest, seemingly unfazed, set her down on the blanket. "When Mommy calls lunch, it's time to eat. Look at all the good food she fixed for us."

The two-year-old's face froze in a wailing pose. She glared up at him as if stunned by his involvement in her tantrum.

With her distracted, Paige set a plate with cut-up pieces of chicken and fruit in front of her. "Mmm. Yummy. Try it, Pipe."

She must have been more hungry than angry because she stuffed several bites into her mouth.

"Thank you," Paige said to Forest.

"Sure thing." He dropped onto the blanket beside her.

The waves rolling in and out and the sun sparkling off the shimmering water created a blissful scene as they ate their picnic delicacies.

Soon, the sand became too much of a draw for Piper, and Paige let her go play. That gave her and Forest time to sit close, both facing the water.

"I've wanted this forever, it seems," he said. "You and me. A lovely beach."

"Me too." She snickered. "Minus the sitting on the beach part."

"You want this with me now, right?" He swept strands of hair off her face, gazing deeply into her eyes. "Us being together. Sitting on the seashore."

"Sure." With him staring at her so adoringly, almost like he was lovestruck with her, she'd agree to almost anything. "I want what we have as a couple, and as a family. No more holding onto the past."

"Mmm. I agree with that." He met her lips for a brief kiss.

She wanted to linger in his arms and enjoy his kisses. Kind of like sugar, once she tasted it, she wanted more and more. But she couldn't let herself get too distracted. As much as she'd like to throw caution to the wind, her priority was watching Piper.

When Forest jumped up and sat down next to their daughter, playing in the sand with her shovel, Paige smiled at the duo. Forest as her husband, and Forest as her daughter's daddy, were both wonderful parts of him. Amazing parts of her new life with the man she loved, would love for the rest of her life.

Stuffing everything back into the basket, she cleaned up their picnic mess. Then, grabbing her camera, she set the dials and moved down the beach. She squatted and peered through the lens, observing Piper and Forest playing together. A gulp filled her throat. Tears made her focal point blurry. She snapped the picture anyway. Didn't want to miss out on a single shot of Piper laughing up at her daddy, his twin-colored eyes shining down at her.

Such tenderness engulfed Paige like a wave stealing over the shore of her heart. She'd almost lost the chance to experience this love with Forest. She could have married him but never given him her heart. But she had! Oh, she had. And this beautiful love story between them was just the beginning.

Thank You, God.

Forty-seven

Ruby had never loved heights, but the view from the rooftop of the project house was spectacular. From here, she could finally see the ocean. Tied to the roof with safety ropes, she and Forest had been tearing out soggy chunks of roofing for the last hour. While she worked, she kept thinking about Peter. Praying for him, too. Wishing he'd call or text and let her know he was okay.

She let out a long sigh.

"You okay?" Forest asked from his side of the damaged patch of plywood.

"Just troubled about Peter."

"Thinking of heading back?"

Was she so transparent? "If he doesn't call soon, I might. What if he's in trouble? According to news reports, the storm caused tremendous damage. Heavy losses of boats and severe flooding in the town."

"I can see why you're worried."

She held up her end of the board while Forest used a pry bar to release the other side from the aged nails. Suddenly, the wood came loose, and she nearly toppled over before regaining her balance. Ugh. She'd better be more careful.

The metal ladder clanked as someone tromped up the rungs. Judah's work hat appeared above the roofline, then his chest. "How's it going up here?"

"Got the worst of this section out." Forest stood and flung the board down to the pile where they'd been tossing rotten wood.

"Your phone's been buzzing on the counter, Ruby. I thought you'd want to know."

"Okay, thanks." She took a few steps down the sloped roof. Turning to Forest, she asked, "Do you mind if I check it?"

"Not at all. I'll keep working here."

"Thanks." She moved to the ladder where Judah was already climbing down.

Inside the project house, she accessed her voicemail.

"Hey, Ruby, I'm alive!" Peter's voice rumbled in her ear. "The boat and I are a bit battered, but we made it through the worst of it."

Static made her pull away from the phone.

"Hurt. Ankle. Drink. Sor—"

What did he say? Was he hurt? She replayed the message but couldn't make sense of it. Tapping the screen to access his number, the call went straight to voicemail. She hung up and texted him.

Got your message. Glad you're safe. Call when you can.

Gripping her cell phone, she sighed. *Thank You for watching over him.*

Judah entered the living room, stopping by the doorway. "Is Peter okay?"

"He's alive."

"Great news."

"Yep. The connection broke up, so I don't know what's happened. Or the extent of the damage to the boat. But he called."

"Excellent. I'm glad he's all right, and that he contacted you." He pulled out his cell. "I'll text Paisley. We've been praying for him, and you, too."

"Thank you, Judah."

She stared at her phone for five minutes without any text or call coming in. Time to get back to work. But she'd keep her cell in her overalls' pocket just in case Peter called again.

Forty-eight

Morning light revealed the extent of damage not only to Peter's boat but to other ships in the harbor as well. Debris floated like ice cubes bobbing in the churning sea. The winds were letting up, but not enough for him to work safely outdoors. The weather report wasn't good, either. More bad weather was expected.

Groaning, he stood at the window of the cabin door, nursing his coffee mug, staring at the dismal gray clouds. Nothing to be done but wait it out. He'd slept off and on through the night. A few crashing sounds awakened him. Whether the noises came from his boat or another, he didn't know. He forced himself not to follow his impulse and rush outside to check on anything.

The ache in his ankle, and the flashback of the pole crashing next to him, reminded him of the swiftness of accidents, even the fatality of some. He wasn't ready to die. Not by a long shot. And not without making things right with his wife.

Every time he woke up in the night and felt the emptiness of the bed beside him, he knew he had no one to blame but himself. If he'd tried harder to reconcile with Ruby, to be more understanding of her point of view, tried harder to communicate with her, maybe things would have turned out differently.

The buildings onshore still appeared dark. The local radio announcer said the electricity had been off for hours. Might be off for days. Good thing Peter had enough gas to last a while.

He fixed eggs and bacon for breakfast on the propane stove, the comforting smells filling the confined space. Only the homey scents caused the ache of loneliness and missing Ruby to worsen. They usually took turns fixing breakfast in their little galley.

This was their time to be a couple before the workday began, she'd said once upon a time. Did she miss sitting across from him at the table that was just big enough for the two of them? Even while he ate breakfast, he imagined her eating eggs and toast, laughing over something she read or heard on the news. Their knees bumping.

Sigh.

Could he be happy living this life alone? Being the fisherman he always wanted to be, but doing so without the woman he loved by his side? He groaned. The internal ache in his chest, in his spirit, made him almost physically ill.

Buying the boat, owning the business, and living on board had been a heady adventure. But meaningless if his wife wanted out. What would he do then? Sell? Go on without her? It would be a solitary life, working out on the sea alone. Plenty of fishermen worked by themselves or hired a deckhand. But, man, he'd have to hire two workers to replace Ruby. His Ruby.

She was such a huge part of this lifestyle. Of him.

He guzzled his coffee, washing down his food.

A mental replay zipped through his brainwaves of Ruby tugging on his arm, playfully begging him to take a day off—*"Please, this once, let's go somewhere and hold hands and act romantic! One day away from the boat wouldn't kill us."*

At the time, he didn't see the point. He had important things to do—always things to do. Work came first. Their livelihoods depended on it. Why couldn't she understand his responsibilities? Goodnight. They owned a boat. If he missed a salmon opening, or if something broke down, the whole burden rested on his shoulders.

Her pleading and cajoling, saying they needed time away for fun as a couple ate at him now.

Boat swaying, breakfast finished, and with nothing tangible to do to get his thoughts off their marital problems, he groaned and rubbed his forehead. What should he do while he waited out the next phase of the storm? He had a crossword puzzle he could work on to pass the time, but even that seemed meaningless without Ruby here to share it with him.

A quick check of his cell phone showed no bars. If it were working, he'd call her. She might be worried. Thinking of him.

Ruby, I wish you were here with me.

But maybe it was a good thing she wasn't here last night. What if she'd been the one outside checking the decks? What if the rigging had hit her in its descent? He shuddered.

He heard a loud rumble. Thunder? The storm was picking up again. How long would it take for the thing to finally wring itself out?

Forty-nine

Judah and Mom stood in the kitchen, sipping their morning coffees and discussing the work that was left to be done at the project house.

"The roof is the big thing hanging over our heads," he said with a grin. "Still lots to do upstairs and outdoors."

"But it's all coming together. I saw Ruby and Forest up on the roof."

"Neither of them are thrilled about that part of the project." He chuckled.

Heavy footsteps pounded across the porch. They both turned as Callie strode into the kitchen with Kathleen on her heels.

"It's here!" Callie clutched the *Basalt Bay Gazette* against her chest, her arms covering most of the front page.

"What does it say?" Mom clasped her hands together. "Who won? Tell me. Don't keep me in suspense."

Kathleen beamed so widely she looked about to burst with the news herself.

"You won!" Callie pulsed one fist in the air. "You, Bess Grant, are the interim mayor of Basalt Bay!"

"Hip-hip-hooray for Mayor Bess!" Kathleen cheered.

Mom laughed and accepted the ladies' hugs, all of them chattering and laughing.

As soon as Mom broke free, Judah hugged her too. "Congratulations, Mom."

"Thank you. I can't believe it. I mean I hoped, but this? Oh, my."

Callie spread the newspaper over the butcher-block island. Mom's picture filled the space beneath the headline, "Grant Continues Legacy."

"What will Edward say about this?" Mom asked in a hushed voice.

"Who cares what that toad says?" Callie huffed. "The people of this town chose you. We decided who we want to lead us. That wasn't him or his flirtatious minion!"

"Callie!" Kathleen said.

Mom covered her face with her hands for a few moments, then lowered them. "Should I call Mia and Clyde and say something kind or sympathetic to them?"

"It works the other way around," Judah offered. "You might get a congratulatory call from them."

"That's right." Kathleen nodded. "Maybe they'll give concession speeches."

"What should I do?" Mom asked.

"Go celebrate." Callie hugged her again. "Party today. Work tomorrow."

"What a gob of work it will be. Fun, too." Kathleen ran her hands over the new countertops. "Judah, you precious man. Thank you for all the work you've done for us!" She hugged him fiercely.

"You're welcome." He was getting paid for the work, but it was nice to hear gratefulness for his part in the project, too.

After a few minutes of discussion about his mom's new job, Judah headed upstairs to the planning room to look over his to-do list.

"Judah, I need to talk with you." Ruby followed him into the room, her facial expression saying there was a problem.

"Sure. What's going on?"

"I'm afraid I have to leave."

"Oh?" That would be a kick in the kneecap to their project. Ruby was a great asset to their team. He was counting on her help with the rest of the remodeling. The roof, too. "Did you hear something bad from Peter?"

"No, but I'm worried. The one broken message came through, and the storm is still raging."

"How would you even get into Ketchikan? Are planes flying in?"

"No." She let out a soft moan. "I thought I'd head to SEA-TAC via Portland. Then fly in with the first available flight."

"Do what you have to do." He shook her hand. "We'll miss you, Ruby. Our motley crew wouldn't have gotten nearly the work done here without you. The ladies will move in sooner thanks to you."

"It felt great to be a part of a team again."

"What's this?" Callie bustled into the planning room. "You're leaving us in the lurch?"

"Callie—" Judah warned.

"It's Peter." Ruby nudged her braid over her shoulder. "Otherwise, I wouldn't go. I wouldn't leave the work unfinished."

"Did you hear bad news?" Callie asked, her tone softening.

"Actually, no news. Other than he's alive."

"Well, see there. That's good." Callie embraced Ruby. "You know what I think? I think work is the best remedy for waiting. Not sitting idle in an airport. I'm not saying that because I'm impatient for this house to be finished, either." She turned toward Judah. "Give us the room, will you?"

"I don't—" He bit back a negative reply to her bossiness. "Yes, ma'am." He met Ruby's gaze. "Talk to you later." Then he trotted out of the room.

Fifty

Ruby watched Judah exit and braced herself for whatever Callie might have to say. Since being in Basalt Bay, she noticed the woman had a way of telling people what to do and just what she thought of their actions. But she had a loving side too, like the warm, maternal hug she just gave Ruby.

"Now"—Callie strode to one side of the table—"I have a proposition for you."

"You do?"

"Bess, Kathleen, and I have discussed this, and we'd like you to stay on here with us."

"Stay on? What do you mean?"

"This may come as a surprise, but the girls and I are going to open our home to other women who may be in need of friendship or encouragement, perhaps a refuge during a storm in their life." Callie gripped the top of a folding chair. "Does any of that sound familiar?"

Ruby tucked her hands into the pockets of her overalls. "Yes. More than I like to admit."

"Just what I thought." Callie nodded. "No judgment or condemnation, mind you. We'd be here to offer support and friendship."

Ruby didn't know what to say. Since coming to the project house, and with all the work she'd done, she never imagined herself living here. "You're saying I could stay—"

"Indefinitely. Until you felt ready to"—Callie stared at the ceiling—"get back together with Peter, strike out on your own, or what have you. You'd be welcome and loved for as long as you wished to remain here."

"That's a generous offer. You ladies have already been so kind to me." Could she stay here? Not go back to Ketchikan? Or Peter?

"Why sit around the airport waiting for news when you can wait right here among friends?" Callie shuffled to her and clasped her hands. "We are your family. We love you and Peter. We want what's best for both of you. But you came here for a reason, didn't you?"

"Yes." She gulped, not wanting to explain anything to Callie. But she was feeling sad and worried about Peter. Missing him, too. Would his aunt be a sympathetic listener?

"Sometimes, getting something off our chest helps, but it's up to you." Callie pulled out a chair and dropped into it. Patting the table beside her, she eyed Ruby. "Why did you come to Basalt Bay? Don't get me wrong, I'm glad you did. Otherwise, we wouldn't have seen our Peter. The man stayed away from us for twelve long years." Moisture puddled in the older woman's eyes.

"I know." Ruby sat down next to Callie. "I came here to learn about his past and to find out what caused the wall around his heart." She sighed. "He and I have grown distant."

"I'm sorry to hear that."

The woman's kind response drew more from Ruby. "There's something in him that runs deep and locks me out every time I try to reach him."

"Heartache runs through our family like a drippy faucet. But before I say anything else, what do you think about moving in with us?" Callie wiped the back of her hand beneath her nose. "You don't have to make a decision right now. I'm just eager to hear. Probably being pushy—sorry about that."

"The idea is lovely. I'm thankful, believe me. But so much depends on—"

"Peter," Callie finished.

"Yes."

"Do you see yourselves reconciling?"

"I still love him, so I wish for that, yes." Ruby took a long breath. "But sometimes love isn't enough."

"Do you think learning about our family will give you the insight you desire?" Callie's dark eyes shadowed as if a cloud passed over them.

"It's my prayer." Ruby broke a loose thread off her overalls.

For the next twenty minutes, Callie took her down a road of family history. She told her more information than Ruby needed or wanted to hear, but with each story, she understood her husband's personality, and the mechanics of the Cedars family, a little better.

Callie spent the most time describing Penny, Peter's mother, who she said was a melancholy, self-absorbed artist with a short fuse when it came to doling out punishment. Ruby shuddered at the mental image of Peter as a little boy sitting on the pantry floor waiting to be released from his prison. Her heart ached for the possibly hurting boy in him now.

"I went there to check on the children, but Pauly resented it." Callie wore a far-off look as if lost in her storytelling. "I loved Peter and the girls, but I was kept at arm's length."

"I'm sorry."

"As am I."

"And now?" Ruby smoothed her hand over Callie's wrinkled one, sensing the woman's sorrow. "Are things any better between you and Paul?"

"Not even. I still hope for reconciliation. Pray about it every day." Callie patted the table. "But we're supposed to be helping you find out what made those walls around Peter. Not me and Pauly."

"You're part of his family, his upbringing, too. A good part, I think."

"I hope so, but he left so quickly after graduation." Callie dug through her sweater pocket and pulled out a tissue, twisting it between her fingers. "I always wondered why."

They talked for a while longer, then Ruby stood up. "Thank you for talking with me. I think I'll go for a beach walk to clear my head and consider your invitation."

"Okay, sweetie. Let me know what you decide."

After hiking through the thick brush down to the beach, tossing rocks into the sea, and then beach walking as she pondered the things Callie told her, Ruby came to a decision. She needed more time away from Peter to sort things out. Her rushing back to Ketchikan, even if a plane were flying there today, wouldn't help anything improve in their marriage. She'd be jumping right back into the same frying pan. Nothing changed.

Although she doubted Peter would like her plan, she was going to accept Callie's invitation and stay at the project house with the three ladies for the winter. By the time spring came, hopefully, she'd know what to do next.

Fifty-one

Paige ran the paint roller over the walls of the gallery, working opposite her handsome business partner. Stealing glances at Forest, she was amazed at how much she loved spending time with him, even when they were working. For several hours they'd been painting the interior walls a soft cream color that would be a great backdrop for all the art pieces. Her shoulders ached, but the task was satisfying. So was the view of the good-looking man beside her.

She grinned at him. Too bad he didn't glance her way. He looked so serious, rolling the paint roller over the walls around the now enclosed glass window, his brow furrowed. What was on his mind? Was he tired? Working too much? Between his tasks with Deputy Brian, the project house, and now helping her paint the gallery, maybe he was exhausted.

She was tired too, but others had stopped by to help this week, lightening the load. A few locals, thanks to Bess, volunteered with removing damaged Sheetrock and the warped plywood flooring. Others came by to install new Sheetrock and apply tape and mud to the walls. Even installing new plywood and vinyl flooring. The teamwork had been amazing.

Paige was thankful for all the neighbors and friends who donated their time. In the future, she planned to help other business owners too. They were a community. One person's success was a step-up for someone else.

At Judah's prompting, she'd called in professionals to check for mold and to double-check all the electrical stuff. So far, everything passed with flying colors. The glass guys installed the big window. No more wind gusts were billowing in through plastic sheeting. A local carpenter replaced the front door and frame. It wouldn't be long until she announced her grand opening.

Amid all that, she found love. Or maybe love found her. Forest was all she could hope for in a husband, partner, and friend. She loved him. Wanted to be with him, close to him, even when he wore such a serious expression.

"Are you okay?" she finally asked.

"Yeah, I'm okay." He met her gaze. Shrugged.

"Where'd you go for a while there?"

"Just thinking." He set his roller down on the tray and shuffled toward her, his demeanor changing from somber to happy. His smile aimed at her sent butterflies frolicking through her middle. That look on his face usually meant he was going to kiss her.

Clasping her roller handle, he set it down. Tenderly, he stroked wisps of her hair back that escaped her red bandana. His thumbs smoothed over her cheeks, his eyes sparkling. "Were you staring at me like you wanted me to kiss you?"

"Maybe"—she dragged out the word.

He leaned up and pressed his warm mouth against hers. A zillion bolts of electrical current shot through her.

She scrambled down the ladder and melted into his arms. Probably should have warned him about getting wet paint on his clothes. But didn't. She settled her cheek against his jacket. "Thanks. I needed this. Being with you."

"Me too." He kissed the side of her head. "Sorry I've been so quiet. Just rehashing case stuff."

"It's okay." She smoothed her palms over his shoulders. "I know your job is entitled to *some* of your thoughts."

His grin bordered on laughter. "If it were up to me, we'd leave this work and head home. Then all my thoughts would be yours. We could sequester in our honeymoon suite for a month."

"A month? Might be difficult to explain that."

"Not when I can't get enough of—" He kissed her again.

She sighed, wishing she could agree to leave and head back to the house with him. But the walls wouldn't paint themselves.

His irises turned from jade to gray-green. "We have to keep working, huh?"

"Yeah. Sorry. Not my first choice."

"No?" His lips covered hers again.

She sure liked his kisses.

Noticing some paint smudges on his gray sweatshirt, she snickered. "What would you say to us doing something else later?"

"Something else?" His eyebrows rose, a spark in his gaze.

"Like going on a date."

"Sure. I'll go on a date any time with you, baby."

"How about if we go to a nice restaurant? Forget work for a little while."

"Sounds great! Still have the cute black dress?"

She laughed, surprised he remembered. "I do." Although, years had passed since she last wore it.

A few hours later, after removing all the paint off her skin, and slipping into the black dress she'd worn in Vegas, she sat across from Forest in Claude's Fine Dining along the waterfront in Florence.

"You look amazing in that dress." Grinning, he squeezed her hand gently. "I'm glad you suggested this. We need to get away by ourselves more often."

"We are newlyweds, after all."

"That we are." He winked at her.

Their salmon dinners arrived, and Forest whispered a prayer of thanks for their food. Over salmon slathered in caramelized onions and baked potatoes with sour cream, they laughed and chatted about happenings at the project house, in the town, and concerning their families. With every conversation, it seemed their lives, their hearts, were blending more and more together.

Setting her fork down, Paige scooted forward in her chair. "What do you hope for? Like what are your goals?" She wanted to get to know him even better.

"I want you," he whispered huskily. "A family. More of this. Us."

A good kind of chill skittered up her back. "What about your love for detective work?"

"What we have is worth more to me than any job or money or goals." His gaze locked on hers. "I want to be here for you,

Piper, and any other children we may have. Being a part of this family is more than I could have hoped for. More than I ever dreamed. But, yes, I'd like to continue working as a detective, too. Hopefully, that can happen from Basalt Bay."

She nodded, letting his words sink in. He wanted a family with more kids. He wanted to be here for them. For her.

"What do you hope for?"

His softly asked question caught her off guard since she was still pondering his answer. She slid her hand over the silkiness of her black dress, glad she'd still been able to fit into it.

"I want all that life has for us together. You, me, Piper, other children, and God in our lives, too."

"And your art."

"Yes, but it's not something I hope for." So few people understood the depths of how she felt about art. But if anyone should get this about her, it was her husband. "Art is part of who I am. It's like an extension of me in the way my arms or legs are. This urge to experience life through painting or a lens has been with me forever. I never had to force myself to paint or draw. It's like breathing. It just was."

"I love and respect that about you. The gallery is a way of sharing that part of yourself with others, too, isn't it?"

Oh, Forest.

"Yes. And you're a beautiful, tender-hearted man for seeing that."

He chuckled. "No one's ever called me beautiful before."

If their blueberry topped cheesecake hadn't arrived just then, she would have leaned across the table and planted a whopper of a kiss on his mouth.

Later, Forest pulled the car into the parking lot at City Beach in Basalt. "Feel like a beach walk?"

"Uh, not really. I wore heels. Besides, isn't it too cold?"

"Probably." He turned off the engine and faced her. "If the weather were warmer, we could remove our shoes, hold hands, and walk barefoot across the sand. Sounds romantic, huh?"

"Being with you, wherever we are, sounds romantic." Walking on the beach? Not so much. But why spoil the mood and tell him that? "You know, I've never held a guy's hand and walked on the beach."

"Seriously?"

"You'd be my first."

"Okay, then. Tomorrow morning? You and me. Walking barefoot in the sand and holding hands."

"It'll still be too cold for bare feet." She chuckled. "It's fall, Forest."

"At least walking and holding hands." Leaning over the console, their gazes met in the moonlight, and he kissed her slowly, tenderly, making her brain fuzz up.

Oh, yeah. She'd walk barefoot in the sand with him. She'd do anything he asked as long as he kept kissing her like this.

Fifty-two

Peter spent most of the day fixing the busted rigging on his boat. Not an easy task. The wind still gusted with annoying ferocity, albeit not as harshly as before. The crippled city had a plethora of downed trees and no electricity, making it difficult to get to any stores for supplies.

As he worked on the pole, thoughts of Ruby staying in Basalt with his family assaulted him. If he asked her outright to come home, would she? Would he want her to come back if she didn't want to?

Another idea had been churning in his mind too. What if he were to winterize the boat and return to Basalt for a couple of months? Leave his boat? Man, that would be tough. Miss part of the winter trolling harvest? He groaned. Missing any fishing openings went against his grain. But as the idea came back to him again and again, his stubborn determination to do things one way, his way, softened.

Wasn't his marriage worth some sacrifice on his part?

His hometown wasn't his favorite place to hang out, but it would give him and Ruby time to work on their relationship. He wouldn't have to come north until early next year. Could he leave the *Lily Forever* to return to his wife? He gulped.

Ruby was the most important person in his life. He'd do anything for her. Even wintering in Basalt Bay? Returning to port for her? For them?

Yes. *Yes!*

With the decision made, a grin stretched across his mouth. A more peaceful feeling than he'd experienced in weeks crept through him. He let out a colossal sigh. Soon, he'd get to see Ruby again.

This meant he'd be with her for Christmas in Basalt. He still hadn't given her the ruby necklace, the one he was holding onto to give her when they made up. It'd make a nice Christmas present, too. He closed his eyes, imagining himself placing the wrapped package in her hands, kissing her.

He should call and see what she thought of him joining her. Holding up his cell phone, one bar showed. He tapped Ruby's name and limped into the galley. Nothing. He held up the cell, swaying it in the air like those old "can you hear me now" commercials. "Useless piece of trash." Tempted to toss it in the drink, he headed back onto the deck.

He tapped her name again.

"Peter? Peter, is that you?"

"It's me."

"Are you—?" A crackling sound smothered her words.

"Rube, you're breaking up. I'm okay. The storm passed."

"It's good ... your voice." A breathy sound came through the speaker. "I've been—"

"Listen, I'll call when I have better reception. Power's down." He swallowed. "Can you hear me?"

"Sort of," was followed by crackly static.

"I'm thinking of heading back to Basalt Bay," he shouted into the receiver.

Silence.

"Ruby?"

"—to stay. Your aunt asked me to bunk—"

More static.

"What was that?"

Did she say Aunt Callie asked her to bunk at the project house?

"Rube?" He held the phone up toward the sky. The connection was lost. Groaning, he tapped her name again. It went right to voicemail. "Of all the—" He punched "End."

He returned to the broken rigging he'd been working on before. He took out his pocket knife and scraped some gunk off a bolt. Was Ruby telling him to stay put? Did she mean they didn't have a chance at reconciliation?

Ack. He cut his finger on a sharp edge of metal. Bleeding, he hobbled into the galley, holding up his finger and grumbling. Why couldn't things go easier for once? He ran water over his finger in the small sink, dried and bandaged his wound, then covered it with a plastic wrap to keep it from getting dirty.

Back outside, his phone vibrated. Must have gotten a signal.

Scrambling to get the phone out of his pocket, he hit "accept" before paying attention to Caller ID. As soon as he heard the older woman's voice, he gritted his teeth.

"Peter?"

"Aunt Callie? Is something wrong?" He pictured Ruby hurt. Or Dad being rushed to the hospital. His aunt had never called him before.

"Everyone's okay. How are you?"

"Surviving. Surprised by your call."

"I got your number from—" Static. "—you might not like."

"What now?" His voice came out sharply.

"I invited Ruby to stay with us."

He'd figured as much.

"It's not because she's right—" Her voice faded out. "—you both."

"Look, this is a bad connection. Thanks for the heads-up."

"One more thing."

Peter sighed, hating his aunt's pushy sense of entitlement to tell him stuff he didn't want to hear.

"You should—" Crackly sounds. "—things right." Her voice rose. "I'd like to see you make a go of it."

"That makes two of us," he growled.

He despised her telling him what he should be doing. Tempted to flat out tell her so, her next words beat him to the punch.

"Ruby is worth any effort it takes on your part to win her back." Every word of her sentence came through clearly.

Every ounce of fight left him.

The phone went dead.

Fifty-three

A strong knocking at the door awakened Forest. He slipped on a T-shirt and jogging pants and ran into the living room. The pounding came again.

"All right. All right," he muttered, opening the door.

Deputy Brian stood on the front porch holding a newspaper, a deep scowl on his face.

"Morning, Deputy. To what do I owe the pleasure of this early morning visit?"

"No pleasure." Brian thrust the paper toward him. "I saw this at the diner. Thought you should see it."

"Thanks, I think." Forest grabbed the edition of the *Gazette*. "Want to come in?"

"No. Sorry about this." Brian chin nodded at the paper then headed for his squad car.

Concerned, Forest strode into the kitchen. He dropped into a chair and held up the newspaper. The front-page headline— "Detective Leads Double Life"—punched him in the gut.

"Whaaaaat?"

He skimmed the article, catching phrases—"Detective marries local while double-timing another," "fathers child … abandons her mother," "questionable associations," "can we trust such a man," "is this the type of person we want for—"

Who wrote this garbage? He found the byline. A. Riley. Who was that? He flipped the paper to the information section. Milton Hedge was listed as the publisher. Was A. Riley his pseudonym? An editor?

Forest raked his fingers through his hair. Was this what the note on the rock meant? *"Watch what you're doing. Or all of Basalt Bay will hear about your mistakes."*

He groaned.

An anonymous source had supposedly provided details for the article.

Anonymous, my foot.

Was Mia behind this? Evie? Craig wouldn't jeopardize his early release. Was Edward trying to make him look incompetent?

What was Paige going to think about this? She was the one who didn't want to be in the gossip spotlight. Isn't that one of the reasons they married quickly?

"Who was at the door?" Paige shuffled into the room in her slippers and robe, yawning. "Boy, I slept in." She flung her arms around his shoulders as if nothing was amiss—not knowing the world just dropped out from beneath his feet—and kissed his cheek.

"It was the deputy. Bad news."

"Oh? What happened?" She sat on the chair next to him, her soft gaze on him.

He loved her so much. Wanted to protect her from anxiety and pain. He could tell her it was nothing. That's all this was, right? Silly nonsense. But it was a small-town paper. The gossip would be rampant by lunchtime.

"Forest, tell me, what's wrong?"

"This." Tapping his finger against the headline, he scooted the paper across the table. He strummed his fingers over his scruffy chin and watched her take in the words, her mouth dropping open, her eyes widening, a look of dismay crossing her face.

"I can't believe it."

"Apparently, I'm the worst cad who shouldn't be working as a detective." He exhaled. "Shouldn't be living in Basalt Bay."

"Oh, Forest," she said, still reading. Then she lifted her chin, giving him a brave look. "This isn't you. I know you. They're wrong about this stuff. Just plain wrong."

He'd never been lambasted in a newspaper before. But Paige's words, her support, made his next breaths come easier. Not quite so painful.

Then she was on his lap, her arms wrapping around his shoulders, the side of her head against the side of his head. They held each other like that for a while, and he felt such relief that she'd taken the news like this. Like she didn't believe anything bad A. Riley had written about him. Like she'd support him, stand by him, no matter what.

"Thanks, baby."

She leaned back, their gazes meeting. "What are you going to do about it? This is insulting! Inflammatory. You could sue the newspaper. Or sue A. Riley."

"It's a he said, she said thing. No proof. However, I wonder who's behind this. Even if I asked, I doubt the editor would give up his source."

"We can talk to Milton Hedge. He's a decent guy. Or you could write a counter argument." Paige slapped her hands against the tabletop. "I bet this was Mia's doing." She jumped off his lap. "Who else would claim to have the inside track on this investigation? Doesn't that sound like her?"

"Hard to say."

"We have to do something! Make them write a retraction." She stomped across the small kitchen, her robe flaring behind her. "What if this is revenge? What if Mia did this because she lost the election? Because she lost Edward's ear?" She groaned. "That woman is a troublemaker. Paisley is right about her."

"Paige." He stood in front of her. "Someone is fighting dirty, that much is obvious. Maybe it's Mia. Or Evie. Maybe Edward. But I can't fight back dirt with dirt."

"Why not? Forest—"

He chuckled at her passion and feistiness. "Thank you for being on my side, though. That means the world to me."

"I am on your side. I'm your wife."

"I'm so glad you are." He pulled her to him and wrapped her arms around his shoulders again.

"Milton should be ashamed of himself. He shouldn't have allowed this submission without checking the facts, without asking for your input. I'm sure if we talk to him—"

Forest kissed her, stopping her tirade.

"We have to do something," she said.

He leaned his forehead against hers. "We can't talk to him about this or accuse his editor of slander. I can't discuss an ongoing case with anyone."

"You're just going to let it go? Let her get away with this?" She huffed but stayed in his arms.

"I can't comment. No doubt, I'll face an inquiry with Sheriff Morris." He smoothed back strands of hair over her ear. "I'm sorry for any trouble this may cause you. You know, with wagging tongues and all."

Paige grimaced. "It's nothing Paisley and I haven't experienced before."

Forest hated causing his wife and her family more turmoil.

"Are we still going to walk on the beach this morning?" she asked in a quieter tone.

"Do you still want to? I mean, with this—"

"I do. A walk might clear our heads." She kissed his cheek. "How about you fix me another one of those great breakfasts while I clean up? Can you try to forget about this article for a little while?"

"That sounds good." A relief, even. He knew how to compartmentalize work stuff most of the time. Tomorrow would be soon enough to discuss this trouble with Sheriff Morris.

As Paige exited the room, she glanced over her shoulder and smiled sweetly at him. In his thoughts, her expression translated to "I'm glad you're my husband. I'll always stand by you."

And he thanked God for that.

Fifty-four

After dropping off Piper at her grandpa's, Forest and Paige strolled hand in hand alongside the waves rolling up in front of Basalt Bay, leaning into the breeze. Even though the newspaper allegations hung over his head, he smiled at her, glad for this time alone together.

"This is nice. I like being here with you," she said.

"Yeah?" Warmth spread through his chest, and he brought their forward motion to a halt. Wrapping his arms around her waist, he drew her to him. "And this? Do you like this, baby?" He skimmed his mouth over her cool mouth, forgetting the morning's problems a little more with each soft caress.

"Mmm. I like that a lot." Giggling, she met his gaze. "Can I tell you something?"

"Anything." He felt distracted by her fingers exploring his neck, twirling in his hair.

"I want to do something to keep a promise to myself."

"What's that?" He leaned back. Her cheeks were pink. Her eyes bright. Drawn to her, mesmerized by her, he met her lips again. "I love you."

"Love you too." She clasped his hand. "Before we got back together, even before you came to town, I told Paisley what I'd do if a man ever loved me as Judah loves her." She took in a sharp breath. "Forest, you do love me like Judah loves Paisley, don't you?"

"Of course I do! If you doubt, I'll have to do something to convince you otherwise." He leaned in to kiss her again.

She put out her hand, touching his chest. "Let me say this first. I told her if a man ever loved me like that—"

"And I do."

"And you do, so I'd sing and dance in the street."

"You'd—" He gazed up at the sky and laughed. It felt good, comforting even, to let out a hearty laugh.

Paige chuckled too. "Would you dance with me, Forest?"

"Forever." His breath caught. "Oh, you mean in the street?"

"Or here. We have the whole beach to ourselves."

"I'll dance with you in the street or on the beach." He smiled. "Or in our bedroom."

"Oh, you." She swatted playfully at his arm. "Because you love me and I love you, I'm going to dance and sing with all that's in me. It doesn't matter if it's in the street or on the beach or in our house." Tapping his chest, a determined look crossed her face. "It doesn't matter what anyone else says about us, either. We know the truth. We're a real couple. In fact, we're wild about each other."

He swallowed a tug of emotion. "Yes, we are. Thank you for saying that." He placed her left hand on his shoulder, his hand at her waist, their free hands clasped. "I will be your dance partner for life. Whenever we dance, I'm going to remember this moment with you here on the beach."

"It's a celebration dance for me."

"For me too."

Grinning widely, Paige burst out the lyrics to the Monkees' "I'm a Believer," and boisterously danced with him across the beach with the waves rolling in close to their feet.

The beauty and love of this woman, his wife, filled him with a glorious euphoria. He was so happy, so moved by her display of tenderness and fun and love. When she reached the line about the guy not leaving the woman he loved even if he tried, something gripped his chest, reminding him of his promise to never leave her again. A promise he was sticking to forever and always.

He paused and kissed her, deeply, lovingly.

Then they were dancing again. Only this time, their frolicking morphed into a slow dance with both humming the tune to "I Will Always Love You." On the final high note, Forest tipped Paige back and kissed her, branding this moment, her, them, with the passion he felt in his heart.

"I will always love you," he whispered.

"I will always love you, too." She kissed him softly. "I hope we keep dancing and singing about our love."

"We will, baby."

Their kisses left him breathless, hopeful, and completely enraptured with his wife.

Epilogue

Sweaty and worn out from all the work she'd been doing in the attic, Ruby took a break outside and lifted her face to the rain, letting moisture drip down her cheeks.

A truck pulled off the road in front of the house and parked. It wasn't Judah's pickup. Was the rug installer due this morning?

A man with wide shoulders and wearing a dark green rain slicker stepped from the truck. Ruby's heart pounded hard. Peter? He didn't say he was returning to Basalt Bay.

She took off running down the brush-strewn driveway. The raincoat-clad man met her halfway up the path before lifting his head. When his dark gaze met hers, lightning bolts flashed through her.

"Peter! It is you." She came to a fast stop in front of him.

"Hey, Rube. It's me." He stretched out his hands.

They didn't embrace, didn't span the two feet between them that felt an ocean wide. If only he'd take the initiative, wrap his arms around her and kiss her like he meant it. Or she could throw herself into his arms and kiss him. But she didn't want to make the first move. So they stood like mannequins, staring at each other, appraising each other.

"Want to come in? Have some coffee?" A mundane question. But she had to start somewhere.

"Coffee sounds great."

Inside the house, Ruby removed her raincoat, placed it on a peg on the wall by the door, then went straight for the coffeemaker. She fixed two cups of black coffee while Peter removed his coat and hung it up. Then they sat down on barstools at the butcher-block island. He clasped his mug between his hands in a familiar gesture.

"You weathered the storm, I see."

"Yeah, it was rough. The *Lily Forever* is secure. If another storm hits, I won't have to rush right back."

"That's good. How long do you plan to stay this time?" Her stomach tightened in anticipation of a knockdown drag-out argument about her returning to the fishing vessel with him.

"I'm staying in Basalt Bay for the winter."

"You are?" She nearly dropped her cup. "Christmas too?"

"Mmhmm." He took a casual slurp of his coffee. "Plan to stay with Dad."

"Does he know?"

"Yep. I called him."

"Well, I—" She gulped. "That's great." Utterly shocking, but great.

Peter was staying for the winter. But why? Dare she hope … to reconcile with her?

Sipping her coffee, she eyed him. Slightly slouched shoulders, messy reddish-brown hair, scruffy whiskers like he hadn't shaved for weeks, and dark eyes staring right back at her.

"I'm glad to see you, Peter, but why are you here?"

"Returning to you, my wife."

His throaty response sent chills racing through her. His smile was to die for. Peter smiling at her? Saying nice things to her? Amazing. But she needed more information.

"Returning to do what, exactly?"

The clinks of their mugs as they set them down echoed in the room.

"I want to make things right between us, Rube." He reached his rough, workworn hands across the wooden surface of the island and snagged her fingers. "I'll do anything to fix the harm I've done. To get you to love me again will be the greatest gift I could imagine. If that takes me living here for the winter, I'm okay with that. I just want to be near you."

"Oh, Peter." Emotion clogged her throat.

"May I take you on a date tonight? So we can talk. Spend time together."

A breath rushed out of her. "That would be lovely."

Gazing into her husband's shimmering eyes, so much needed to be said between them. Many things needed to be worked out, but Peter's return felt like a brand new beginning for them.

Thank you for reading *Port of Return*!

What happens next in the Grant/Cedars saga?

Watch for *Sound of Rejoicing*, Part 7, coming in Winter 21-22!

If you would like to be one of the first to hear about Mary's new releases and upcoming projects, sign up for her newsletter—and receive the free pdf "Rekindle Your Romance! 50+ Date Night Ideas for Married Couples." Check it out here:

www.maryehanks.com/gift

Thank you to everyone who helped with this book!

Paula McGrew ~ Thank you for caring about my writing and knowing the heart of these stories. My work is better because of you.

Suzanne Williams ~ Thank you for always working with me and creating sweet artistic covers.

Kellie Griffin, Mary Acuff, Beth McDonald, Joanna Brown, and Jason Hanks ~ Thank you for reading *PORT* and giving me insights and critiques for how to make it better. I enjoy hearing about the things you like in the story and the things you want to see happen in future books, too. You guys are amazing!

My family—Jason, Daniel & Traci, Philip, Deborah, Shem, & Lala-girl—Love to you all!

The Lord—who gives me creative ideas and inspiration!

(This is a work of fiction. Any mistakes are my own. ~meh)

Books by Mary Hanks

Restored Series

Ocean of Regret
Sea of Rescue
Bay of Refuge
Tide of Resolve
Waves of Reason
Port of Return
Sound of Rejoicing (Winter 21-22)

Second Chance Series

Winter's Past
April's Storm
Summer's Dream
Autumn's Break
Season's Flame

www.maryehanks.com

About Mary Hanks

Mary Hanks loves stories about marriage restoration. She believes there's something inspiring about couples clinging to each other, working through their problems, and depending on God for a beautiful rest of their lives together—and those are the types of stories she likes to write. Mary and Jason have been married for forty-plus years, and they know firsthand what it means to get a second chance with each other, and with God. That has been her inspiration in writing the Second Chance series and the Restored series.

Besides writing and reading, Mary likes to garden, do artsy stuff like mosaics, go on adventures with Jason, and meet her four adult kids for coffee or breakfast.

Connect with Mary by signing up for her newsletter at

www.maryehanks.com

"Like" her Facebook Author page:

www.facebook.com/MaryEHanksAuthor

Thank you for reading the **Restored** series!

maryehanks.com